MIKE O

A Man and Music

MIKE OLDFIELD
A Man and His Music

by
Sean Moraghan

BRITANNIA PRESS PUBLISHING

First published in Great Britain in 1993 by Britannia Press Publishing,
a division of Britannia Crest International Ltd.

British Library Cataloguing in Publication Data. A Catalogue record for this book is available from the British Library.
Moraghan
Mike Oldfield. A Man and His Music

ISBN 0-9519937-5-5

Printed and bound in Great Britain by Biddles Ltd, Surrey.
Distribution: Bookpoint Ltd, Oxon.
Cover photograph: Rex Features Ltd.

Britannia Press Publishing, Britannia Crest International Ltd.
44 Chalk Farm Road, London NW1 8AJ.

CONTENTS

PART ONE

PART TWO

PART THREE

FOREWORD

Mike Oldfield shot to fame in 1973 with his debut LP, *Tubular Bells*. Nothing quite like it had ever been heard before: a continuous, highly melodic, multi-instrumental, multi-overdubbed piece of music. The album received enthusiastic critical acclaim, won Oldfield many appreciative fans, and went on to sell millions of copies worldwide.

Tubular Bells had been turned down by all the major record companies, until, finally, Richard Branson's newly formed Virgin label issued it as the record company's first release. Its unexpected success simultaneously launched both the label and the career of the then little-known nineteen-year-old musician.

Oldfield, however, then an extremely introverted personality, was not prepared for, nor interested in his new found fame, and retreated to the country, where he would compose and record subsequent popular work.

Often drawing on previously published, but not readily available information, this book traces the career and assesses the music of the gifted musician, composer and studio technician: from his troubled, musical childhood, through his early instrumental album successes, his fine guitar work for other artists, his subsequently varying musical quality and critical and commercial standing, his later songwriting (which produced *Moonlight Shadow*, the biggest-selling single in Europe in its year of release) and 1992's *Tubular Bells II* (which went straight to number one in the chart in the first week of its release).

Throughout, it is generally Oldfield's music and career, rather than his personal life, that is more the focus of the book. The author hopes he has illuminated all these areas, however, and conveyed his enjoyment of, and fascination with the music to both fans and skeptics alike.

A full discography, videography, and bibliography is included.

The author would like to express his thanks to the writers and publishers of quoted material; and to Jonathan Williams, for advice and encouragement.

Sean Moraghan

PART ONE

Chapter 1

A Musical Childhood

Mike Oldfield's childhood was not a very happy one, and this circumstance provided the impetus to his becoming involved in making music, to which he resorted as a means to comfort himself.

He was born on 15th May 1953 in Reading, Berkshire, where his father, Ray, was a doctor. His mother, Maureen Liston, came from Charleville, a village in County Cork in the Republic of Ireland, and emigrated to Britain in the 1920's. Mike was the youngest in a family of three, with a sister, Sally, born in 1947, and a brother, Terry, born in 1949.

What was so traumatic for him was his difficult relationship with his parents, particularly with his mother. Things were so awry that he was later to observe quizzically of himself that he was not really able to love his parents, describing plaintively by way of explanation: *"my childhood was domestically turbulent. I needed domestic security, and it wasn't there"*. The problems were due to the effects of his mother's mental illness on all of the family, but particularly on himself: *"My mother was a drug addict and kept falling over and going into hospital and I didn't like it so I invented music to escape into ... used in as a way of retreating into my own little world"*. He complained of her situation: *"it was pills, tranquilizers, electric shock treatment. I felt so helpless. That was why I became so immersed in the guitar. By the greatest stroke of good fortune my father bought me one and taught me a few chords when I was seven. Every day I'd come home from school and lock myself in my room and play"*. Playing music allowed him to create a vivid alternative world of sound and melody, a childhood sanctuary in strict opposition to the real world and his painful feelings. He was to continue this practice through the early LP recording he made as an adult: his emotional state, which continued to be quite disturbed, still required it. This motivation was to account for a good deal of the emotional content and larger significance of his recordings.

Ray Oldfield appears to have tried to make up any shortfall in parenting which resulted from Mike's mother's emotional problems, and, accordingly, Mike appears to have experienced a more beneficial relationship with his father, his resentment at his parents notwithstanding. As well as encouraging him to take up the guitar, his father shared with him his interest in star-gazing and flying, imbuing Mike with a lifelong enthusiasm for these pastimes.

After he took up the guitar, Mike began to listen to, and to learn from contemporary popular music, *"I suppose the first things that I liked were by The Beatles, really. After that I started liking Bert Jansch and John Renbourn when I was about ten or eleven. I started playing on (the) 6-string guitar that my father gave me ... and the first thing that I learned to do was a claw-hammer pick. I was really knocked out with it. I could just about play 'Angie', the Bert Jansch version of the Davy Graham tune. It involved a lot of finger-picking"*. His models, Jansch and Renbourn, were the two foremost guitarists of the British folk music revival of the 1960's; Jansch was the more melancholic of the pair, and perhaps the more technically pioneering, creating a folk guitar style which came to be called 'folk baroque'; the quite complex instrumental, *Angie*, was his most celebrated piece. Besides making recordings, both artists played live, and it is likely that Mike also saw them perform in the folk clubs that had been set up in Reading (as in many other towns).

Although his unhappiness acted as the stimulant to his music making, Mike was by nature musically gifted, and he subsequently became involved in a number of childhood and teenage musical activities. From the age of ten he was composing long instrumentals for acoustic guitar and tape recording them. He played instrumentals, rather than songs, because, he explained in 1976, *"when I was ten I found my guitar was a better way of communicating than words. I still feel that way"*. As he suggested, he carried this sentiment - one born out of his childhood introversion and poor verbal communication skills - onto *Tubular Bells* and his other early solo LP's, which were almost exclusively instrumental.

Soon he was performing solo in a Reading folk club, and trying to copy Bert Jansch's guitar technique. He was only eleven, although, as he recalled, he did not look it: his voice had broken, and he had to shave; *"I was big for my age, a premature adult. The skin on my back split. I've still got the marks"*.

When he was about twelve or thirteen, he made a switch over to electric guitar, and subsequently formed a small group, playing the guitar instrumentals of The Shadows, and some early rock 'n' roll material, at youth clubs and dances.

For some reason he then decided to give up music, and for a period of about six months he seems to have replaced it with painting.

"Then I persuaded my father to buy an old 12-string acoustic guitar for me. I used to play things like Gerry And The Pacemakers' Ferry 'Cross the Mersey. Eventually I wanted another 6-string, but I couldn't persuade my father to buy me one, so I took half the strings off the 12-string and made it into a 6-string. I used that in a duo with a friend of mine. We used to play at a couple of folk clubs in Reading. We did some original songs that were quite involved. Most were the typical adolescent poetry - the painful stuff". The duo had to come to an end when the Oldfield family moved to Hornchurch, in Essex.

There Mike attended a local grammar school, which he described as *"abysmal"*. Music was taught on this school's curriculum, but, remarkably, for a youngster who actually liked classical music, as well as folk and pop, and who, as an adult composer was to borrow some musical approaches from it, he did not enjoy these lessons, and was to finish near the bottom of his class. He explained: *"they taught classical music along strict guidelines and it was very restricting. There wasn't any room for experimentation and I just found it frustrating"*.

He sought a different sort of musical education just before he left the school, when he and his sister Sally travelled to Olympic Studios in London to see Rolling Stone Mick Jagger recording. The trip had been arranged by Jagger's girlfriend, Marianne Faithful, with whom Sally had attended the same Catholic convent school, and who had played in the Reading folk clubs. Faithful also managed to get Sally, who sang and played acoustic guitar, some time in the studio, later, to record some tracks, none of which saw release.

Mike left school abruptly on his fifteenth birthday, because they wanted him to cut his long hair, of which he was quite proud: *"One afternoon I had an argument with the headmaster and I just stormed off and never went back*". He departed with only one O' level to his name, unable as a result to follow his only, somewhat unrealistic career ambition - to join the RAF and fly with the Red Arrows display team.

He was rescued by his sister, who invited him to join her to play professionally as a folk duo. The pair worked out some songs together, called themselves Sallyangie (after Sally and *Angie*, Mike's favoured Jansch tune), and went on to play live in the summer of 1968.

In May they appeared in Paris, just as student radicalism broke out into street confrontations with the gendarmes; at one gig, tear gas spilled into the venue, but Mike, even then a somewhat emotionally removed professional musician, was upset, not at the turbulence around him, but at its disruptive effects on the quality of his performance.

Back in Britain, Sallyangie were lucky to be spotted by John Renbourn, then a member of Pentangle, who recommended them to the group's record company, Transatlantic, one of the major folk labels of the time. Mike and Sally got a contract, and recorded an LP, *Children Of The Sun*, on which they sang and played guitars.

Sally has the more prominent vocal role on their LP, Mike occasionally joining her on choruses or verses and singing the odd verse himself. Sally's singing is quite mannered, her high-pitched, trilling delivery being sometimes irritating.

Lyrically, the duo's songs are wordy and over-sweet. They are done in a 'high-nonny-no' style, and also reflect the influence of Pentangle. Mike's imprint appears to exist on some of the songs, although it is not known how much of the lyrics he wrote; many of these evoke physical details, which on his own, mature songs, have inordinately important place, often almost overshadowing a song's human situation.

The album includes two extremely brief, half-minute acoustic instrumentals by Mike, *Milk Bottle* and *Changing Colours*. On these the young musician uses the guitar for its sound, rather than for its melodic potential. His guitar accompaniments for the rest of the material also display some juvenile dexterity.

Listened to today, the album is less interesting for its own merits, which are not particularly enduring, than it is as Mike's first recorded performance.

After the LP was released, in November 1968, the pair played some more live shows. They later made a single, *Two Ships/Colours Of The World*, which was issued in September 1969.

Like their album, the single was not a great success, and this and the following factors made Mike unhappy with the duo. Transatlantic, for example had tried to give them an image which he hated: he and Sally had to play the 1969 Cambridge Folk Festival dressed up in green velvet and satin. Mike had also become unable to stomach their own somewhat syrupy sound, commenting, *"I didn't like what we were doing at all, apart from two long instrumentals, which I used to do at every gig"*. (Mike recorded these in the studio at the time, but later had no idea what became of the tapes). After a year together, the duo split up under the weight of Mike's discontent and the nature of his relationship with Sally, Mike concluding: *"Probably the main reason it didn't work out was those little-brother-big-sister squabbles"*.

By this time, as a result of his childhood family experiences and their continuing effects upon him, Mike had developed definite emotional problems. There is some evidence to suggest that, while he was not a fully-fledged manic-depressive, he certainly had such tendencies. Further disillusioned by his experiences with the duo, he had a nervous breakdown after they broke up. He later explained that in order to counter the state of incipient madness which he was suffering, he tried, typically, to create another, more peaceful state of mind by playing his guitar, this being the only thing which comforted him, allowing him to alter his mood and create feelings which were the exact opposite of those he was going through. It was at this time that he composed a very gentle acoustic tune which he was later to recall when he came to record the second side of *Tubular Bells*, in 1973, when, adding this to sympathetic organ, he made a particularly beautiful passage, inspiring in the listener as well as in himself feelings of melancholy contemplation and joyful release.

After he broke up with Sally, Mike said he had a lean year living off his father and trying to run a four-piece rock bank he had set up with his flautist brother, Terry. The group was called Barefeet, after Sallyangie's bare-feet stage act. Mike played electric guitar (a Fender Telecaster which used to belong to Marc Bolan), and wrote songs. The group, however, was not fated to last longer than the duo, folding in February 1970. Mike later characterised the band as not very good; they played live, until, he explained, *"we packed up after on disastrous performance"*.

Chapter 2

With Kevin Ayers and the Whole World

The day after his band broke up, Mike auditioned as the bass player for a band being formed by Kevin Ayers. Ayers had left the then highly talented and inventive Soft Machine, with whom he had been the bass player and occasional songwriter, to go on and record a fine solo album of his typically sardonic, whimsical songs in 1969. He was forming the group so that he could perform his songs live. Mike got the job, despite the fact that he had only recently picked up the bass, which he had never played before. Looking back when he had become established as a successful and assured multi-instrumental musician, he commented: *"It's not as easy as it looks. It's a whole different concept (to the guitar), and it was fantastic training to learn how to do it"*.

The band, The Whole World, was a diverse crew led by dark-eyed, blonde-haired Kevin on memorably deep, bassy vocals, rhythm guitar and winsome smile, with jazz musician Lol Coxhill on saxophone, comic songs and jokes, avant-garde composer

David Bedford on organ, Mick Fincher on drums, and Mike on bass.

Ayers was born in Herne Bay, Kent, on 16 August 1945, but was brought up in Malaysia, spending a warm, happy childhood in the colonies. His family later moved back to the colder climes of England, to London, where he crammed his General Certificate of Education. The subsequent impetus of his musical career came about, circuitously, as a result of his being arrested for possession of drugs: *"It was one of those classic 'plant' scenes where the policeman puts this parcel in your hand and then says "'ello, 'ello, what 'ave we 'ere" and then the next thing you know you're in court ... Anyway the judge ordered me to leave the evil influence of London".* He moved to Canterbury, and there met modern-jazz-inspired drummer Robert Wyatt, at whose house a group of enthusiastic young musicians would gather which subsequently evolved into Soft Machine: Wyatt, Ayers, Mike Ratledge and Australian Daevid Allen, a general oddball and one of the earliest British experimenters with LSD.

Soft Machine went to London, became part of the emerging psychedelic music scene and recorded a commercially unsuccessful single with London-based guitar pyrotechnician Jimi Hendrix. They turned their attentions to France, where they played and recorded a set of demo tracks later released as *Jet Propelled Photograph.* Kevin later re-recorded the title track with The Whole World as *Shooting At The Moon.*

When the band returned to England, Daevid Allen ran into passport and visa trouble and was refused entry into the country. The band reduced to a trio, went on to tour with Jimi Hendrix in the US, where they also recorded their first LP proper, *Volume One,* an odder, more quirky piece than their debut, particularly in its adventurous instrumentals.

During the tour, however, Ayers began to feel that the group's music was getting further away from ideas which he wanted to pursue. He was very much in favour of instrumental experimentation, but felt that the band was leaning too much in a jazz direction for his taste.

He got hold of some advance money for a proposed solo LP and disappeared to Ibiza for a few months to write songs before returning to England to record *Joy Of A Toy* in September 1969. Among those who played for him on the LP was David Bedford, whom the manager of Soft Machine had recommended as an arranger.

Bedford (born 4 August 1937) was a classically-trained composer, whose avant-garde work of the early 1960s had been greeted with a great deal of critical praise. For financial reasons, he worked as an arranger and school music teacher. In his compositional work, Bedford was primarily interested in sound and the varieties of effects on listeners which could be achieved by introducing random or chance elements, experimenting with tone colours and combining the sonorities of various instruments. This concern with sound had already led him to become interested in both listening to contemporary rock music (such as The Who) and scoring for rock instruments in some of his pieces.

It was in his capacity as an arranger, however, that he became involved in the series of Implosion concerts at The Roundhouse in London, a set of shows which presented some of the bigger acts of the current rock underground. The manager of Soft Machine, who were on the bill, heard some of Bedford's work for the concerts, and, knowing that Ayers was looking for an arranger for his solo album, recommended him. Bedford arranged the LP and also played some fine piano.

When Kevin then decided to form a band and perform material from his LP, he asked Bedford, whose work for him he had admired, to join him in a proposed group. As someone so interested in sound and in rock music, he was ideal for the type of band which The Whole World would become. Kevin discovered Lol Coxhill busking under a railway bridge, and then recruited Mike and Mick Fincher. The group went on to play in March 1970. They would become one of the few oases of genuine talent and inventiveness in the otherwise largely desolate landscape of the early 1970s British rock scene.

The Whole World's live shows were to feature a very strong element of individual and collective improvisation, sometimes homogeneous, sometimes clashing. The band's sonic explorations for their early gigs were based on material from Kevin's LP and also his Soft Machine songs *Why Are We Sleeping?*, *We Did It Again* and *Jet Propelled Photograph (Shooting At The Moon)*, with Mike mainly playing bass.

The improvisation was actively encouraged by Kevin, in his role as self-appointed leader of the band. While not himself particularly adept in this department, he had a gift for recognising good musicianship in others (as his quirky collection of the players in the band demonstrated) and he liked to spur them on in their own instrumental trips. Knowing that Mike also played guitar, for example, he prodded him in this direction, as the latter explained: *"I was a relatively timid performer before I met Ayers but after a couple of weeks he had me doing these screeching solos and somersaulting round the stage"*.

Given that Kevin also played guitar, the pair worked out an arrangement which held for the early part of the band's existence:

"what we used to to do is flop over" said Mike, *"I'd play bass most of the time and Kevin would play rhythm guitar. Then we'd switch and he would play bass, and I'd have a lead solo at the end of the set. I would do a completely unaccompanied solo then, and depending on my mood I used to let it feed back and I would do somersaults all over the floor"*.

A reviewer of one of the band's very first shows was more taken with the presence of composer David Bedford on organ, and wrote: *"When I heard them at the Country Club last Thursday he played it with a brick, much to the surprise of his associates"*. Commenting on the band's overall performance he continued: *"The sound is occasionally a bit anarchic, but it's the kind of warm chaos which draws you into it and the band is a highly recommended listening experience"*.

For Mike, his experience with the band, both musically and personally, was to be a mixed one. On a musical level, he would absorb some instrumental and compositional ideas from the band's work which he would redefine in his own later work, and he would become more skillful on bass and guitar. On a personal level, Kevin was a friend to him, even if they subsequently argued about the band's musical direction; Mike was attracted to Kevin's energy, which contrasted with his own continuing despondency, and Kevin enjoyed taking the young man under his wing and teaching him how to drink, wine being among Kevin's major enthusiasms. Mike also made a useful contact in David Bedford, and enjoyed discussing classical music with him; for Bedford's part, he recognised Mike as a good musician, and the pair employed each other's services on their own later respective recordings.

After gigging, Kevin and the band recorded a session for Radio One DJ John Peel, later to be broadcast in June. Peel was to become a strong fan of the group, and later signed individual member Lol Coxhill to make an LP for his avant-garde record label, Dandelion. This session presents the earliest existing recording of the band. Kevin sings *The Interview* and *Derby Day*, but the most interesting pieces are the group performances of *We Did It Again* and *Lunatics Lament*. The former begins with Mike playing some jagged guitar, and continues with David on organ and Kevin on bass, the latter providing a useful grounding for the flurried surface activity; Lol incongruously sings a comic song about currant buns, while the music goes on and on behind him creating a vortex of sounds; he sings *Pretty Little Girl*; and then he and David get together to perform their one-act mock-melodrama *Murder In The Air*. All of this, remarkably, happens within an extended version of *We Did It Again*. Mike features prominently on the new, delusional and vaguely hostile *Lunatics Lament*, playing a great, burning guitar solo: by this time his electric guitar playing had flowered into a highly personal, alternately very driving or very delicate style.

In June, the group went into the studio and recorded the album, *Shooting At The Moon*. This, their only full LP legacy, is a sparkling, yet now little-known gem of the period. Most of the album consists of Ayers' songs, which he sings in his warm, deep voice, and which are supported by excellent solo and collective playing; one track, *The Oyster And The Flying Fish*, is a duet between Ayers and folk-singer Bridget St John which the pair had originally intended to record for an album of children's songs. There are two purely instrumental pieces, *Underwater* and *Pisser Dans Un Violon*.

The album encompasses a great variety of musical approaches and effects, many of these benefiting from David Bedford's arrangements and playing, and his interests both in sound and unorthodox playing techniques. It is as if he told the band, as he often instructed his classical musicians, to improvise as they saw fit; he has also told the latter to 'sklitter' on their instruments, which pretty much characterises what he and the others do in the instrumentals. The LP's emphasis on sound effects and repetition, its occasionally tongue-in-cheek approach, its strange mock-choruses, and, most importantly, its segueing, or linking, of music from one track to another, would be absorbed by Mike, and he would use these elements in his own work later, particularly the latter feature, which formed the main compositional basis of *Tubular Bells*, and, indeed, all his instrumental work.

Mike plays mostly bass on the album. He said later that his approach to the bass was to try and extend its relatively simple function with a playing technique that was more communicative. Tracks like Kevin's amorous *May I?* and *Rheinhart And Geraldine* amply illustrate his attractive approach in action, the latter featuring his sprightly, jumpy bass runs, the former opening with a very rounded bass riff which carries a sensitivity not usually associated with the instrument.

Despite Mike's also playing guitar in the live setting, Kevin appears to have preferred to take control of that element for their LP, Mike featuring only on *Lunatics Lament*. Soon after the LP was recorded, however, Kevin realised that Mike was a better guitarist than he was, and left him to take more of the guitar parts.

When *Shooting At The Moon* was subsequently released in late October 1970, Sounds' reviewer Steve Peacock was among those who were enthusiastic about it, praising the band's effortless slide from one mood to another, and noting *Lunatics Lament* and *Red Green And You Blue* as among the best tracks of an excellent album; he said of the latter: *"For me this is a perfectly constructed song, with a lilting rhythm, sensitive bass playing from Mike Oldfield, a hazy vocal and a sweet, fluid solo from Lol"*.

After the LP was finished, Lol Coxhill went off to record

himself busking under railway bridges for his solo album.

He rejoined the others again to play live. On 18th July they appeared as part of a free concert at Hyde Park. On this occasion, and possibly earlier, drummer Mick Fincher was replaced by Kevin's old friend and colleague Robert Wyatt, who had joined the band temporarily, after feeling slightly constrained in Soft Machine. At least part of the band's performance was recorded for Lol's LP: one new piece appeared on his set as *A Collective Improvisation*. Mike plays some thin-sounding guitar at the start of it, but most of the piece becomes based on the activities of David Bedford and Robert Wyatt.

Later in the same month, the group, with new drummer Dave Dufort, travelled to Holland to play. Lol's LP includes another live track, *Vorblifa-Exit*, recorded near Rotterdam. It begins with the band backing Lol, with Mike on guitar. The band then stops, and Lol goes into a long soprano saxophone solo, after which the band rejoins him. It all sounds very jangly and cheerful: Dave Dufort's drums clatter like pots and pans, while Kevin's bass rumbles along in the lower registers. Mike's guitar is not terribly prominent, simply forming one element of the band's instrumental backing. The piece ends on a strange note, with an incredible series of varied squeezing and wrenching effects which David Bedford creates on organ.

As well as performing with the band, Bedford had continued to compose his own work. His experience playing in a rock group was to influence his material as he had influenced that of the band. Over the previous month or so, and during the next, August, he wrote *The Garden Of Love*, a setting of William Blake's poem from *Songs Of Experience*, a dark and insightful collection that Bedford liked very much. He scored the piece, in his own easily understandable space/time notation, with The Whole World in mind; it was to be for organ, swanee whistle and bird warblers, which he would play, for two electric guitars (Mike and Kevin), saxophone (Lol) and drums (Dave). There was also to be a quintet of flute, clarinet, horn, trumpet and double bass, and 'six beautiful girls for dancing and turning pages'. Bedford's work was to be premiered at the Queen Elizabeth Hall in London in late September.

Once Bedford was free to play live with the band again, in early September, The Whole World played more gigs. On the 13th they appeared in another series of the Implosion shows at The Roundhouse. Two songs from the show have survived on a bootleg tape. The first of these, *We Did It Again*, reveals Lol Coxhill to have assumed an eminent musical role in the group: The Whole World seems at time to have simply been like his backing band. Kevin repeats the refrain over and over until the crowd become quite spirited, while he also lets out the occasional catalytic scream. Everything then quietens down, and Lol plays on, with David Bedford as his accompanist. Throughout, Dave Durfot's drums are a constant focus around which the other musicians' improvisations can revolve. It is mad, powerful stuff, presenting moments of surprise and delight when the individual activities coalesce.

Bedford's organ then comes to the fore, and the band, now playing like some heavy, acid rock group, go into a slow version of *Why Are We Sleeping?*, Kevin's narcotic Soft Machine song of foreboding and despair. In the middle of it Lol sings another of his little songs, and later Mike plays guitar, in a similarly aggressive style to that which he had employed on *Lunatics Lament*, while Kevin plays Mike's original bass line for *Clarence In Wonderland*. Lol later plays a sax solo and Mike some screeching guitar.

In September, Kevin and the band also recorded a new single, *Butterfly Dance*. This is strong stuff lyrically, while musically it moves along at steady speed, ably propelled by the drums and percussion of Mick Fincher, whom Kevin appears to have recruited again just to play on this song, rather than to rejoin the band. Mirroring their occasional arrangement live, Mike plays bass for the first part of the song, while Kevin plays guitar; then the pair switch over, and Mike plays guitar, Kevin the bass.

The B-side for the single, *Stars*, is simpler. Mike accompanies the verses on thin, watery guitar. The drums are by Dave Dufort, who was to remain the drummer in the band until the beginning of its demise.

The premiere of David Bedford's *The Garden Of Love* took place at the Queen Elizabeth Hall on 26th September. The quintet with whom The Whole World played was formed of members of the London Sinfonietta. (The performance was taped and broadcast by Radio 3 as part of the series *Music In Our Time* on 17th October).

Some idea of the nature of the never studio-recorded composition might be gained by describing it, crudely, as a combination of the kind of instrumentals Bedford strongly influenced on the band's LP with the style of his own later *Star's End* (1974). The piece is approximately twenty minutes long. The first fifteen minutes consist of music alone, during which the band members follow the parts written for them by Bedford, but also include their own solo and collective improvisations. Mike is the more prominent guitarist than Kevin, and picks odd, typically delicate sounds from his instruments. At one point the six dancing girls also become involved, taking over the keyboards and bashing them with their fists and arms while the band drink beer on stage. Bedford intended the musical climax before the vocal setting of the poem to be purely improvisational, and the group get stuck into some noisy, weird avant-garde stuff, after which they pause, and Kevin sings the poem. Then, the audience having already been informed that they are welcome to join the girls to dance in the aisles for the final few bars, the band, with Lol's sax to the front, plays on in a marvellous cacophony.

All this does not seem to have been what the audience expected, given Bedford's more formally 'classical' previous work. The musical director of the London Sinfonietta, (the quintet Bedford had employed), together with a few other audience members so disliked the rock music element of the piece that they walked out of the hall. The Musical Times' reviewer commented afterwards:

> *"If it is true that on the contemporary scene nothing succeeds like excess, then this score's densely matted later stages - with random tone clusters on electric organ and electric piano, the pop group's amplification remorselessly close to ear-splitting level, the saxophonist doodling a bald imitation of John Coltrane, and many other felicities - must be accounted a triumph".*

In the following month, October, The Whole World began to play another series of gigs in town halls and universities around England. Another audience tape exists which features four pieces which they played at the Central London Polytechnic on the 10th. This begins with Kevin alternately laughing and screaming his head off, before the group goes into a fairly standard rendition of *May I?*, on which Mike plays bass. (Mike may have remembered Kevin's cathartic screaming when he created the 'caveman' section of *Tubular Bells,* it providing him with a similar, but much more urgently needed emotional release). *Clarence In Wonderland* is next, Mike again on bass. This is a new version of the song, with two extra verses. The band's live performance of *Underwater* is so improvised that it has only the barest relationship to the LP recording. Mike has switched to guitar. At first his contributions are embedded within the general instrumental effects. Later, however, he emerges to play his guitar so that it sounds like a demented church bell chime, spinning faster and faster. Everything then flows back into *Clarence* again. *We Did It Again* is Kevin's chance to come to the fore again after the band's instrumental work. He really enjoys himself on this one, chanting the refrain hypnotically and, given the title and subject of the song, directing various comments towards the female members of the audience. Mike now plays guitar in a staccato style, after which the whole band comes in, making the proceedings very noisy and lively.

After this London date, the group travelled to Brighton's Sussex University, to Cambridge, Wolverhampton, and to Manchester University. After returning to London, the band played at The Lyceum on 12th November, with singer Bridget St. John on the same bill.

By early November The Whole World were being described by one critic as *"one of the most interesting outfits on the club circuit"*, their live shows being justly characterised as *"an orderly chaos out of which can spring, without warning, moments of real revelation"*. Kevin commented: *"We play as a band, but also people will come forward so that it becomes completely them for a moment - their own little fantasy - and then they come back in again"*. This is certainly an apt description of how the group performed.

His aim with the band's shows, he explained, was to create a party atmosphere and a sense of celebration, the latter being a feature he felt contemporary groups did not attempt. This sometimes created difficulties, however, he had noticed ruefully: *"David tends to have this distinction between "serious" and "funny". You have your funny bit which is Lol telling a joke or singing a funny song, and then you have your serious bit which is playing the music. I don't really have those divisions, which makes for a bit of a problem - I might do something ridiculous in a part that is apparently serious, and they'll think it's a mistake or that I'm trying to mess them up or something. In fact, it's just a device to stop things from getting serious or heavy. Or it's just that I'm too drunk to remember what it is I'm supposed to be playing"*.

This was not the only problem within the band. Kevin's domineering style of leadership, and his role as self-appointed musical director sometimes annoyed the others.

He revealed that the band also had trouble with clashing personalities. *"We've just had a very bad period for about a month that was building up mainly because of lack of understanding, and fears and things. But we've had a minor storm and as always it clears it, and there are signs that we're coming out of it. It needs a lot of attention. It's like a little family - you have to keep catering for various people's needs and demands"*. Some of this tension came about as a result of a growing desire in Mike for greater musical independence within, and control of, the group.

During a break from their recent touring, Kevin and the band made an In Concert recording for Radio One at the BBC's Paris Theatre, in London. The show was broadcast in November. Mike played bass on *Lady Rachel*, a song from Kevin's *Joy Of A Toy*, bass on *Oh My*, a duet between Kevin and Bridget St. John, and guitar on the new and never recorded *Love Is*. The latter is a revelation in terms of Mike's input. At first his playing is confined to some fragile accompaniment to the verses; he plays opposite trumpets arranged by David Bedford, acting as a foil to them. Then he breaks into a long, skirling, spinning solo, a more prominent and intense emotional contribution than most of the others he had previously made to the group's music. He gets great support from the rest of the band, who provide a rock solid backdrop to his thin, bare, constantly searching guitar.

The Whole World resumed playing gigs, including an appearance in the second half of November at a free concert for the drugs information organisation, Release, following its reopening after a raid by the police.

The band's promoters also set up a large concert at Liverpool Stadium for the end of the month. The concert was to showcase three of the promoters' interests: The Whole World, The Edgar Broughton Band, and The Third Ear Band.

In early December the group flew to Holland again, for a ten day tour.

Before departing, the group had been recording a proposed new single, the version of *Clarence In Wonderland* performed live at the Central London Poly in October. Work on it seems never to have been completed, perhaps because of the trip abroad. A short fragment of the work in progress subsequently appeared on Lol Coxhill's double album, retitled *The Rhythmic Hooter*.

By the beginning of 1971, David Bedford had, sometime previously, recorded with Lol Coxhill for the latter's solo set. He played piano and sang with Lol on songs from the 1930s and 1940s that Lol had long been fond of, like *Pretty Little Girl* and *Two Little Pigeons*. Once these and other studio tracks were done, Lol's *The Ear Of The Beholder* was finished. Lol then prefaced his work with a strong spoken introduction. *"This is the first record I've made under my own control entirely, without anyone else telling me what to do in certain places"*, he said, in an obvious reference to Kevin Ayers' directions concerning how he should play in live performances of The Whole World's material.

The double LP includes the two live Whole World performances at Hyde Park and Rotterdam, and *The Rhythmic Hooter*. Lol's saxophone playing is the most important feature of the track. Mike plays some guitar. The bass line that emerges just before the track is cut abruptly is Kevin's playing of Mike's part for *Clarence*.

The rest of Lol's set consists of his own saxophone pieces, a whole side of him jamming with local musicians in Holland, recorded while The Whole World were on tour there, and the vocal and piano duets with David Bedford, among them *Don Alfonso*, the humorous tale of a recalcitrant bull-fighter.

After Lol had finished his solo work, The Whole World again performed David Bedford's *The Garden Of Love*, this time with members of the BBC training orchestra, at a gallery in Bristol on 14th January.

They then resumed regular gigs, appearing at The Temple, in London, on the 29th of the month, and at another benefit for release in London, sharing the bill with Soft Machine, Daevid Allen, and Scottish poet and harmonium player Ivor Cutler. They also played The Guildford Festival, in Surrey, on 7 th March.

It appears to have been later in March that Mike and David Bedford worked on an LP being recorded by The Edgar Broughton Band. The latter shared the same record label, Harvest, and live appearance management as The Whole World, and both parties were thereby on terms of acquaintance. The Broughtons were a wild-looking bunch, with their long hair, full beards, and Afghan coats. They were a real oddity at the time, in that they still espoused and acted upon some of the political and social rhetoric of the hippy movement long after those elements had faded in favour of the strictly musical values of that movement. They played many free gigs, turned up unannounced to add themselves to the off-stage bills of festivals, and played live in some of London's more disadvantaged streets out of the back of their van. Musically, they played a fairly standard brand of heavy rock, although for the eponymous LP on which Mike and David worked, Bedford added brass and string arrangements to three tracks. On one of these, *Thinking Of You*, Mike, curiously, plays mandolin, where he can be heard faintly simply accompanying the song's verses; this was the first hint that Mike could turn his hand to instruments other than his regular bass and guitar. The hard rock of The Broughtons and others was to interest Mike, and in later years, he would adapt the general musical style and incorporate it into his own work.

In April, The Whole World began to disintegrate slowly. This happened partly because of Mike. He had always taken the making of music intensely seriously, and he was uneasy with the often drunken playing, chaotic content and what he viewed as the sometimes unnecessarily frivolous nature of much of what they were doing - the group's music was, in his own words, *"too unfocussed"*. Mike's tendencies were towards music that was more polished in sound and performance. (There was nothing necessarily wrong with such an ideal, but it was one which he would develop, much later, during the second creative period of his own career, to a point where he often sacrificed feeling to clinical, professional technique). Mike told Kevin that he would leave the band unless Kevin rectified the situation by ceasing to drink, ceasing to play any of the guitar parts, and Lol Coxhill was dropped from the line-up. As a music press journalist later observed, Kevin had come to rely so much on Mike's guitar work that he gave in, *"and the result was that the humour, spontaneity and surprise element all went out of the band"*.

Taken aback by the sudden and uncharacteristic ultimatum from his talented but normally withdrawn young guitarist, Kevin agreed to stop drinking and playing, and told Lol he had to go. *"I was fired"*, Lol said soon afterwards. He seemed unaware of Mike's role in his dismissal: *"I think Kevin just wanted to change the whole style of the band and that was it. I'm really glad to be out of it really, because I was getting a bit fed up reading in various magazines that I was a very funny man who was quite a good player, when I think it was rather the other way around. I was in a position where I was told where to be a funny man, and I don't like to do it to order very much"*.

Kevin decided to disband The Whole World as such and continue as more of a solo artist. He still retained Mike and David Bedford, however, whom he augmented with bass player Andy Robertson and drummer William Murray, whom Mike appears to have introduced into the band, Murray being a friend of his brother, Terry. Kevin and the others played Llanelli Technical College on 29th April; Chelmsford, on the opposite side of the country on the following night; and the Festival Of Life for the Campaign For Nuclear Disarmament on Easter Sunday.

The last gig that the reconstituted band played was at The Temple in London on 10th July. It was a particularly miserable experience for Kevin, and after it he broke up the group. He felt that The Whole World had started well, reached a peak, and that its second incarnation wasn't going to get any better. *"In fact it got worse. I stopped playing and just sang, but I felt a bit of a twit without an instrument. I got more and more drunk and despairing, and the gigs got worse. There were practical hang-ups ...we weren't getting paid"*. He had grown tired of the constant gigging, especially all the hanging around before they went on stage, and he was finding that shows had become mundane and had lost the sense of celebration that he sought.

Kevin also felt that relations within the band had deteriorated beyond repair: *"It was getting very bad - it just wasn't working, particularly between Mike ... and myself. He wanted more and more to do his own ideas"*.

Mike explained: *"We toured for over two years, but I found that a bit miserable ... we didn't have much money and we travelled around in the back of a Transit van with no window. You tend to get a bit miserable and get a bit drunk and wish you were somewhere else"*. Again, this had repercussions on the standard of the band's performances which he disliked: *"We were trailing everywhere to gigs, but technically and creatively the music became abysmal. People would get drunk, we'd struggle to find the right notes, so we'd turn up the amplifier and the feedback and do somersaults"*.

But most importantly, Mike wanted to pursue his own musical ideas: *"by the end of it I really wanted to start my own group, to start making my own music, and to play guitar. But at the beginning I was very happy to be a bass player. It was a very good experience"*.

He was also having continuing emotional problems, and not just the pain he felt over his childhood experiences. *"I got mixed up in drugs, too, because it was fashionable and everyone was so bored. Pot, LSD, all of it... Towards the end I had a total panic attack. I couldn't carry on. I was rarely meeting any honest, sincere person, only people who were on drugs or without hope. The music business seemed like a wilderness. I knew I'd got to change. Kevin rented a house in Tottenham, and we all lived there. He lent me a tape recorder and I started work on Tubular Bells"*.

Chapter 3

Tubular Bells

One of the main reasons why the demise of The Whole World came about, as Kevin and Mike indicated, was because the latter wanted increasingly to pursue his own musical ideas. There was one in particular, which he had long had, *"about doing one long piece on an album"*. He visualised this long composition as being, unusually, completely instrumental, with an orchestral effect.

He had been encouraged in this towards the end of the group's existence by composer David Bedford. Like Kevin and Mike, Bedford had come to find the travelling, sleeping in the band's van, and the hours on end sitting around in dressing rooms wearing. It was in long hours such as these that he would talk to Mike about the piece he wanted to create: *"I suggested composers he could listen to and suggested books on notation because he wanted to learn how to write it down - I was involved only marginally in the very, very early stages. He bought some of the records I suggested - Delius and Debussy - but ... I'm sure he would have found those pieces anyway"*.

When the group had broken up, Mike had got Kevin's two-track tape recorder and borrowed an organ (probably from Bedford). Although he already had a few bits and pieces that he had composed, when he switched on the organ the first thing that he played was the sequence that appeared at the beginning of the later LP. He then just started to build it up from there, adding his electric guitar and bass, and, later, his acoustic guitar, recording what he was doing on a home demo tape.

After he had left the band, Mike remained in London, where, without the income from regular Whole World gigs he was soon reduced to penury. He was living in a 'horrible flat' in Victoria, *"and having to sneak into the kitchen to scrape up the remains of other people's meals"*.

Sitting alone in his room on one occasion, in what he afterwards characterised as a *"very sensitive condition"*, he heard Sibelius' Fifth Symphony which led to his inspiration for some of the mood he wanted to create on his piece. He explained: *"I'd had a very painful growing up... and I had so much energy, not knowing how to use it. I saw much unbelievable beauty in Sibilius, not tranquil, but a huge and powerful beauty. It seemed to me what life ought to be like and wasn't"*. Listening to the last movement of the piece, the most melodic and exhilarating, he experienced briefly what he later called *"a very wonderful state of mind"*; this only lasted about ten minutes, but, he said, it had *"a tremendous effect"* on him. Accordingly, he decided to attempt to recreate a similar state of mind through his own composition. He wanted to do so in order to replace his continuing state of emotional disquiet with a comparably beautiful and energetic state to that which the classical piece had all too temporarily instilled in him.

Sibelius was not his only source of inspiration, Mike recalled: *"I looked in my record collection and I thought, there is nothing there that I really want to listen to today, so I made some music out of all the bits and pieces that I'd liked in other music"*. He did not simply copy the latter, but borrowed the general ideas behind the parts that he liked, and reworked them to his own taste.

As well as working in his London flat, Mike also returned to the Oldfield family home in Hornchurch, and did some recording there. (His finished demo tape included the sound of his mother's vacuum cleaner in the background).

The technical process by which Mike made his demo was unorthodox, as Melody Maker journalist Karl Dallas later explained:

"he didn't just produce simple mono tapes, building up the texture of sound by "bouncing" from one track to another, which is the normal way you can do these things on any reasonably sophisticated recorder ... he did the whole thing in stereo, using bits of cardboard to block off the erase head

and pressing buttons that were never intended by the engineers who designed it".

Mike explained: "I'd always loved orchestral music, but I was never any good at methodical learning, so studying composition was out"- David Bedford's books on notation do not seem to have worked out for him- *"That and a boyhood fascination with gadgets, led me to try and do it all with a tape recorder"*.

When it was finished, Mike took his twenty-minute tape, and went on to do the rounds of the record companies. These included Harvest EMI, the label The Whole World had been with: *"to begin with they were very interested, but something happened. Maybe somebody didn't like it or thought it was too big a chance to take"*. He then brought it to CBS, who told him that the long, completely wordless instrumental just wasn't marketable. *"At one point I was almost in complete despair. I'd go and drown my sorrows in a pub and sit for hours meditating on my plight"*. After CBS's rejection of his tape, he said, *"I decided I wouldn't go to any more, and got this tall, forceful Scotsman to take it to WEA for me. Apparently they liked it but weren't too sure"*.

Still living on the breadline, Mike turned his thoughts to earning a living. At one point he considered applying for what he termed 'artistic asylum' in the Soviet Union, because he had heard that they provided state subsidies for musicians. Instead, he took up session work. It was in this capacity that, in September 1971, he arrived at Virgin Records' just opened Manor studio, deep in the Oxfordshire countryside. He was with minor American artist Arthur Lewis and his band, who went there to record demo tracks. Luckily, Mike brought along his tape.

The studio was the latest business venture of young entrepreneur Richard Branson and his partner Simon Draper of the Virgin Records chain of stores. Branson had set up Virgin in 1969, as mail-order record retailers, offering substantial discounts on all LPs. Careful attention to otherwise poorly available material drew a great number of rock record buying public, so that Branson was then in a position to set up a group of record stores. These carried on the discounts policy, and did well, as Branson explained, *"by halving our profit margin and doubling our sales"*.

At the instigation of acquaintance Tom Newman, an ex-musician and now an aspiring producer, Branson's next enterprise was to branch out into studio ownership. He bought a sixteenth-century manor house at Shipton-on-Cherwell and proceeded to have the coach house converted into a recording studio, designed by Newman. From the start, this move had been envisaged as part of the parallel development of a record label.

Mike's week-long session at The Manor with Arthur Lewis did not go well, mainly, he felt, because Lewis was not very talented.

But afterwards, Mike played his demo to some of the studio staff, who brought it to the attention of Tom Newman and Richard Branson. They liked it and asked if they could keep it because they were not at this stage ready to go ahead with their plans for the record label, but wanted to hold on to it so that they could consider it in the event that they decided to proceed.

Meanwhile, Kevin Ayers had returned to England to record an LP, following a not entirely successful stay living and performing with David Allen's group, Gong, in France, and he wanted to use again the talents of his ex-Whole World colleagues Mike and David Bedford. It is not clear when exactly recording took place, but Kevin seemed to indicate that his album was wholly or partially complete by mid-October 1971. Mike may have started to work with Kevin in September, shortly after his visit to The Manor. Kevin explained to Steve Peacock of Sounds the reason why he had re-enlisted Mike in terms which glowingly praised the almost entirely unknown musician: *"I'm using Mike a lot... because I really dig his playing — he's the best guitarist for me after Hendrix; absolutely brilliant"*.

Kevin's LP *Whatevershebringswesing*, featured Mike, David Bedford, Dave Dufort and William Murray. Despite the presence of some of The Whole World among the players, the album is a melancholy affair. Kevin was, he himself explained, simply quite miserable at the time.

Mike plays on three of the LP's tracks, the first and most remarkable of which is *Song From The Bottom Of A Well*, which dramatically closes the first side, and which justifies Kevin's praise for Mike's guitar playing skills. The song exemplifies Kevin's fall into a pit of despair, for which the well is a metaphor. He sings, slow, throaty, and brooding, over Mike's incredible, wrenching, machine-like guitar noise. At the instrumental break Mike makes his guitar scrape and scream, and, later, makes it sound like an abbatoir blade, as it rises ever higher and sharper until, suddenly, the track is cut. Mike's extremely frantic playing style is unusual for him, and he has never since repeated it.

The second side of the LP starts with the gentle title track, which Mike begins by playing a soft bass riff, to which he then adds his electric guitar. Kevin sings about his searching for a friend so that he can put the recent past behind him. He is joined by Robert Wyatt on harmony vocals for the chorus, in which he exhorts everybody to drink some wine and let the good times draw near. These sentiments, however, are delivered in such a manner that the possibility of 'good times' seems rather remote. Mike plays a long, sad, delicate, gently melodic break that matches the mood of the song well. Kevin, particularly pleased with it and his bass part, praised him for them with an LP cover credit.

Mike features again on *Champagne Cowboy Blues*, a drink-sodden song about the need for love to be free from jealousy. It is interrupted by an excerpt from the happy, uptempo music of the title track from Kevin's first LP, *Joy Of A Toy*, in what is obviously Kevin's nostalgic reminiscence of the good times. Mike accompanies the song on guitar,and plays a suitably depressed solo.

The album also features some bass that was originally by Mike, but which is played now by Kevin. This occurs on *There Is Loving/ Among Us/There Is Loving*, which uses Mike's bass part from what had been The Whole World's *Butterfly Dance*.

When the record was released, in January 1972, Sounds' Steve Peacock praised the title track as *"a beautiful piece of writing, nicely paced, with a spot on vocal harmony by Robert Wyatt, and a superb guitar solo by Mike Oldfield"*.

Like Kevin, David Bedford was also recording an LP in October 1971, for the Dandelion label, and he asked Kevin to sing on one track, and Mike to play bass on the title track, *Nurse's Song With Elephants*. The latter was inspired by another poem from William Blake's *Song's Of Experience*.

The bulk of the piece, like that of *The Garden Of Love*, consists of a section of music followed by a vocal setting of the poem. The former is played on several acoustic guitars. Bedford gets the musicians to use the sounds of the guitars in unconventional ways. Fingers slid across strings and picking and strumming are valued for the sounds they produce, not for a melody. The odd sounds they produce in this way are arresting. They confuse and break down one's preconceived notions of music, melody and the guitar. Any attempt by the listener to find a clear melody is made to collapse, and one has to open oneself in a different way. If this is done, the music becomes very sensually affective.

Then a guitar melody does appear. The effect of this, after such a long time, is remarkable. Mike's bass - so typically rich and resonant - begins, and a sadly uncredited female vocalist sings the poem. A new and delightful acoustic guitar break follows, with Mike's bass in the background, and the second verse of the poem is repeated with Mike's bass the only accompaniment.

The contact Mike had with David and Kevin at this time continued when, for an Old Grey Whistle Test television performance towards the beginning of 1972 Kevin temporarily reformed the Whole World line-up with David, Dave Dufort, Lol Coxhill, and Mike, on bass. They gave a fairly regular rendition of *May I?*.

Kevin then took the former band members into a studio in February to re-record *Lady Rachel*, from his *Joy Of A Toy* LP. The new version, however, is inferior to the original, sounding lethargic. Mike's bass is minimal and David Bedford's flute, brass and string arrangement does not add anything to the song, which had been fine without one.

The re-arrangement of *Lady Rachel* for orchestral instruments seems to have been a result of Kevin's long held desire to add a medium-sized orchestral ensemble to the rock instruments and do grander versions of some of his old songs. Accordingly, he retained Mike, Bedford, Coxhill and Dufort, augmented them with bass player Archie Leggatt, and got Bedford to create new arrangements for two French horns, two flutes, two violins, a trombone, a cello and a double bass for a Radio One In Concert set. This recording has since been released. Unfortunately, as with the re-recording of *Lady Rachel,* the orchestrations overwhelm the genuine character of the original material, and the band were generally tidier in their playing than in their heyday; the recording, is not, therefore, a good reflection of the more anarchic approach of their early live performances. Although *Whatevershebringswesing* is featured, Kevin plays Mike's guitar part for this, and Mike only appears on *Why Are We Sleeping?*. He fingerpicks his electric guitar delicately, almost as if he was playing Spanish guitar. His particular style here is noteworthy, because he was to re-employ it later on the last tune of the second side of *Tubular Bells,* where he played very similar guitar phrases.

Soon afterwards, Kevin was planning on touring with the group and ensemble. It is not clear if Mike fancied this again; in any case, the cost of the venture proved prohibitive, and David Bedford had part-time teaching posts in London (at Queens College girls' school and Lincoln Art College) so he could not tour, although he did do the occasional gig with Lol Coxhill. Kevin went on the road instead with a new electric band, Gong's guitarist Steve Hillage taking the place Mike had had with Kevin.

Mike went his own way again. He did occasional jobs here and there, including playing a couple of gigs with blues-rocker Alex Harvey, and even playing guitar for the American hippy musical Hair in London's Shaftesbury Theatre.

He was involved in the latter when, in September 1972, Virgin Records' Simon Draper called him. They had decided to go ahead with their record label, and Draper approached him as their first possible signing. The young man was invited to The Manor, where Draper gave him a week's trial period to see if he could come up with something worthwhile.

Using his original demo tape as a guide to recording, Mike worked with studio staff members Tom Newman and Simon Heyworth. Newman was an interesting character, with a Russian

Jewish father and an Irish mother. He was an unusual colleague for Mike in that his was the exact opposite of Mike's painfully introverted personality. He was full of extravagant ideas and had a wonderful sense of humour, while a journalist later described Mike as *"a depressive who at that time hardly spoke to anyone"*. With Newman, however, Mike soon found he could be a little more at ease, and he was to come to love the former's grandiose and whimsical nature. The three worked hard during that first week and got most of the first side of what was then simply called *Opus One* recorded and rough-mixed. Mike commented afterwards that Draper and Branson approved of it, and that things therefore became a lot easier for him from then on.

At last, Mike was to be able to experience the feeling of being able to pursue only his own varied musical ideas, unhindered by those of others; *"I'd been frustrated in my efforts to be creative for several years, and I'd finally got the chance to do what I liked"*.

After having approved of Mike's work, Richard Branson sat down with him and typed out a contract, under which Mike was to make ten albums for Virgin, for which he would be paid a royalty of five per cent.

Once the trial period was over, Mike used up all the spare studio time that was available for the next six months. What happened was that he was allocated a particularly small room at The Manor (where everyone who came to record was accommodated in more lavish terms free of charge) and was allowed to go into the studio in the odd hours when no-one else had booked it, or late at night. He thus avoided having to pay the standard studio fee of £20 an hour, which he was in no position to pay. Working like this was also convenient for Newman and Heyworth because they, too, lived in at The Manor.

The recording of the LP, as distinct from the later mixing, took three weeks. During the last fortnight, Mike had also to compose the second side of the record. For this he included some of the parts of his demo tape that had not formed the basis of the first side, and the acoustic guitar piece he had composed when he was fifteen as his way of influencing his distressed emotional condition. In all, recording the LP involved a previously unheard of 274 overdubs and about 2,000 drop-ins (to correct bum notes and for minor repair work).

"The main problem was linking up the various bits and pieces I had worked out. It was David Bedford who showed me how to do that", Mike said. *"There are basically two linking themes, one quite high notes and another a very low pulse going dum-dum, dum-dum, coming at you all the way through"*.

The finished LP was mixed several times, and, Mike recalled

several years later, that was an enormous job because computerised mixing desks had not yet been devised. Newman, Heyworth and himself mixed it four times, each occasion taking a couple of weeks.

This technical work with Newman and Heyworth marked his first experience of studio production. But it was a side of recording to which he took immediately because of a latent concern with the varieties and qualities of sound, and his own perfectionist streak: music had not only to be played perfectly, it had to be similarly recorded. In subsequent years he would take over control of the production as well as the playing side of his recordings.

As well as composing and recording the remarkable piece, Mike's equally surprising achievement lay in his playing the entire thing mostly alone. And all of these things represented a quantum leap in his musical development that could not have been imagined given his previous work,. fine though that was. Mike played acoustic and electric guitars, piano and organs, and some fairly simple, orchestral percussion, such as timpani, glockenspiel, and, of course, tubular bells. He worked solo for several reasons: he could not afford to pay musicians to play for him; his natural talent for music meant that he had been able to pick up instruments other than the guitar (for which he possessed the greatest abilities) and play them with reasonable proficiency; and because he did not want to trust the music to people who would not have the deep emotional stake in it that he had.

Despite its heavily solo nature, however, the record was enhanced by a handful of other people. Vivian Stanshall, the most eccentric member of the comic rock group The Bonzo Dog Doo-Dah Band acted as a mock master of ceremonies for one section, and drummer Steve Broughton, of Mike's one-time musical acquaintances The Edgar Broughton Band, played on another; both men had been recording at The Manor at the same time as Mike's LP was being made, and had been invited to take part. Mike also brought in his sister Sally, who, along with Mundy Ellis (once Richard Branson's girlfriend and then the manager of The Manor House) comprised The Girlie Chorus (whose name Mike drew from a similarly titled chorus on one of the tracks on The Whole World's album). Lindsay Cooper, from the group Henry Cow, who were also recording at the studio, played some string basses, and a little flute was provided by Jon Field, whom Tom Newman brought into the proceedings, Field having played in Newman's 1969 psychedelic band July.

The nervous tension that resulted as a byproduct of playing, recording, mixing, caring about and living with the LP had often been relieved by Tom and Mike's playing wrestling matches on the lawn of The Manor, and enhanced by their emotional states, made weirder by their illicitly drinking a good deal of Virgin's cellar-full of Jameson whisky. It was during one of the pair's more formal drinking sessions in the pub, towards the end of recording, that Mike had hit upon the idea of bringing in Vivian Stanshall as an MC, to announce the entrance of a series of instruments. He and Tom also decided to have him at the end of the LP, doing a drunken commentary on what he saw in various rooms in The Manor, over an unusual recording of *The Sailor's Hornpipe.* Microphones were placed in various rooms and stairways in the house, the tape machine was turned on, and the trio set off, Stanshall babbling, Mike on mandolin and Tom on acoustic guitar, all equally sozzled, the sound of their music and their footsteps appearing and receeding as they enter and leave the rooms and move around the microphones.

Mike liked it, but Virgin, company publicist Al Clark later explained, thought it a little too offbeat to include on an album by an unknown artist, and Mike and Tom replaced it with an instrumental version. Virgin's decision was an example of the record company's attempt to mould Mike's LP to a form they felt would stand more chance of some commercial success; Mike recalled in 1980 that at the French international music fair, the Midem Festival, in January 1973, *"there was a big debate about whether Tubular Bells should have words on it. It would have flopped if it had. There's no point in me writing lyrics because I can't sing, but I think I can compensate by playing instruments very lyrically".*

Mike had definite ideas about what he wanted to achieve on his album. At the most basic level he has said that he wanted to make something on his own that sounded large-scale and orchestral in some of its effects, and that he wanted to prove that he was more than just a bass player.

His motivation was, in fact, far deeper and more personal than this. He explained: *"I suppose you could say that I had a vision of what I wanted to do, but it was a vision of security and warmth and safety because I felt so unsafe".* Mike composed the piece partly as a way of escaping the still painful feelings about his life that his childhood had left in him, just as he had sublimated his childhood unhappiness by immersing himself in his music, which he said he used as a way of retreating into his own little world. With his LP he similarly wanted to create a world of music, a sanctuary in opposition to the real world and his current painful feelings: *"I was creating a musical environment where I knew all the things there and I felt secure"*, he said later. *"That music was an escape. I created a reality for myself, a different world, a world of sound. It was more comfortable there than in real life. Tubular Bells reflected my complete rejection of reality".*

Mike's feelings infused the music of *Tubular Bells* and following compositions with a highly emotional undercurrent, and they account for some of their impact: they are in part a catharsis of feelings of pain, longing and release through varied melodies, sounds and moods, both gentle and energetic. In this fashion they affect the open-hearted listener, producing in him or her contrary feelings of melancholic contemplation and joyful release.

By the end of recording and mixing, Mike was so tired that he was unsure whether or not he had been successful in his aims for the record. On the release of the LP he was able to look back at it with more equanimity, and said, *"What I was trying to do was create an atmosphere of complete tranquillity. I haven't succeeded entirely in what I wanted to do, but it works pretty well, I think"*.

The LP was finished by December 1972, and then cut at Apple. Some word of the content of Mike's record was given at this stage to the New Musical Express, to whom Virgin described it as *"classically orientated and very melodic"*.

The album was scheduled to be released in February 1973, but Virgin held up the release to bring it closer to a promotional concert of the piece which they wanted to take place at the Queen Elizabeth Hall in June.

Tubular Bells comprises two long twenty-minute sides of continuous instrumental music. But it is a whole made up of many parts: the first side is made up of ten tunes presented in different ways for twenty three sections, while the second side consists of only eight tunes in seven sections, one tune being a modification of that which precedes it.

Great effects are achieved by segueing the tunes. Not only does one delight in each of Mike's beautiful melodies, but also in the way in which each transition between tunes is done. One is sensually affected by each of the ever-increasing number of parts, in a heightening of awareness and emotion, until one has been led to a deeply satisfying experience of the whole.

The technique of the addition of one or more instruments to each section is equally attractive. Overdubbing of the same instrument, or Mike's recording of speeded-up or slowed-down instruments also creates striking and unusual varieties of sound effect.

The record begins with a piano and glockenspiel tune, in uncommon 9/8 time. This has a particularly hypnotic quality: a style of playing that Mike uses often on the LP. Mike may have absorbed this technique from similar effects on *A Rainbow In Curved Air* (1970), by American minimalist composer Terry Riley, whom Mike said he had heard before he made his own album. But to suggest that Mike's piece as a whole is a copy of Riley's is unfair - Mike's work is so much more varied that Riley's and depend far more on sectional tunes. David Bedford later defended Mike from such criticism, explaining that in Riley's work, repetitive musical figures were used principally for their hypnotic effect, while on *Tubular Bells* Mike employed such a technique as the basis for so much more, so that to fault the piece on such grounds was not valid.

The piano tune which opens the LP is augmented, in succession, by bass accompaniment, and staccato flashes of organ. After a while, there is a transition to another piano tune with mandolin-like guitars, followed by piano and acoustic guitar, and another piano and glockenspiel part.

The first side of the album is played mostly on piano, with, surprisingly, Mike's electric guitar appearing less prominently that one might have imagined it would following his guitar work for The Whole World. But after a swirling transition, which seems to miraculously dissolve what has gone before, there is a rough electric guitar section. There follows a bassy-sounding part with slowed-down organ, and piano takes over again, in two tunes with acoustic guitar. This guitar is well done, in a characteristic mixture of strength and delicacy.

A bridge made by introducing bass leads to a section using speeded-up electric guitars, a rough electric guitar and a brief choral-style backing. A sudden climax, and a new electric and acoustic tune races along. This ends as abruptly as it had begun, to be followed by the sound of a single bell toll. After a quiet acoustic part, bass and electric guitar begin the 'finale'.

Owing to Mike's visualisation, while he was in The Whole World, of the piece that eventually became *Tubular Bells* as a composition intended to last one side on an album, the 'finale' appears at the end of the first side. This consists of the gradual addition of instrument upon instrument in a single tune, with Vivian Stanshall announcing the entrance of each. Mike's inspiration to add Stanshall sprang from his familiarity with the latter's similar introduction of instruments on the Bonzo's own *Intro and Outro*. Stanshall announces 'grand piano', 'reed and pipe organ', 'glockenspiel', 'bass guitar' (a new riff added to an original bass) and 'double speed guitar'. (The latter was to become one of Mike's favourite devices, as he explained in 1979: *"I do quite a lot of stuff at half-speed. I then play it back at the normal speed and get a funny effect; a different insight ... That's how I get a mandolin-like sound"*). This is followed by 'two slightly distorted guitars', 'mandolin', 'Spanish guitar, and introducing acoustic guitar', 'plus ... tubular bells!', the bells clanging loudly while the female chorus moans quietly in the background. (The famous bells are a set of eighteen tubes of different lengths which hang vertically and which when hit with a hammer each give out a different note). This section is followed by a coda, a lovely acoustic guitar part, which has a particular 'live' quality.

The second side of the record begins with two organ and acoustic guitar tunes. The first of these demonstrates again the hypnotic and repetitive quality that is such a notable feature of this and subsequent LPs. It is restful and tranquil and is among the most beautiful parts of the whole record. The little piano tune that is added on top of it is incredibly sensitive. Here the music most clearly appears as a self-comforting exercise for Mike, and it has a similar effect on the listener. There follows the guitar tune that Mike composed when he was fifteen as a way of influencing his feelings. The organ that goes with it is particularly gentle. Wonderful female choral-style vocals enter, soothing all cares, like a mother's lullaby.

Then there's a Scottish kind of tune played on electric guitars that sound like bagpipes. This acts as a useful prelude to the following 'caveman' section, because its dark timpani pattern sounds hauntingly primitive, like something that might have been played at the dawn of man. The Scottish piece then changes into the caveman part, with Mike grunting and growling in a parody of speech. Steve Broughton plays rock-style drums, and Mike some unusual piano and rasping guitar. Mike continues to howl intermittently and the whole thing ends in a screaming climax. This section is one of the more obvious examples of Mike's cathartic musical therapy, a release of his energy and frustration, just as the quieter, acoustic sections are, in part, releases of sadness and yearning.

All goes quiet after this and there is a long, warbling organ and electric guitar piece, a sad, swirling thing. It is another really special part of the record - there are points where the guitars eddy like waves, which are almost sublime in their effects, as one balances precariously within a characteristic Oldfield admixture of sadness and joy. This effect is extended by the organ, which opens out, fan-like, like an aural sunrise.

The album closes with the jolly, strictly instrumental version of *The Sailor's Hornpipe, played faster and faster on mandolin, acoustic guitar, organ and string basses. Its presence does tend, however, to disrupt the reasonably unified mood which this second side of the record has managed to create.*

At some stage during the LP's recording the working title of *Opus One* was jettisoned in favour of *Tubular Bells*, after the bells at the finale at the end of the first side. The album was subsequently packaged in its distinctive cover of a seascape and tubular bell, which suggested the sometimes ethereal nature of the music, while the blurbs on the back of the sleeve hinted at some of the occasionally humorous spirit of the LP.

Tubular Bells was released on 25th May 1973, the first record on the new Virgin label. It was issued with Gong's *Radio Gnome Invisible Part 1*, the German rock band Faust's collection of live and rehearsal material, *The Faust Tapes*, and *Manor Live*, a session record featuring among others, Lol Coxhill, and Ollie Halsall, who was afterwards to become Kevin Ayer's guitarist.

Critical reaction to the remarkable LP was enthusiastic. Sound's Steve Peacock wrote a feature on the Virgin releases:

It is not often that you get in a batch of the first releases from a new record company and find among them an album that not only strikes you with its freshness of ideas and excellence of execution, but surpasses your expectations of the artist concerned. But Mike Oldfield's *Tubular Bells*... does all that and more.

Peacock, who had been a strong fan of The Whole World, continued;

Unless you were a devotee of Kevin Ayers' Whole World or are a close scrutineer of session credits, Mike Oldfield may be an unfamiliar name, but knowing that he was making a solo album, I was expecting to hear a good album that features some outstanding guitar playing.

I was not expecting two uninterrupted sides of complex, interlocking carefully woven music that works its way through an enormous dynamic and emotional range.

Peacock concluded: *"I can't think of another album that I'd as unhesitatingly recommend to everyone who's likely to read this"*.

The article carried a Virgin publicity photograph of Mike, the first photograph of him that most of the general public would have seen, the young man with long, windswept hair and sparse beard and looking slightly truculent.

The reaction of Al Clark, then of the NME, was similar to Peacock's. His expectations of an LP by Mike were also coloured by his knowledge of Mike's past work with Ayers:

having no further evidence of his abilities, it was not unreasonable to expect his first album to consist of, at best, one dexterously protracted guitar solo, or, at worst, a collection of songs delineating his juvenile fetishes.

But, Clark continued; *"Tubular Bells rapidly evaporates such notions"*, and he felt, Oldfield is consistently inventive within established territory, so that, without departing from a framework familiar to rock-oriented ears... he achieves a multi-layered intricacy which is absorbing at every level.

He finished,

Tubular Bells...is a superlative record which owes nothing to contemporary whims. It is one of the most mature, vital, and humorous pieces of music to have emerged from the pop idiom. One hearing should provide sufficient proof.

Radio One DJ John Peel said that it was the finest record he had heard in many years, and was so impressed that he reverentially played the entire forty-minute piece on his show.

Meanwhile, the date for the concert premiere of *Tubular Bells* had been fixed for 25th June, a date that was approaching rapidly. The concert had been Virgin's idea, the record company having conceived of it as a promotional device at a time when they were by no means sure that the LP would be a success. Mike had complied with the scheme, but afterwards became beset with terrible doubts about the feasibility of trying to reproduce live the effects of the studio-created, multi-overdubbed LP. The arrangements for the concert had already been long set up when he told Richard Branson that he did not want to do it. Branson, having become, with Newman, one of Mike's few trusted friends, tried everything to cajole him into participating, without success, until, desperate, he offered Mike his Bentley; Mike agreed.

Mike subsequently managed to become a little more enthusiastic about the concert, as he sought and worked with musicians whom he felt were capable both of playing his music and learning it quickly. Given the large amount of organ on the record, he approached Steve Winwood, who had been recording at the Manor, and played him the LP. Winwood liked it, but after agreeing to take part, had to withdraw as a result of other commitments.

Mike recruited members of the group Henry Cow to play at the concert. He felt he was fortunate in this, because he had actually worked with them previously, having engineered for them a couple of times while he had been at The Manor. (The first such occasion hadn't been auspicious: he wiped almost a complete track by mistake).

The completely gathered ensemble consisted of Mike (electric guitar), Kevin Ayers (bass), David Bedford (piano), Steve Broughton (drums), Vic Stanshall (M.C), Pierre Moerlen (percussion), Steve Hillage (electric guitar), Ted Speight (acoustic guitar), Mick Taylor of The Rolling Stones (electric guitar), Fred Frith of Henry Cow (electric guitar), and the other members of that band, John Greaves, Tim Hodgkinson, and Geoff Leigh (instruments unknown, but probably bass and two wind instruments respectively). David Bedford also arranged a choir and string section for the performance.

Almost all of these musicians came as a result of Mike's recent musical contacts and activities. Broughton, Stanshall and Field had appeared on his album. Bedford and Ayers were of course old colleagues, and Kevin brought with him both Pierre Moerlen and

Steve Hillage, both of whom he knew as a result of his temporary association with Gong. Mike knew Ted Speight from the latter's playing on a track on Lol Coxhill's *Ear Of The Beholder*. It was Richard Branson who asked Mick Taylor to become involved, sensing a small publicity coup in procuring one of the Rolling Stones.

Mike taught each of the musicians their part individually, then got them all together for rehearsals. He commented, *"Mick Taylor was very good, he learnt it by ear, quicker than anybody else. David Bedford was important because the piano was central in the music. He did a lot of work on his own, learning it off the record. I only saw him a couple of times before the final rehearsal and he'd written it all out"*. Bedford had in fact scored the entire LP.

Mike was very nervous about the upcoming concert: *"I'm terrified"*, he said. *"I don't know what is going to happen"*. He was not concerned with the gathered musicians' technical ability: *"The actual notes are quite simple. It's getting them to understand what I want. That's the bit that's going to be hard"*. He was anxious that the emotional nature and cathartic element of the music would be missed by the musicians, and that they would not be able to create the appropriately intense degree of feeling in the music, as he had done on the album.

Before the concert, Mike had begun to come before the attention of the music press, as a result of their unanimous critical praise for *Tubular Bells*. During these and later interviews, his insecure personality came more to light. He was interviewed for the first time by Karl Dallas for the June 23rd issue of Melody Maker. Mike mentioned very briefly his musical history with Sallyangie, whom Dallas had once seen live, his leaving the Whole World, and the genesis of his album and the forthcoming concert. But, Dallas reported,

when it came to transcribing the interview I did with him from my cassette recorder, I could hardly hear the replies to my questions, so hesitant and quiet were his replies. It was a friendly interview, I felt, even cosy, as he sprawled on his bed in his pad at the Manor recording studios where he seems to have taken up almost permanent residence, but after it was all over he confessed: "I feel as if I've been raped".

Mike's reaction at the end of the interview and his inability to talk other than in a whisper demonstrated a measure of his disturbed emotional condition.

The live performance of *Tubular Bells* took place on 25th June in the grandiose setting of the Queen Elizabeth Hall, one of the bastions of London's classical music culture. The concert consisted of the two parts of the music, separated by a half-hour interval. Among those in the audience were Mick Jagger, drawn probably as a result of Mick Taylor's appearance, John Peel, and the rock press journalists.

The latter afterwards thought that the concert had been generally successful, and singled out performances by Mick Taylor, Mike and Kevin Ayers for commendation, although there were quibbles about occasional mistakes and the varying sound balance.

Mike's experience at the concert was not good. He said later that he knew before the event that all the musicians were capable; *"the only question was whether we'd be able to create any atmosphere. I know we did in the second half, I'm not too sure about the first. I'm too frightened to listen to the recording of the concert"*. A few years later he confessed: *"The concert didn't please me.....I felt dejected as we played the final bars"*.

A description of himself at this time which he gave several years later suggests that his disappointment with the concert was due as much to his then troubled emotional state as it was to any real musical deficiencies. *"I just couldn't feel happy"*, he explained. *"If people said they liked me, I hated them. I remember when I did that thing at the Queen Elizabeth Hall...I stood on the stage at the end of the concert and looked at the audience. And they looked at me. And do you know what they did?...They actually applauded. I was amazed. I hated that concert. I thought we were terrible. I'd never had such a bad time on stage. And people came backstage after the concert and said they'd love it. I couldn't believe it. The only way I could even begin to enjoy it was by reminding myself how bad I thought it had been. I used to feel bad about everything. The more they loved it, the worse I thought it was. And that made me feel happy"*.

Tubular Bells meanwhile, had not only received critical acclaim, it was also becoming a popular success. It entered the album chart in mid-July and started its rise to number one. Mike had not expected the LP to be a particular success, and was, in any case, psychologically unprepared for, and bewildered by it. The album subsequently spent fifteen weeks in the top thirty, thirteen of these in the top ten, and remained in the ratings for two hundred and forty seven weeks. To date, it has sold over sixteen million copies worldwide.

Mike had made another, short, recording since the album had been finished. This was *Froggy Went A-Courting*, an introverted and childlike version of a traditional song, done in the same sensitive and overdubbed style as his LP. He and Bridget St. John sang, while he also played guitars, mandolin and bass. He was very fond of the song and wanted to have it released, but Virgin did not like it, and shelved it indefinitely.

He had also had ideas for a future album, and said in July that when he found somewhere to live he was going to set to work.

(Having finally moved out of The Manor, he was currently staying on Richard Branson's houseboat in London's Little Venice). He said of a new LP: *"it's got to be better than Tubular Bells, for my own sake anyway. Tubular Bells was really the first thing I'd done and it could have turned out so many different ways. A lot of it was just the first things I thought of"*. The ideas he's got at the moment were quite different, he said. *"I want the actual melodic structure of it to be more subtle and continuous. I think the first side of the album was bitty and quite a lot of it was based on fairly ordinary rock patterns"*. He now seemed over-acutely aware of faults which he felt existed on the album, complaining again: *"a lot of it's based on very ordinary clichés with just a slight twist or two - to give you an example, there's that bit near the beginning with a blues guitar riff with that organ on top of it. If it hadn't been for the organ part that wouldn't have been worth doing, not for me anyway. And the melodies are all a bit obvious, no subtlety there really. Also there's a lot of silly bits, which are OK, but they could have been more imaginative silly bits. I got quite upset about that really because bits they'd pick out to play on the radio or something, they'd pick the silly bits, and they only work when they're balanced by good bits either side. They (Virgin) were even thinking about releasing a silly bit as a single"*.

He said, revealingly, that, for him, the most important part of his album should have been the comforting organ and acoustic guitar section at the start of the second side. But he felt that it had not really worked well enough, although he thought that, at the concert, he was a little more successful in reaching the mood he had desired. Accordingly, he was later to go on and record a new LP that was almost a large form reexploration of that single organ and guitar part and its elusive mood. Mike was also to avoid including any humorous bits, and went on to do as he had planned in creating a generally more subtle, continuous piece of music.

Whatever about the faults Mike saw in *Tubular Bells*, the artistic achievement and critical and popular success of the album launched his career as a solo musician and composer. It also gave the insecure young man some encouragement for his future. *"It's a good start"*, he said in another interview in which he was reported as speaking at a pitch barely one decibel above a whisper, *"I just hope I can keep going and get better. I don't know"*.

Chapter 4

Success, Sanctuary, and Other Stories

In autumn 1973 Mike retreated to a country house on the Heredfordshire side of the border with Wales. He was attracted there by a dislike of London: the city acted as a constant background irritant to his sometimes fragile mental state. But where he had moved, he said, there was *"a lot more room to breathe and be normal"*.

Mike was pleased with the house. Inside and out, it was intended to resemble a ship; although the main rooms were big, with ceilings about twenty feet high, there were small bedrooms like cabins, and an outside balcony which was meant to represent a ship's bridge.

The house was situated on a large hill, and surrounded on all sides by National Trust land. This was of remarkable beauty and physical interest, with Offa's Dyke a few miles away and Radnor forest to the north. It was hilly, rolling country, and Mike's house looked out directly onto a high land formation known as Hergest Ridge, which straddled the border.

After he had bought the house, with proceeds from *Tubular Bells,* Mike returned briefly to London around the end of the year, to record a good TV studio performance of the first side of the album for the BBC's Second House programme. He played with a handful of the musicians who had appeared with him at the Queen Elizabeth Hall. The music was later wedded to some appropriately heady and romantic film images (like buttercups waving in the breeze) when it was broadcast in January 1974.

By that time the album was not only doing well at home, it was also making headway in the US, where it looked like being a similarly unexpected hit. This American success was somewhat ironic: when Richard Branson had brought the master tape of the then just completed LP to the 1973 Midem Festival to play to US record labels, he had met with the same uniform lack of interest that Mike had had to endure when he was bringing his original demo tape around the British companies. Branson found only one label representative who was willing to buy the rights to a US release of the album - and then only on condition that vocals were added to it - while the rest of the American companies did not even bother to put in a bid for the LP. In the end, however, it finally saw release through Atlantic records.

The US release came about almost entirely as a result of the tireless enthusiasm and promotional efforts of Richard Branson, who had now become Mike's manager as well as being his record label's boss. Branson's further efforts determined some of the extent of the success the LP was to reap after release: he managed to persuade the director of the satanic horror movie The Exorcist to use a four-minute excerpt from the album as the main theme for the film's soundtrack. Having already sold a very creditable two hundred thousand copies before the release of the film, with the latter's support the LP went on to do even better, and by March it entered the US Top Ten, subsequently rising to number one.

After he had moved into his house, it took Mike a long time to get down and compose a new album. He felt he was being pressured by Virgin, who were ringing him regularly, urging him to quickly produce a potentially lucrative follow-up LP, preferably something similar to *Tubular Bells.* They also wanted him to do interviews, to promote the LP, and to consider the idea of touring. Mike, however, was exhausted and bewildered by his recording work and its successful aftermath. It also struck him that some of the ideas he had had in the wake of *Tubular Bells* might not turn out as well as he had anticipated. Fortunately, his simply living in the country, and working there, suggested new ideas to him, and when he finally came to explore these, inspiration came to him reasonably easily. He would work on the composition for a few hours each day, going downstairs to play piano for a couple of hours; nothing worthwhile might emerge for weeks, he commented, until he might make a breakthrough. He also discovered that he did not necessarily need an instrument as a channel for inspiration: taking one of his then frequent country walks, for example, he suddenly became aware that he had been humming a tune to himself, one which he continued to call to mind on subsequent walks.

Mike's conscious and unconscious reactions to the physical landscape around his house greatly influenced his work and its later recording, the resulting album turning out to be generally peaceful and pastoral in mood. *Tubular Bells*, he felt, was composed in a harsh, urban environment, and he thought that some of the music reflected that. But the area around Hergest Ridge was *"smooth, uncluttered...lots of open countryside, smooth hills, a general feeling of smoothness and well being and non-hysteria, just a much nicer environment"*.

The work was also inspired by the music he was listening to at the time: lots of classical music, particularly choral music, and Delius, a composer of what have been called orchestral landscapes of Britain; Mike's LP, *Hergest Ridge*, is just such a piece.

He recorded home demo tapes of his ideas in a makeshift studio in his house: a room whose walls were simply soundproofed with egg boxes. *"I did two weeks working on it every day for the first side and two weeks for the second side - like keeping a diary in a way. I suppose there were five or six bits where I came to a full stop and didn't quite know where to go next, but finally it turned out quite coherent"*.

The experience of working on this second composition was a valuable one for Mike: he commented that he now knew enough to reject many ideas he would have used previously, that he was more aware of what was worth keeping and building on, and was more conscious of making the various tunes and bits and pieces that he decided to record relate better to each other.

After the demo tapes were finished, Mike started proper studio recording with Tom Newman at The Manor at the end of February. Most of the album was recorded very quickly, and by the middle of March the first side was finished and the second almost half done. Melody Maker's Steve Lake had a chance to watch Tom's working relationship with Mike at this time, observing, *"Newman keeps the session flowing smoothly and with an abundance of wit, and he seems at the Manor at least, to be the only person that can really communicate with Mike"*. Tom would point out mistakes of suggest a novel approach. At one stage he told Mike,

"The bass notes there make the sound too cluttered, why don't you just strum it, skiffle style?"

Oldfield looks surprised, but tries it, Newman is right. Mike climbs the wooden stairs to hear how it sounds on tape. One arm around his lady, Maggie, he listens in silence, and then nods.

The pair's relationship was not always smooth, however, as Tom Newman recalled: Mike was by now a little more confident, both personally and technically and Newman felt that his own presence was not as needed as previously; differences of opinion would lead to rows. The jovial spirit which had occasionally relieved the long work on *Tubular Bells*, then, became diluted, although the producer did recall a funny moment when Mike decided to climb into a grand piano to play a bit of sleigh bells.

Although recording had previously gone well, Mike was a week after Lake's visit, at the end of March, found by NME's Roy Carr to be *"in a state of stagnation and acute frustration"* about some of the results. He had removed one whole section of recorded music and was trying, Carr said, *"to work up some enthusiasm"* to finish the LP within the next two weeks. Mike said *"I'm going through a bad phase at the moment, things aren't going quite right for me. Nothing is turning out the way I want it and, at the moment, I'm not quite sure how to go about rectifying it"*.

The recording of a second album by Mike Oldfield had aroused a good deal of music press interest, and emissaries from the three main music papers sought Mike out in March. Sounds' Steve Peacock visited him at home soon after he had begun recording at The Manor, but found him to be more interested in talking about his hobby of flying model planes than about his music. Conversation itself proved to be onerous for Mike, and Peacock wrote afterwards that *"Interviewing Mike Oldfield ...is something like hard work: you feel like a dentist trying to extract a tooth with each question"*. He observed that Mike was *"genuinely one of the few people who seem totally out of place in the music business"*.

Mike's reticent personality surfaced again when Steve Lake visited the recording sessions at The Manor. Lake said of him: *"He's without doubt the most introverted artist I've ever met. In the thirteen hours I was at The Manor, he spoke barely a handful of sentences"*.

To Roy Carr the best selling your composer seemed to appear *"anonymous"*, and he characterised him as *"docile"* and *"about as animated as a day-old corpse"*. Mike's personality emerged at its most clearly bleak in his interview with Carr as he struggled to sort out the recording difficulties he was experiencing. Carr's casual remark about the misfortune that was said to befall anyone associated with The Exorcist caused an extreme reaction in Mike, who became quite disturbed, trembling and saying that such news frightened him.

Mike was certainly not a happy person. He said of himself at one point: *"Basically I'm very insecure. In fact, I'm a bit worried about what's gonna become of me"*. He confessed that he rarely got enough satisfaction from his long, complex recording work: *"If I do get any sense of achievement from what I'm doing, it's when I'm mixing the thing. After that I'm so exhausted I couldn't really care less about things. I'm a bit too dazed to know if I'm really satisfied or dissatisfied with what I've done"*. His new role as a composer lay heavy upon him, and he even talked about joining some group as a guitarist. He didn't fancy being pressured by Virgin into playing his music live again, feeling that other musicians would not be sympathetic or capable enough for him, and that it would be impossible to recreate live the complex, multi-overdubbed studio effects he employed. He also wanted to have his own studio somewhere in the country, where he could work entirely at his own pace.

One of the effects of Mike's childhood experiences had been to leave him with low self-esteem. As a result, his reaction to his success was the most unusual of his feelings. As he told Roy Carr, disconsolately: *"I always thought that once I had made my own album, held the cover in my hands and read my name, I'd think it was wonderful. But, do you know, it's not like that at all"*. Perversely, a reader's letter in one of the music papers, calling *Tubular Bells* the biggest load of rubbish ever recorded did affect him: *"Believe it or not, that letter made me feel quite good inside. The fact that somebody hated it was great, but quite honestly, I can't understand why that one letter had such a wonderful effect on me. It gave me much more satisfaction than any of those positive reviews I read"*. He said sadly of success: *"I really wish that it had changed me more than it has. I'm not very happy with myself as a person. I'd like a different brain, you know, I'm tired of the one that I've got. I find life a strain"*.

Meanwhile, the musical careers of Mike's old associates, David Bedford and Kevin Ayers, were continuing to develop, and Mike became involved with them again. By March Virgin had signed Bedford to their label and he was to record an LP of a composition then entitled *The Heat Death Of The Universe*, a piece which had been commissioned by the Royal Philharmonic Orchestra. Bedford asked Mike to play bass on the album, Mike Taylor to play guitar, and Steve Broughton to play drums. It was also intended that the same line-up would perform with the RPO at a live concert of the piece scheduled for early November. The LP recording was planned to be made before then.

Kevin Ayers had left Harvest and been enthusiastically recruited by Island Records. He used the money from the deal to buy and renovate David Allen's house in the Rhone valley, and after about a year he returned to England and recorded *The Confessions Of Dr Dream And Other Stories*. Sometimes in February or March Mike guested on one track, *Everybody's Some Time And Some People's All The Time Blues,* whose sad mood he picks up with his sympathetic, twangy guitar curlicues. The LP was later issued at the end of May.

Mike's own *Tubular Bells* was still doing very well in the US, and by April he had been booked by an American TV channel for a live in concert programme. This was probably arranged by Richard Branson or Virgin, not Mike, who was not well disposed to playing live; as a result, the event never went ahead.

It seems to have been around this time that Mike played on a track for Robert Wyatt's *Rock Bottom,* recorded at The Manor after Wyatt had been signed by Virgin. Wyatt's making the LP was something of an achievement: the drummer had written it during a six-month stay in hospital, after he had fallen out of an apartment window at a party given by Gong in the summer of 1973 and broken his back, leaving him paralysed below the waist and permanently bound to a wheelchair. The LP was an avant-garde, jazz-tinged affair, with Wyatt employing his own unusually sensitive and gifted vocal style, singing or making vocal noises or 'drones'. On *Little Red Robing Hood Hit The Road,* Mike comes in with a slow, piercing break, alternately scratchy or ringing, sending out pinpoints of sound around a main pattern, occasionally, 'dipping' in a strange and fascinating way. The track ends with Scottish poet Ivor Cutler intoning one of his typically bizarre pieces over a screeching viola accompaniment by Fred Frith.

In May Kevin Ayers and his band went on tour. Kevin planned to include a special concert at the Rainbow Theatre on 1st June, and he asked musical friends Brian Eno, John Cale, Nico, Robert Wyatt and Mike to play with him. Rehearsals for the show took place over three days in May.

The sell-out concert began with solo sets by Eno, Cale and Nico respectively, after which Kevin and his band performed, Robert Wyatt on percussion. Kevin then introduced Mike, to appreciative cheers from the audience, and Mike played with the ban on *Whatevershebringswesing,* with a long, ragged version of his memorable original guitar part. He made the odd mistake, but his guitar often 'sang' characteristically. Mike was better amplified and more assured as the ensemble played *Everybody's...Blues,* giving a beautiful, straining performance. After an interim when Mike left the stage while the others played some more, he returned to play with Kevin and Ollie Halsall, the trio building up a repetitive guitar refrain on *Dr. Dream Theme.* This segued into *Two Goes Into Four* and *I've Got A Hard-On For You,* with the trio strumming acoustic guitars.

A few weeks after the event, Island released well recorded selections from the event, as *June 1st 1974.* This included Mike on

Everybody's...Blues and *Two Goes Into Four*.

On 28th June, Virgin issued Mike's first single, the so-called 'theme' from *Tubular Bells*. They did so in order to counter an American single of highlights from the record as it had appeared on The Exorcist, which had been selling well in import shops. The official single was issued on the 28th to capitalise on the BBC's repeat of the Second House film of *Tubular Bells*, broadcast the previous night.

Rather than have an unrelated chunk of the LP released as a single, Mike had gone back into the studio for a week and re-recorded an excerpt from it. The music was drawn from the middle of the second side of the album, but its new treatment is different in structure, instrumentation, and mood. Mike made it into one unified, self-contained tune, in three instrumental settings. It is based on acoustic and electric guitars, and, surprisingly, on oboe, the use of which may have sprung from the latter's appearance on the on-going recording of *Hergest Ridge*. Oboe makes the tune quite pastoral this time. But what is most striking about the music is its tranquillity - as if Mike was now achieving more exactly the kind of peace-inducing atmosphere he had needed on *Tubular Bells*, and which he was to create on *Hergest Ridge*. Recording the single was thus an opportunity for him to make another attempt at getting the much desired effects upon his mental state which he felt he had only partly managed to create the first time.

The delightful *Froggy Went A-Courting* was put on the B'side of the single. It is sung in a soft, deadpan manner by Mike himself, Bridget St. John also appearing. Mike plays electric guitar, bass, simple piano, and speeded up mandolin, and is backed by an unnamed drummer and saxophone player, the latter closing the song with some mad saxophone doodlings. The charm of the song lies in its sweet, nursery-song lyrics, the gentle, happy vocals, and the general mood of child-like innocence and naivete, in which Mike seems utterly immersed.

The first 20,000 copies of what was called *Mike Oldfield's Single (Theme from Tubular Bells)* came in a picture cover, with a lovely black and white photograph of a wistful looking Mike, sitting on his haunches, feeding birds on the lawn of The Manor. The single went on to reach number thirty one in the chart.

By the end of June, the recording of *Hergest Ridge* was almost finished. *Spanish Tune*, a one-sided promotional single, was taken from the album and released on 7th July to increase radio and public interest in the forthcoming LP.

By this time Virgin had set 5th and 6th August for the recording at Barking Town Hall, Essex, of David Bedford's piece, which was now know as *Star's End*. (*"At one stage I wanted to call it The Heat*

Death of the Universe", Bedford recalled, *"but the Orchestra didn't like that"*). A public performance of the work was to be held on 5th November at the Royal Festival Hall, with Mike and Mick Taylor, Chris Cutler replacing Steve Broughton.

Virgin also decided to make an orchestral version of *Tubular Bells*, to be recorded from 6th to 10th September, at Barking Town Hall. The idea for an orchestral treatment came from Bedford, who was quite taken with the composition his former colleague had created. He had in 1973 re-scored part of it as *Variations On A Rhythm Of Mike Oldfield*, a percussion piece, to be played by three musicians on a remarkable eighty-four instruments, such as milk bottles, vacuum cleaners, jugs, and so on. He then finally persuaded Mike, who had been quite indifferent, to allow him to re-write and record *Tubular Bells* with a full orchestra. Bedford fancied the idea out of curiosity - just to see how it would turn out as a sort of 'classical' piece - and also out of a long held desire to break down the barriers between rock and classical music and their respective audiences. Virgin took up the idea enthusiastically, seeing in it the opportunity to tap a whole new market for Mike's composition.

To further extend sales of the original LP, Virgin issued a quadraphonic mix of it in early July. The sound quality of the release was nevertheless not very good.

The recording of David Bedford's *Star's End* took place in early August as planned. The piece, which had taken six months to write, was an example of his strong interest in astronomy. *"It's a depiction of the history of the universe"*, *he said*, *"from the first big bang, through settling down and civilising the galaxy to a state of complete entropy"*. This was a state in which *"everything runs down and you can't get energy once it's used up...It's what physicists used to think would happen to the universe, this head death, where everything would be the same temperature and everything would be totally disorganised and chaotic. There wouldn't be atoms coming together in any way. So I tried to translate this into music so that a straight four-in-a-bar rhythm would be the maximum order, and my way of writing down rhythms so that they are completely chaotic would be complete chaos. The thing changes from one to the other and back"*.

Bedford had felt that an intelligent combination of the sonorities of electric rock and orchestral instruments would suit the composition and so had scored the piece for orchestra, electric guitar, bass and drums. *"I wanted to have a marriage of electric and classical instruments and not just have them playing rock riffs. I won't mention any names but most of the marriages between rock and classical have been souped-up Mantovani-style orchestrations....boring, pretentious and unimaginative. I believe in using instruments as they have been built to be used, and electrical instruments sustain and bend notes"*.

Mick Taylor had become unable to participate, and he was replaced by Steve Hillage. At the sessions there was some trouble from his fuzz box, and possibly for this reason, he did not appear on the final LP, Mike, as well as playing bass, subsequently overdubbing the guitar at The Manor later in the month.

By this time, Virgin had planned orchestral performances of *Tubular Bells* and *Hergest Ridge,* to be scored by Bedford, at which it was proposed that Mike would play guitar. The concerts were planned to take place in late November or early December.

Now that *Hergest Ridge* was about to be released, Karl Dallas of Melody Maker arranged to meet Mike in mid-August. It was Dallas's second recent attempt at an interview: he had previously hidden a small microphone about his person and tried to do it all surreptitiously, feeling that outside a formal interview situation Mike might open up more; Mike found him out, however, and the interview came to nothing. This time he did not fare much better, and he found Mike *"not a terribly impressive figure, withdrawn, mumbling into the sparse beard on his chin"*, offering *"little in the way of spontaneous conversation"*. A long question of Dallas' on whether the various sections of *Hergest Ridge* were related to different parts of the Ridge itself brought forth a bald *"No"* from Mike, who then, Dallas reported, *"shut up like a clam"*.

If he was not able to talk to his quarry, Dallas was nevertheless able to observe him. He thought him little altered by fame in any way other than having become very financially secure. Apart from his having bought a Mercedes and his spending money on his model planes, he noted that Mike lived *"fairly frugally"*.

During the visit, Mike and his sister Sally, Richard Branson and his girlfriend, and Dallas travelled to a restaurant in Penhros, where they spent an evening. There happened to be a resident musician there, Leslie Penning, who played recorders, harpsichord and hurdy-gurdy. Mike subsequently took out an acoustic guitar and mandolin, and with Sally, the trio jammed together in front of an audience of dead-eyed American tourists on traditional folk songs like *She Moved Through The Fair* and *Barbara Allen*. Penning had no idea who Mike was, and after the group had all drunk several bottles of wine he told him: *"I understand you're quite famous but I know nothing at all about the sort of music you play. Nothing"*. Nevertheless, the pair played some mandolin-and-recorder or guitar-and-harpsichord duets together over the course of the evening. Mike talked to him about *Angie,* the tune he had learnt as a child, explaining to Penning, who was a classically trained musician, that it had the same harmonic structure as a certain piece of baroque music. The evening was not to be the last time that the pair would play together: Mike would visit the restaurant for further sessions, and a year later he invited Penning to record with him.

It was not until Dallas was about to leave Mike, the following day at The Manor, that he felt that he got close to him. The latter was overdubbing guitar onto *Star's End* when Dallas commented appreciatively on Bedford's work. Mike was surprised and pleased at Dallas's views, and, afterwards, Dallas felt that, through them, he had passed some sort of test. In subsequent years Dallas would be the only journalist to whom Mike would reveal anything remotely personal.

It was around this time, while he was at The Manor, that Mike also laid down guitar on *Ma Song*, a track which was recorded this month for his producer Tom Newman's LP *Fine Old Tom*. Newman had been recording the LP on and off since 1972, when The Manor opened, and he was to finish it late in 1974, by which time Mike would also play on two other tracks for him. *Ma Song* was a kind of parody of a rhythm and blues song, but with a skiffle beat which hinted at Newman's original musical experiences: when he was fifteen his parents had thrown him out of the house for joining a skiffle group and having an Everly Brothers haircut. Although the song, like others on the LP, was a piece of musical nostalgia, it was filtered through current hippy musical perspective, with lots of overdubs, instrumental embellishments and humorous bits, such as Tom's nasal trumpets. Being R'n'B, Mike played what Newman characterised as a *"Keith Richards type guitar solo"*; it was a short, untypical break, without the usual sound of his guitar, nor his usual style of playing.

At the end of August it was announced that Robert Wyatt would play a live show at which Mike and others would appear, at the Theatre Royal, Drury Lane on 8th September, On 24th August NME carried an unusual publicity shot for the gig on its front cover, with Wyatt, Mike, and the other musicians reclining nonchalantly in a wheelchair each.

By this time the finished *Hergest Ridge* was pressed and ready for release. Alas, as Virgin's Al Clark observed, first pressings of the LP were done on poor standard vinyl as a result of the dearth of quality vinyl which was byproduct of the mid-1970's oil crisis; this was particularly damaging to *Hergest Ridge*, the frequently deficient sound that resulted from this situation obscuring the often subtle music. With this drawback, Mike's second LP was released to the waiting critics and public on 28th August.

The first side of the piece begins with an unusual, expansive organ drone, and glockenspiel. There are also incredibly faraway-sounding washes of organ. This mysterious sense of 'distance' was to become a characteristic quality of Mike's recordings. The beginning of the side is accompanied by a very slow bass pattern. The organ and bass tune is then gracefully changed into a nice mandolin and organ part. Already it is clear that Mike has learned to make the transitions between tunes less abrupt than they had sometimes been on *Tubular Bells*.

The music continues in the same always calm vein, with the perhaps intrusive sound of electric guitar now generally kept in the background. Nevertheless, throughout the LP, guitar often twinkles and shines in its new position away from centre stage, sometimes still rising to dizzying heights of feeling and expression.

Trumpet, arranged by David Bedford, calls out later and is subsequently introduced as part of a very unified organ, oboe and guitar part that is remarkably peaceful and pastoral. Here we are at the very heart of the mood of the LP.

Really deep bass introduces a wonderful sleigh bells section. There is some great rough electric guitar here that emerges to prominence out of its established background role.

The side concludes with a choral section and piano. The choir, organised by David Bedford, had been introduced earlier, but its entry here is particularly grand and impressive. The music ends with Mike and Terry Oldfield playing a noticeably wobbly organ and flute coda.

The second side of the record is rather like that of *Tubular Bells*, beginning as it does with a blending of Spanish guitar and organ tune. Here you can hear Mike's fingers sliding over the strings as he finds the chords. Swirling and diving electric guitar is added, and a cymbal crash is used as a bridge into a new section, this time on acoustic guitar and trilling mandolin. Swathes of sound wash against us. There's subsequently a fuzz electric guitar and timpani part very like the Scottish tune on *Tubular Bells*. This is built up and then, suddenly, removed.

It is followed by a very striking staccato-style organ pattern with flute. Guitars sounding like screeling bagpipes are used as they had been on the first LP. There's a dramatic and winning key change during the organ playing, a disarmingly simple device that resonates with great effect out of all proportion to its nature.

The only real clash of sound on the LP occurs in a noisy organ and electric guitar section with Sally Oldfield and Clodagh Simmonds wailing in the distance. The noise resulted partly from the poor quality of the vinyl, which is most noticeable here, but mostly from the fact that the tune had not been composed under the effects of either Delius or the countryside, but a full two years earlier, when Mike called it *The Martian Song*. It was now included on this LP under the influence of the heavy rock of Led Zeppelin, which Mike had also been listening to, using it to match his mood when he was feeling depressed. After a repetitive, cacophonous electric guitar refrain, a great solo burns through. The whole tune is played again and again like an aural mantra, even coming to several false endings but starting up again. It is repetitive, but by the end quite exhilarating. Generally, however, repetition, resulting from the small number of tunes on the piece compared to its predecessor is sometimes a slight fault.

The LP ends with another typically quiet acoustic guitar and organ part. Strings and voices are added, and the whole thing fades and then stops altogether.

What Mike was creating for himself in making *Hergest Ridge* was another musical sanctuary. The music represented a flight from the real world into a more pleasant re-creation of the countryside in music. *"It was really like Herefordshire"*, he enthused afterwards, commenting revealing, *"just the texture of it is so comforting"*.

The idea of *Hergest Ridge* as a sanctuary stretched to the cover of the record, which showed a bit of the countryside (with one of Mike's gliders and Bootleg, one of the two Irish Wolfhounds from the Manor) made up to look like an enclosed round world of its own. The publicity blurb for the LP also caught some of Mike's intention for the album, calling it *"a motionless point in chaos"*.

The critics' reaction to the LP was harsh, in complete contrast to the reception with which they had greeted *Tubular Bells*. Melody Maker's Steve Lake admitted that the second album was more unified than the first, but felt that, as a result, this made for a less interesting experience. He disapproved of the (natural) similarities it shared with *Tubular Bells*, and characterised Mike's compositional ideas as entirely predictable. *"Mike Oldfield is safe"*, he wrote,

His compositions couldn't offend even the most conservative mentality, and they make ideal background noises for driving the car, painting a wall, and doubtless, shopping in the supermarket.

He thought that Mike had now exhausted his limitations, and that the only people to benefit from the LP would be Virgin Records' accounts department.

NME's Ian McDonald, who said he never liked *Tubular Bells*, recognised that the new LP was a more homogeneous and better organised piece than its predecessor and that Mike had obvious gifts with melody and the guitar, particularly in investigating tone and timbre with the latter. He observed that Mike's compositional practice was a rock musician's idea of the classical practice of variation, but complained that what Mike did was merely repeat a tune several times in different instrumental settings, without significantly developing the tune itself. He condemned *Hergest Ridge* as immaculately escapist, erratic, uninventive muzak.

Sounds' Steve Peacock included in his review a partial retraction of the praise with which he had welcomed Tubular Bells, saying that he had been carried away. as to the new LP, he noted doubtfully that Mike's music was a succession of tunes *"which follow one another in a rather random pattern that assumes its logic - you feel - more by accident than design"*. (If this was the case, however, it did not detract from the effects of the music). He was also disappointed that *Hergest Ridge* was so close in style and technique to *Tubular Bells* (the LPs were, not surprisingly, often similar). David Bedford commented on this criticism when he met the reviewer at the end of the year: *"What on earth could he have done except write another piece of music in the style at which he had arrived? Which is what he did. There's nothing you can do to satisfy people's expectations after a gigantic, enormous seller like Tubular Bells. If it does sound like Take Two, as you say, then it's Take Two two years later, and he's learnt how to put tunes together so that they lead on from one section to the next rather than suddenly jumping into something else, which is what happened in Tubular Bells. Formally speaking, as a 40 minute piece, it's far more successful in compositional procedure than Tubular Bells. But maybe it's not so interesting - who knows?"*

Mike was shaken by the lack of critical appreciation of *Hergest Ridge* and the retraction of critical favour for *Tubular Bells*. He recalled many years later how at first everybody had loved his debut: *"And then everybody hated it. And I found that a bit bewildering"*. He rightly protested a few years after *Hergest Ridge* that his second LP was *"Not Tubular Bells' Part Two. It's involved and complex because I'd been accumulating so much more inside me. Influences like Ravel and Stravinsky, Led Zeppelin and heavy rock"*.

Despite the critics' reaction to the LP, Mike's still increasing public ensured that it reached number one in the album chart. It was soon replaced at that position by a resurgence of interest in *Tubular Bells*, so that, for a short, remarkable period, Mike held both first and second placing.

Soon after *Hergest Ridge* was issued, the recording of the orchestral version of *Tubular Bells* took place. David Bedford had made few changes to the original piece, but he felt that the orchestral rendering would *"put a new slant on lots of bits"*.

Mike, who was to play a small part on guitar at the end of the piece, was dubious about the whole idea and found it hard to become very interested in it: *"if it had been my idea and I'd organised it, I might have been more enthusiastic, but it was out of my hands. It would have happened anyway"*. He was generally unimpressed by the orchestra's playing, and indeed, the latter do not appear to have been wholly keen on the piece; on the first day of recording Bedford had had to counter their vague hostility to it by doing some straight talking: *"I had to explain that in fact that piece was legitimate....and any sloppy playing or mistakes would be bound to be noticed and slammed by the critics... You have to lose your temper once to make them sit up"*. As time went on the orchestra do seem to have warmed a little to the piece Bedford reported: *"I heard somebody in the coffee break ask "what do you think of it?" and the reply was "well, it's beginning to grow on me"". I think that's the general attitude now"*. Nevertheless, by the end of the sessions there was a large editing job to be done, selecting the better takes from what Mike and visiting journalists concluded were generally lacklustre performances.

Robert Wyatt's Drury Lane show took place in the middle of the sessions for the orchestral *Tubular Bells*. Mike contributed to four songs. Karl Dallas noted that the first appearance on stage by the reclusive young composer sent an excited thrill through the theatre. He played first on Wyatt's *Instant Pussy* and *Signed Curtain*, his scattered electric guitar making occasional appearances as one of the accompanying instruments on the former, while on the latter he emerged a little more to the foreground, his guitar shining and twinkling, shifting and changing, playing his own solo he had created for the song. Later on he played his original, screeching break for *Little Red Robin Hood*, and the show culminated with Wyatt's version of the Monkees' *I'm A Believer*, and *The Laughing Policeman*, with Mike playing a little jangly bit in the background.

Playing guitar at this gig, in what was essentially a band situation, seems to have given Mike an idea about forming a band of his own and perhaps playing live. This prospect caused some excitement in the music press, but Mike appears to have only been toying with the notion, and the idea was easily smothered by his doubts about finding suitably sympathetic and capable musicians and creating a live sound that matched the quality he could achieve in the studio.

Towards the end of the RPO's recording of *Tubular Bells*, Karl Dallas managed to get Mike to talk to him. Dallas recalled: *"Eventually, I came straight out with it, and asked him when he was going to stop buggering about and give me a proper interview...to my discomfort (since I had no tape machine with me) he agreed straight away. "OK", he said, "Let's do it know""*. Being unprepared, Dallas got Mike, and David Bedford, to settle for the following day.

Bedford's comments on Mike's music were particularly observant. He pointed out that, as a composer, Mike was a great individual - his pieces could never be mistaken for anybody else's, and in his work there was a very particular individual musical voice. Bedford also characterised the fine melodies which made up Mike's compositions: they were not classical melodies because they were not capable of much development or extension; rather, Mike simply accompanied them with one or more different instruments, a factor which meant that they were always changing in texture. His melodies, then, were just tunes. They had a distinct pastoral feel to them, he had noted, almost like Delius. He concluded that it was as if Mick's music was a mixture of every type of music to which the young man listened, which then became mixed up in his head, emerging as something different to the original influences.

Mike commented on the absence of words on his compositions, and his consequent concentration on purely instrumental works. He felt that he had a kind of mental block against them, for some reason. He countered this, however, with his style of playing guitar and other instruments; with his guitar, he recognised, he could say things which had an equal validity as words or lyrics.

Although it was not reported at the time, it appears to have been on this occasion that Mike told Dallas that he had no idea what he was going to do after *Hergest Ridge* and that he thought it unlikely that anything new he might record would be, in this own words, another *"epic work"*. Remarkably, he later commented that having made *Hergest Ridge* it seemed to him that he had come to the end of composing music. He may have felt that having left the band situation (with Kevin Ayers) and made his own solo album and recorded a follow-up, he had done everything he had originally intended, and more. It is probable that the critical backlash that greeted his second LP had also put him off stepping in the line of fire again. Mike did not, of course, stop recording LPs, but in the months ahead he switched his attention to shorter pieces of music.

During his interview with Dallas, Mike mentioned his nervous breakdown at fifteen and his making music that would alleviate his feelings. It was the first time that he had mentioned the deeper motivation behind what he had recorded: his need for music as therapy. After he had met Dallas, the personal nature of what he had said seems to have upset him, and he told Richard Branson that it was the last interview he would ever do.

Sometime during September, possibly while he was involved with the orchestral *Tubular Bells*, Mike overdubbed acoustic guitar backing and a little twirly, purely decorative electric guitar onto *Sad Sing*, another track for Tom Newman's LP.

In October, continuing his recent working relationship with David Bedford, he recorded a version of *Don Alfonso*, which Bedford and Lol Coxhill had recorded for the latter's *Ear Of The Beholder* some years before. The recording seems to have been made as a result of a commission from Virgin, who wanted something short from Mike for a sampler LP of their acts which they were putting together.

David Bedford takes on all the vocals and plays accordion, Mike plays several guitars, Kevin Ayers, who had been visiting The Manor, plays wine bottles, and Chris Cutler the drums. While Bedford declaims the lyrics in a humorous, overblown, mock BBC announcer kind of voice, Mike accompanies verses with one guitar style and the choruses with another, as well as playing a chunky bass solo. His guitar reaches a pinnacle on the final chorus, after which he adds another guitar in the distant background and a second lead solo which is interchanged with the original solo, and they curl around each other to fade. The full six-minute piece was put out on the Virgin compilation, *V*, while an edited version was issued as a single, both being issued in 1975.

Bedford's *Star's End* was released at the end of October. The work's combination of electric and orchestral instruments achieves a successful marriage of their different sounds, so that Mike's electric guitar and bass complement the roles of brass, wind and strings. The two sets of instruments alternate with each other or merge very effectively in the sound texture, affecting our senses and emotional reactions with their pure sound. The music is slow moving and creates appropriate feelings of great space, distance and expansion; sounds appear and disappear like music heard from a passing train. Mike mirrors the sense of boundaries reached and surpassed with his fluid guitar spinning outwards and upwards, pausing on a level, and moving on again. After short flurries of activity from several sets of instruments, what has gone before is 'attacked' by the intrusion of other instruments; Bedford's favourite technique of glissando on strings, and funeral trumpet makes the ambience weary, as the universe falls in on itself and is dying. After a period of mounting excitement, with Mike on guitar, the latter lets out a high, piercing note, a signal presaging the end. All fades; there is a little piping from one of the wind instruments.

It appears to have been around this time in 1974 that Mike's mother, Maureen, died. Her death, he said, left him *"devastated"*. He felt that, in contrast to his childhood helplessness about her mental condition, he might have been able to help her, explaining that he had a similar set of problems to his mother's, but that he had learnt how to cope with these a bit better *"by turning it all to creative use"*.

Mike turned his problems to creative use by composing when he was feeling disturbed. Experiencing an onrush of mental energy or of depression, he would pick up an instrument, usually a guitar, and try to create some music which either reflected his feelings or counterbalanced them. If he felt manically high, for example, he might play something on electric guitar which had a similarly rising, heady quality, or, alternatively, a soft, acoustic tune to bring himself down. Through composing and playing he was thus able either to counteract or to externalise his emotions, and thereby become sane and objective once more. He described himself as being in a near trance state of total creativity and concentration during such composing and its later recording.

Star's End was due to be premiered at the Royal Festival Hall on 5th November, and Mike was to have played electric guitar, but his grief at his mother's death made the prospect of appearing before an audience unpalatable to him, and Virgin issued a statement that he would be unable to play because he was ill.

At the event his place was taken by Fred Frith, with Darryl Runswick on bass and Chris Cutler on drums. The performance, like the recording, was conducted by the celebrated Vernon Handley. There was a large audience at the Hall to hear the piece. Many of them were fans of Mike's music who had bought tickets in expectation of actually seeing and hearing him live. However, it is not at all certain that they would have enjoyed the concert had Mike played. The promise of his involvement and Bedford's association with rock led the audience to expect something other than what they heard, and Derek Jewell, rock critic of The Sunday Times, reported that the piece went off *"like a damp squib"*. One member of the audience was overheard after it was all over exclaiming: *"Thank god for that"*.

The classical music critics' response was a little more measured, but not wildly enthusiastic. The Sunday Times' reviewer noted *"Vast expanses of picturesque clustering and chattering"*, but he said that Bedford had too sweet a tooth, *"indulging in immense swoony sequences over thudding drums and protracted Delius-like atmospheric conclusions....Star's End has its attractions but it badly overstays its welcome"*. Musical Times damned the piece with faint praise, describing it as *"an expansive piece, made up of attractive sonorities that glide into hearing and then pass away: a pleasant enough trip"*.

Some time during or after August, Mike had found a cottage in Wales and set up his own studio there. The cottage was known as The Beacon, which, given its name, may have been situated near Beacon Hill, about fifteen miles north of Hergest Ridge. In November he made his first recording there, two short pieces: *In Dulci Jubilo*, an instrumental version of a well-known setting of an old German carol, made with Les Penning, and *Speak (Tho' You Only Say Farewell)*, a music hall love song, sung by himself and David Bedford. The former features Mike's time-keeping acoustic guitar and piano, Penning on kortholt and recorder, and former Whole World associate William Murray on military-style snare drum. Out of this Mike's electric guitar bursts out into fiery life. *Speak* is played by Bedford on school-music-teacher-style grand piano, with Mike singing gently and Bedford exaggeratedly, both purposefully slightly off-key.

Bedford's more sober arrangements of *Tubular Bells* and *Hergest Ridge* were performed at the Royal Albert Hall on 9th December. Mike, again, was to have played guitar, but due to the continuation of his emotional upset over his mother's death, his place was taken by Steve Hillage. Tickets for the concert, issued in mid November, had sold out on the first day of sale, again largely on the strength of Mike's appearing. The performance was to be filmed by the BBC for a ninety minuted programme which was to be broadcast simultaneously on TV and in stereo on Radio 3 on 18th January 1975, after it became apparent that Mike could not participate, only the radio broadcast took place.

The beginning of 1975 saw releases of work Mike had done in the previous year. The first of these was *The Orchestral Tubular Bells*, issued on 17th January, a day before the radio broadcast of the live performance of Mike's two pieces. The orchestral treatment of *Tubular Bells* is occasionally stirring and romantic, but it in no way matches the original. The attempt to replace the instrumental variety and dynamic range of the original through orchestral instruments and techniques paradoxically reduces the effects of Mike's recording. One really misses the rich interplay of sounds and styles created by the alternation of acoustic and electric instruments and their various combinations on the original. The orchestral instruments are clearly unable in some sections to create parallel effects of any value, particularly on sections that were very rock tinged. Overall, the piece lacks a sense of Mike's individual musical voice, particularly as it was expressed in his guitar playing, and the orchestra bring not so much a new voice as a general sense of lethargy.

Mike himself plays guitar at the very end of the piece, where his performance is excellent. He first plays his eddying guitars section, but here, on acoustic guitar. He plays the section differently to the original, in an attractive, new deftly ornate mode. Onto this he intersperses tone colours and some very high notes from electric guitar, in a style continued from some of what he developed for Bedford's *Star's End*.

Reviews of the orchestral version of *Tubular Bells* were not favourable to it. Melody Maker, for example, thought that the Royal Philharmonic Orchestra were ponderous to the point of somnambulism, and that taking the piece out of its original instrumental context made it sound tired. The only saving grace, the review concluded, was Mike's guitar playing. Nevertheless,

The Orchestral Tubular Bells subsequently rose to number seventeen in the album chart.

V, the compilation of Virgin acts, was released in late January or early February. This included the full length *Don Alfonso*, Tom Newman's *Sad Sing*, and tracks by Robert Wyatt, Ivor Cutler, African band Jabula, and others.

Tom Newman's album, *Fine Old Tom*, was issued in February. As well as playing on *Sad Sing* and *Ma Song*, Mike appeared on the opening cut, *Suzie*, Newman's pastiche of 1950's rock 'n' roll love songs, playing a little twiddly guitar.

Finally, a shorter version of *Don Alfonso* was backed with In *Dulci Jubilo* and released as a single on 21st February. As a tribute to his mother's memory, Mike added to the B-side's title the bracketed dedication: 'For Maureen'. Surprisingly, the single did not enter the chart, probably because it was a little unusual.

Meanwhile, Mike, who had been upset by the critics' views of *Hergest Ridge*, became motivated by the criticism that had earlier subdued him. As he explained a few years later, *"I said to myself, "Right, I'll show you". And I went on to do Ommadawn"*. By March 1975 he was reported to have been hard at work at The Beacon on a new composition.

Chapter 5

Ommadawn: Towards Catharsis

Mike had actually been recording a new LP since the new year, but had not, however, originally set out to make another album: *"It began to take shape at the beginning of January. I just had two tunes which ran together on acoustic guitar, and it sounded nice, and I developed it all from that"*. (These two early tunes subsequently formed the basis for the first side of the LP).

It was after he had begun work that his motivation for making some of the music emerged. Part of it came from his desire to prove himself to the critics who had dismissed *Hergest Ridge*. But he later formed the idea that the music could release the pain of his life, which was reflected in various frustrating mental problems. He commented years later that he suffered from a life-phobia: *"I was scared of everything - of people, lights, my own two feet!"* His condition meant, he explained, *"I didn't even have the self-confidence to get up and walk out of the room. I was in an awful state. Incredibly insecure....basically it was a reaction against my childhood"*. One of the strongest effects his childhood experience had on him as an adult was his being seized by moments of unaccountable alarm: *"I used to have these moments of blind panic - they were dreadful. Really dreadful. I used to have to stop whatever it was I was doing and just scream... I used to be so frightened. I'd be incapable of doing anything for days. For months. I'd just stop. I just used to think why?"* With all of this went a general inability to be really happy, and sundry other problems, such as an inability to accept praise. As Mike said, *"Things were not all well in my own head"*.

To deal with his situation, he had withdrawn into music, and he would drink and take drugs to keep himself going. *"I used to take LSD every weekend and I'd smoke myself stupid. Great fun. But I definitely went a bit odd. And then I became very odd indeed. I couldn't cope with anything, it was terrible"*.

During the recording of the LP, however, he decided to try and completely release his utterly wearying, painful feelings. He did so by forcing himself to confront his earliest emotions and experiences as a human being: *"I realised that what had been fucking me up was being born. A lot of people get fucked up when they're born. So I decided that I was just going to be re-born. It was the only answer. I had to recreate the circumstances of my own birth"*. He did so through creative visualisation (whether with professional psychotherapeutic help or not is unclear) and subsequently recording an emotional musical re-creation of his birth, a release of his general negativity and frustration. *"The end of the first side of Ommadawn"*, he later told a reporter, *"is the sound of me exploding from my mother's vagina"*.

The recording of this section, involving a long and intense guitar solo, naturally affected Mike deeply: *"It scared me to death when I did it. When I did that electric guitar, I found it really frightening. I couldn't sleep"*.

Given his aim of complete catharsis, his recording of the LP as a whole was characterised by similar emotional energy. He said afterwards that he was 'obsessed' with making it and put an overwhelming amount of effort into it. He explained that he was in anguish, and angry, and that the music was correspondingly almost paranoid and suicidal in its mood and energy; making the album was *"like one of those nights when you get food poisoning and you're up all night being sick...I was really delving into the most miserable parts of my own.....brain"*.

He recorded all of the first side twice, partly as a result of a technical problem. *"I think there was something wrong, probably with the tape before I got it, or it may have been just that I played it so many times, and it started shedding oxide, getting a bit worn out. Nobody knows what happened to it. But it's a jolly good thing that it did happen, otherwise I might not have done it again and it would not have been half so good"*.

Recording was interrupted when Mike became involved with some of his musical friends. Firstly, in June, and perhaps also in the previous month, he played guitar on David Bedford's *The Rime Of The Ancient Mariner*, an adaption of Samuel Taylor Coleridge's famous ballad.

Bedford had come to write an earlier piece of music based on the poem after he had been commissioned to write a children's opera, and hit upon the ballad as 'a suitably action-packed adventure drama.' Looking over a book of illustrations of the poem by the famous 19th century artist Gustav Doré, he decided that since it was also time to record another album for Virgin he would use the poem for a new recording as well as for the opera. The poem, he said, struck him as very evocative and he thought he could adapt it in the manner of a 19th century tone poem.

"The idea of illustrating a story or poem... has been tried before by rock musicians but none have really succeeded", Bedford commented. *"One of the reasons which prompted my decision to base an album around the poem was feeling that no one had succeeded in carrying out the idea"*. He pointed out, however, that his adaption was not intended as a literal musical illustration of the entire poem, but as an attempt to evoke the mood and atmosphere of certain important episodes.

Virgin were pleased with his choice of subject matter for the new LP he was to record for them, although, said Bedford, they did tell him, *"We don't want you to do another orchestral piece because your previous album, Star's End, was incredibly expensive"*. This suited Bedford, however, because, freed from having to teach his musicians what he wanted, he could play the new piece mostly by himself, even though he felt that this might open himself up to criticism along the lines of 'He's doing a Mike Oldfield and playing everything himself.'

Mike plays on several occasions, he and Bedford accompanying actor Robert Powell's fine narration. (The text is taken not from the poem itself, but from the prose summary that the poet added to a later edition of his work). When the Ancient Mariner's ship is driven by storms, Mike plays some suitably discordant guitar. Later, after the Ancient Mariner has killed the albatross and a spell traps the ship, he lends electric guitar colourations, in clean, clear tones and continuous with a whole variety of effects, playing brief twangy sections, more sharp, thin-sounding parts, his 'eddying' style, and snappier, shorter fragments. The Mariner cast into a trance, the ship is driven home by supernatural means, at which point Bedford has his girl soloist and the rest of the choir of Queen's College (where he taught music) enter and sing the sea shanty *The Rio Grande*. This has a clear and ethereal delicacy which makes it very poignant. Mike comes in on guitar, playing a straining, searching, echoey melody of release, which later rises upwards with the choir and continues alone with its own forlorn voice. Towards the end of the piece, when the Ancient Mariner is telling his story, Bedford on piano and Mike on guitar accompany the final narration, Mike continuing on his own, and then twinning his guitar with Bedford's organ, so that they play gently off each other to fade.

Mike laid down most of his guitar for Bedford at a studio in London, where the latter then played him his beautiful arrangement of the sea shanty. Mike was son enamoured with it that he took the tapes to his own studio to compose a suitable accompaniment. Bedford was pleased with the result, recounting: *"I wanted a guitar to go over the last verse so when Mike was doing the other bits I played him the song and he liked it so he did a lot of work on it. He played it through about ten times before putting a solo down. Most guitarists would just shove down a lot of notes but he's playing with the voices which is really nice"*.

Some time afterwards, Mike played with concertina enthusiast and folk singer Lea Nicholson, on *Kopya*, a track recorded at Mike's studio for Nicholson's LP, *Horse Music. Kopya* was a Yugoslavian dance tune, on which Mike played guitar, bodhran, and sleigh bells.

Mike was also invited to add his distinctive touch to *Bandages,* an LP by his old acquaintances the Edgar Broughton Band. He appeared on three tracks, playing guitar and harp.

After playing for others, Mike returned to his own album. Towards the end of his work on it he recorded the African drummers from Virgin act Jabula live at The Manor, and laid this drum track behind the electric guitar at the *"re-birth"* climax to the first side. He then got Clodagh Simmonds to sing some Irish phrases over this at The Beacon. He recalled: *"The bit with the drums and voices on I did twice and I did the voices several times to get them perfect, and Clodagh ended up coming up at twelve o'clock, working through the night and getting back to London early next morning because she had to be back at work"*.

He had simply asked Clodagh if she could sing something or other over the music, and she had improvised some Irish phrases. A week later, said Mike, *"I was looking at the words with another singer who sang on the album, Bridget St. John, and I was trying to think what the title (of the LP) should be and there was this one word and she had spelled it our phonetically and I thought "What a great title". And it just happened to mean idiot and just seemed to fit"*. The word, *Ommadawn,* was the way Clodagh had written Amadian, the Irish word for fool.

Mike's working with Bedford, Nicholson and the Broughtons

meant that by late August several sections of his album remained to be finished. Virgin engineer Phil Newell explained that as a result it was only in the four weeks prior to the deadline for delivery of the tapes to Virgin that things began to take shape. With only a week to go before the pressing date, he went to Mike's to help him to finish the album. One section that they were trying to get done was an uilleann pipe and acoustic guitar duet which Mike had arranged to do with Paddy Moloney, piper and leader of the prominent Irish traditional group the Chieftains. The group were involved in a hectic tour of Britain at the time, but Paddy and their manager used a rare free night to travel to Mike's house, not arriving until late in the evening. Newell later recalled that even though the pair worked on the troublesome section until the early morning, by the time he retired for some sleep they were all worried because nothing worthwhile had really emerged.

Then Mike and Paddy began to get drunk together, and a couple of hours later they woke Newell with the news that they thought they really had something. After a couple of takes, everybody was dumbstruck when the pair managed to play the complete section with such uncanny skill that, even without a timing guide, it finished exactly as the following, already recorded part began. The next morning, Mike gratefully arranged transport to Southampton, The Chieftains' next venue, by way of private plane. Mike and Newell then just managed to finish off the album in time for the deadline.

After the LP was completed, in September, Mike set about remixing it at The Manor in then vogue-ish quadraphonic form.

By this time he had moved house again, close to the village of Througham, near Stroud, Gloucestershire, at the southern end of the Cotswold Hills. He left The Beacon because it had been situated at the bottom of a steep slope down which often bulky technical equipment and instruments had to be hauled. In an old whitewashed barn at his new home he was having a twenty-four-track, quadraphonic studio built.

In late September David Bedford's *The Rime Of The Ancient Mariner* was released. It came in an attractive black and white cover with illustrations by Gustav Doré. Reaction to the fine album from the rock critics was good, Melody Maker, for example, describing it as *"a powerfully evocative modern musical impression' of the poem"*.

Classical music critics were less impressed with the work, and a later review of the LP in Gramophone magazine led David Bedford to engage in a dispute with the critic in the letters page of the magazine. The reviewer had admitted in his assessment that he had a prejudice against the organ as an instrument. Bedford complained that since the reviewer *"refers to the organ as his "bete-noire", what on earth was the purpose of giving him my record to review...since the compositional procedures underlying much of the piece depend to a large extent on the textural interplay produced by the overdubbing of various kinds of electric and acoustic organs?"* He also pointed out that no comment had been made on the choir's singing of the sea shanty, *"or that Mike Oldfield contributes some exquisite guitar playing"*. He concluded: *"In any event, the fact that a critic can dismiss in one short paragraph a piece of music that took three months to write and a further two months to record, particularly when on his own admission he dislikes the main instrument for which the composition is scored seems grotesquely unfair"*. In response, the critic admitted that Bedford was right to criticise him on his main point, but he felt that the choir's version of *The Rio Grande* was a *"dismal"* one, and that Mike's solos, *"prettily played as they are....do less than justice to his musicianship"* compared to what he called his *"brilliant arrangement of In Dulci Jubilo, to say nothing of Tubular Bells"*.

Meanwhile, Mike was remixing *In Dulci Jubilo* at The Manor in October, for release this time as the A-side of a single. He may have done so because Virgin realised that the carol was eminently suitable Christmas market material.

Then, on the 28th of October, *Ommadawn* was released.

As usual, the music is multi-instrumental and made up of sectional tunes. The joins between them have been even further smoothed out since *Hergest Ridge*, particularly by reprising tunes and playing more than one tune on the same set of instruments, which lessens one's sense of sharp changes.

Mike is joined in places by a larger number of musical collaborators than had previously been the case. His brother Terry plays pan pipes, and his sister Sally and Clodagh Simmonds and Bridget St. John sing. Leslie Penning features on recorders and Gong's Pierre Moerlen plays timpani. Paddy Moloney was not the only piper Mike employed: he also used a Northumbrian bagpipe player. The number of outside players was also swelled by the brass of The Hereford City Band, the African drummers from Jabula, and a group of children vocalists.

Throughout, the music is taut and assured, and characterised by the successful mixing of diverse folk music styles, particularly Irish and Greek, the latter influence possibly springing from Mike's brother, Terry, who loved Greek music and culture. Moods vary from the optimistic, as displayed on a tune by Penning on recorders and Mike on acoustic guitar and mandolin, to the reassuring, with a delicate harp and cello part.

Joyful and intense moods are produced primarily through Mike's fine electric guitar playing. This can twinkle like a shimmering star glimpsed in the heavens, can twirl and spin energetically, or pierce and stab like never before, as it does on the re-birth section.

That section begins after Terry's lonely pan pipes play for a while. Clodagh then chants the Irish words she composed for Mike. Their most likely translation is the following set of enigmatic phrases:

> I am the fool singing but
> I sing that power will come to the weak
> I am the fool singing
> The fool singing.

This is intriguing, suggesting perhaps what Clodagh thought Mike himself might feel. She may have seen Mike as someone who would or should take more positive control over his life, as indeed he was to start to do from this time. Mike must have got her to explain the words to her, and, in view of the fact that he used them, he must also have approved of the picture of him which they suggested, hidden though it was in a foreign language (as Mike was to comment later, only Irish people knew what it meant). Mike accompanies the chanting with a repetitive electric guitar riff, and then by a new electric guitar part that screams and pushes forward relentlessly: this is the heart of the re-birth section. The guitar later reaches a peak, ends, and bodhrans, pulsating like heartbeat, play to fade.

After this climax, the second side begins with a disappointingly weary and over cluttered section that meanders nowhere in particular. Later on, Paddy Moloney plays his long, yearning uilleann pipes part to Mike's acoustic guitar backing.

After the music appears to end, a coda, *On Horseback*, a very gentle song by Mike and William Murray, begins. Mike speaks more than sings the song, sounding lost and vulnerable, accompanied on the choruses by the children vocalists. The song lists Mike's simple pleasures, but particularly horse riding, which he liked to counteract occasional storms of emotional anguish. It was Leslie Penning who had introduced Mike to riding, and Karl Dallas recounted that the sensitive, delicately delivered song *"brought back the experience to him so keenly that he had, quite literally, wept, when Mike sang it to him"*.

The inclusion of the song in the context of the whole LP was *"Very important"*, Mike commented afterwards. *"It seems to balance it out. There seemed to be an over-pessimisticness about (the album), especially the end of the first side, even though some people find it makes them happy. Other people, it makes them unhappy"*. The song, he felt, acted as a kind of opposite to the re-birth section.

The album cover was the first to feature a photograph of Mike, by David Bailey. He appears as a melancholy, blue-eyed hippy, gazing with infinite sadness through a rain-streaked window.

Ommadawn was well received by the critics. Mike's attempt to prove himself, and the emotional energy with which he infused the music paid off. NME's Bob Edmands felt that *"the earlier albums seem like dry runs for the real thing"*. Sounds noted that the work *"perfected the technique of the previous two albums, welding rock styles and influences into the structure of classical music"*.

Most commentators noted the modification in Mike's guitar style. Sounds observed that at the (re-birth) climax of the first side *("an urgent, overwhelming piece")*, *"his guitar stabs and snarls with a commanding authority not previously heard"*. Melody Maker's Karl Dallas, in a review headed 'Portrait of a Genius', remarked that Mike's *""singing" electric guitar tone"* had gone, and that at the end of side one he instead played *"abrupt stabbing phrases, sometimes composed of just two or three notes....This is a new Oldfield....There is anger, there are teeth"*.

Some critics struck upon the horse song. Although Dallas thought that it veered towards kitsch, it still worked brilliantly. Bob Edmands said that the song was banal and childish, but that the result was still *"utterly charming and disarming. Instant, beautiful euphoria"*.

When the album had been finished, Mike gave his only interview of the period to Karl Dallas. It was a revealing action, given that the personal nature of what he had told Dallas previously had led him to refuse to be interviewed again; but that experience, as well as Dallas' encounter with him during the weekend he had spent with him in August 1974 seems to have engendered the only bond of trust that Mike was ever to feel with a member of the music press.

The journalist met Mike at his home in Througham, which he noted as *"a beautiful old greystone building, parts of it dating back to the 13th century, with ornamental gardens in the process of being restored"*. It was situated *"at the bottom of a valley at the end of a road which petered out into a dirt track"*. The house was secluded, Mike relishing the fact that there was nobody around for at least a quarter of a mile. Such a locale, however, was not without its difficulties:

Despite the smell of fresh-baked flapjacks emanating from the kitchen, it appeared that there were serious problems on the culinary front, namely in pumping up water from the spring, and all cups of tea had to be trickled from a jerrycan loaned by a friendly neighbourhood villager.

Mike appeared to have become a little more confident after making the album, and he said that he thought he was finding life easier to cope with. *"I don't find everything so bewildering as it used to be"*, he said. *"I'm getting used to being like me, here"*. The catharsis he had intended his record to create had obviously helped; asked if he had come to terms with himself at last, he replied, *"Well, I've only just started, really. I suppose this record was a picture of that....It doesn't sound so frightened as the others. It sounds a bit stronger"*.

It was only in later years, or in odd moments of insight, that his motivation for making music became clear to him. Although he knew what he was attempting to do with the re-birth section, even if he did not explain this for several years afterwards, he told Dallas that he didn't really know why he made music. *"I've no idea what goes on. I don't understand why I do it and what it is when I've done it"*. He told him subsequently, however, that *On Horseback* had the line "Some find it strange to be here". *"I certainly do. And maybe that has a lot to do with why I make music"*.

While Mike was not always clear about his motivation, he was certainly pleased with the latest result, and, recalling that he had said that he could not imagine making more albums after *Hergest Ridge*, said, *"after this I can imagine me doing loads more. I want to get cracking on another one very fast. So this is not the end for me. Obviously Hergest Ridge never was the end of me writing music, but it did feel a bit like it...unless I crash in the car one night I'm obviously going to do a lot more music, an awful lot"*. (As a result of his going on to work with others again, however, it was to be two years before he would even begin another album; nevertheless, when he did record his next LP, he used one of the ideas he had at this time, that of using an orchestra).

Asked again whether he would play live, Mike was still not keen. He said he did not feel any need to communicate with an audience; *"I do person to person, but not with a complete mass of people"*.

Although he did not appear live, *Ommadawn*, like its predecessors, went on to reach a huge public, rising to number four in the LP chart. As before, Mike's personal music therapy extended beyond his own needs to affect deeply those of his listeners.

Chapter 6

Collaborations

After *Ommadawn* was released, Mike's remix of *In Dulci Jubilo* was backed with *On Horseback* and issued as a single on 14th November 1975. Putting the track out as the A-side paid off, the single subsequently doing very well, rising to number four in the chart. A promotional film clip for the single was shot at Mike's home; he was filmed playing each of his several instruments individually, after which these pictures were combined, to present a visual suggestion of the multi-overdubbed nature of the music.

Mike recorded two other short pieces in January 1976. He invited Les Penning to Througham and the pair collaborated on Mike's arrangements of traditional English tunes, *Portsmouth* and *Argiers*. He commented afterwards: *"Portsmouth is one of the simplest things I've ever done. I was flicking through a book of old folk songs one day and came across it. I thought it would be nice to record it"*.

The tune is an uptempo horn-pipe, with Les on recorders and

Mike playing bodhran, mandolin, tambourine and accordion. To this is added background string synthesizer, kettle drums and the two musicians' thunderous stamping feet.

Argiers is a short, slow, gentle tune repeated several times on Mike's acoustic guitar and Les' lonely, clear, pipe-like recorder.

Having already mixed *Ommadawn* at The Manor in quadraphonic form, a strong perfectionist streak in Mike led him to do the same at Througham with *Hergest Ridge.* As well as allowing him to improve the faulty sound quality of the original release, remixing enabled him to eliminate some musical deficiencies he now felt the recording had had. He said afterwards that his main aim was to reduce what he felt were unnecessary additions. He had originally included such elements as trumpet, snare drum and some guitar parts because he was concerned that listeners might have thought that the LP was too repetitive (although he still observed that there was nothing intrinsically wrong with repetition as long as what was repeated was worth repeating). As well as cutting elements, however, he also added some, giving the voices on Side Two more importance that he had the first time, for example. He concentrated very much on improving the backing tracks, he recounted, even going so far as to enhance the texture of single notes, so that he afterwards felt that the revised album was the experiment in texture, in the sympathetic, coherent overdubbing of instruments, that he had originally intended to be one of its main features.

Virgin seem to have decided to add the new mix of *Hergest Ridge* to that of *Ommadawn* and an improved quadraphonic version of *Tubular Bells,* the three records to be released as a boxed set. So while Mike worked at Througham, Manor engineer Phil Newell made a second quad mix of Tubular Bells. (Before Newell had been able to start, he had first to undertake a lengthy search for the master tape of the famous LP, which had gone missing after a party some years earlier. It was eventually discovered under somebody's bed.) Newell recalled of his work that, owing to the use of The Manor's new, computerised mixing deck, the helpful, time-saving technology of which had not yet been devised when Mike and Tom were mixing the original LP, less concentration had to be devoted to the practical technicalities of mixing the work, so that his team's attention was more directed to the musical aspect of the mixing. As a result, he felt that the remixed version was subtler and stronger than both the original album and the subsequent botched remix that had been issued.

Mike may have taken a break from his mixing to play guitar for an LP by his old colleague Tom Newman. *The Faerie Symphony* was recorded at The Argonaut, Tom's own barge studio in Little

Venice, and Mike's contributions sound as if they were made there and not at Througham.

The album was a long-form composition based on Irish folklore and legend. The piece is successful in conveying a sense of an Irish fairyland, especially through the use of flute and flageolet (the latter usefully resembling the Irish tin whistle), and bagpipe-type sounds.

Tom's composition was obviously influenced by the examples of Mike's commercially popular long pieces. He re-employs the faraway production he and Mike had created for the latter's LPs, although it is also in places far sharper and more immediate, and he often mirrors Mike's style of playing, a feature most noticeable on the album's opening track, with his playing Oldfield-style acoustic guitar and glockenspiel. Other elements he borrows are twinkly electric guitar, bodhran-style percussion, choral backing, trombone like the trumpet on *Hergest Ridge*, and even tubular bells.

Yet for all the similarities in sound and technique, the particular emotional and textural feel typical of Mike's work is, not surprisingly, absent. Newman also had the sense to give some expression to his own musical personality, most obvious in his liking for flute, played by Jon Field. Moreover, he made his piece clearly sectional, while Mike tries always to run his own sections together. The most accomplished of these is the track which closes the end of the first side.

Mike appears on two tracks on the second side. The first is *Dance of Theena Shee* (i.e: Dhaoine Sidhe, the fairy people). This begins with what Tom called his 'pizzicato guitars', and features snare drum. Then a full-blown collection of instruments starts up, opposite which Mike plays rough, scraping guitar. On the other track, *The Unseelie Court* (The court of the unkind fairies), he plays in a very different style. Tom's resonant guitar riffing opens this, and drums and flute are then introduced. After a crescendo it all becomes extremely noisy. Mad, cackling laughter suggests the malevolent fairies, as does Mike's long, powerful, screaming break that plays to fade.

Mike did more session work again in July, when he played on David Bedford's *The Odyssey*, a treatment in six main sections, each section depicting an episode of Homer's epic poem. Bedford had already recorded most of the LP in London in June (with producer Peter Jenner, who had worked on The Whole World's album years before), when he went to Mike's house to have him overdub electric guitar for two tracks, *The Phaecian Games* and *The Sirens*.

The first of these portrays an athletic contest at which the hero, Odysseus, is challenged to prove himself; he ends up throwing the discus further than anyone else, and excelling at other sports.

Bedford plays a typically swirling synthesizer pattern and adds another synth tune, which Mike then takes up on a long, piercing guitar part, a skirling, twisting, soaring affair. Later, Odysseus, who has been trying to return home after his victory in the Trojan war, sails past the island of the Sirens, whose sweet, enchanting song no man can hear without throwing himself fatally into the water to join them. But Odysseus straps himself to the mast of his ship and is thus able to listen and survive. Bedford plays synthesizer again, but the better of the features is the eerie choral part sung by the girls of Queen's College. Mike comes in later with touches of delicate, ringing, glistening guitar accompanying the girls' voices. He appears again at the end playing in a particularly fluid style.

Mike's musical (and personal) association with David Bedford continued directly after he laid down his guitar for him at Througham. In August he recorded a guitar piece, *First Excursion*, for which Bedford played a sympathetically spare accompaniment on Mike's grand piano and string synthesizer.

The eight-minute piece is a triumphant marriage of feeling with technique. *First Excursion* presents through appropriately played and treaded guitar, a feeling of physical movement outwards and of a corresponding inner, emotional response. It begins with Mike's guitar already sky-bound. Mike usually builds up slowly to a climax, but here he begins close to one, and remarkably, moves on from there. The piece thus creates a particular sense of a physical, but also an emotional high. This stimulation of ascending emotions is achieved through specific techniques used to create an ascending guitar presence: a fusion of playing rough, fluttering groups of chords, interspersing various guitar harmonics, and adding finger vibratos, which sustain isolated notes at intervals. The latter are intensified through the personal technical and studio processes Mike often used for recording his guitar work. The result of his system, he explained, was that *"you can get your notes to sustain forever"*. He was also able to emphasise certain pitches: *"depending on the angle I hold the guitar at in relation to the speakers, I get feedback harmonics. I used this throughout First Excursion"*.

The piece was quickly placed on *Collaborations*, an LP pressed just five days after the track was recorded as a bonus album for the forthcoming boxed set of Mike's LP, featuring examples of his work with David Bedford and Les Penning.

The Odyssey was released at the end of September. Reaction to the work was mixed, both among rock and classical critics, probably because the apparently simple and straightforward piece also often appeared bland and monotonous, largely as a result of Bedford's extensive use of vast swathes of unvarying synthesizer sound.

The three remixed Oldfield albums and *Collaborations* were released as *Boxed* on 29th October. A single made up of *Portsmouth* and *Speak*, two tracks from the extra LP, was issued simultaneously. The single did well, Mike being pleased to see it reach number five in the chart; in contrast to his apathetic feelings towards the sales of *Tubular Bells*, he was now beginning to value his success a little. *Boxed* itself went to number twenty two in the album chart.

The four LP package came in a sturdy box in the manner of a classical set. A booklet was included with it, giving some of the history of the records' creation, with a commentary by Virgin publicist Al Clark, and photos of Mike drinking his favourite Cotswold beer, engaging in stress-relieving trampolining in his garden, and so on, and with his array of guitars and other instruments at his home studio.

The *Boxed* mix of *Tubular Bells* smooths out the section transitions and takes the edge off the rougher electric parts. There are only two major changes: Stanshall's announcements of the instruments is relegated a little more to the background, so that it simply underlines, rather than overshadows, the more important musical activity; at the end of the second side, Stanshall's original, drunken commentary on The Manor has been restored.

Of the three remixes, only *Hergest Ridge* is significantly different to its original recording. Mike has made it more muted and even more gentle. One's sense of a much desired and elusive emotional sanctuary has also been deepened. The new LP has a stripped down, sparser beauty. There is greater separation between individual sounds: those of the orchestral instruments have been particularly improved, their coming across as more mellow, subtle and refined; Mike's bass and guitar also benefit from further production.

Mike removed some features of the first version. Not all the trumpet is eliminated, but the instrument's first appearance is replaced by new electric guitar or synthesizer. The disruptive noisiness of some passages of the original LP has been toned down, fuzz guitar has been taken off a loud section in the middle of the first side, and the voices removed from *The Martian Song* - unfortunately, this makes the latter too repetitive and unvarying.

There are also additions, among them several snippets of electric guitar; Mike's physical and emotional distance from his original inspiration makes these a little more coolly proficient than enthralling, however. The most radical changes are to the choir, which Mike has made more prominent. He made the production so much clearer than strange 'words', like those of some lost primal language, can be made out. Mike was apparently coming around to the idea of the at least limited use of some sort of lyrics, and this was later to flower on his next LP set, where he had a choir reciting poetry. Both this new attitude of his, and that which he was developing towards his commercial success reflected minor but definite changes in his personality. These appear to have been sparked as a byproduct of his cathartic experience with *Ommadawn*, and the following months and years would see more relaxations in his personality, and, thereby, changes in his music.

It is the LP of collaborations, however, that is the most attractive of the boxed set. The first side isolated a single excerpt from each of David Bedford's Virgin LPs on which Mike had played electric guitar. The second presented some of the short pieces he had done with Bedford, and with Les Penning.

As well as displaying, on *Collaborations*, other, less highlighted aspects of Mike's music, and indicating on *First Excursion*, as Al Clark observed, that there was a lot more of value to expect from him, *Boxed* acted as a summary of his achievements so far. It was a marker as well as a milestone.

Accordingly, it gave rise to retrospective considerations in the rock press of the body of Mike's music as a whole. The most interesting survey, however, was that in *Tempo*, because it was delivered from the perspective of classical music. Reviewer Bernard Benoliel, who had listened to *Boxed* and to Bedford's three LPs, tried to place the anomalous Oldfield in context with regard to contemporary composers of 'serious' music. He commented that although Mike's work could not be compared to that of great contemporary composers in standards of inspiration and technique, it offered in contrast, *"something fresh and alive"*, and it came close in importance to their work through what he recognised as *"its emotional significance"*. Mike's formal technical weaknesses (the absence of attempts to further develop his basic melodies, for example) were often present in the works of modern composers *"which do not have the immediacy of appeal, direct emotional impact"* and what he termed the *"small but definite vein of originality"* typical of Mike's work.

Benoliel felt that *Tubular Bells* was a *"remarkable effort for any composer not yet twenty years of age"*, but that it was marred by the hard rock section on Side Two, where *"the music actually collapses: the texture becomes leaden and damages the effect of the whole"*. He rightly called *Hergest Ridge* Mike's *"most individual and successful composition"*. He thought it more homogeneous than both of his other long pieces, while the use of choir and strings added *"a richness and serenity which heighten the pastoral intensity"*. He felt that the first half of *Ommadawn* was not successful enough in blending its diverse musical styles, but the second was *"more unified and contains some of Oldfield's loveliest, most moving music"*; *On Horseback* was *"a real delight"*.

For this critic, the originality of Mike's music lay in his blending of varied styles, and it's subtlety was less in its actual material than in the way it was presented, as a result of overdubbing, as a texture.

As for Mike's work with Bedford, Benoliel enthused that it demonstrated his *"remarkable gift"* for guitar improvisation. His best contribution was for *Star's End*, which had *"superb"* improvisation by him; *"The ecstatic, orgasmic climax for guitars...and orchestra...is for me the high point in all this music....yet what would all this be without Oldfield? - for at this point in the score the guitar part gives only chord changes and indications for the bass line"*.

From around the time that the retrospective collection was released, Mike was already working on loose but reportedly radical ideas for a new LP. He took time off, however, to turn out another short piece, an electric guitar version of the overture to Rossini's opera *William Tell* (more popularly recognised as the theme from the old 'Lone Ranger' TV series). The piece allowed him free rein to play lots of electric guitar. To this he adds acoustic guitar and tambourine, mandolin, a bit of synthesizer, and clattering bodhran. The most effective of these various background accompaniments is the glockenspiel, which plays with the guitar in the middle of it all. The guitar itself is remarkably clean, in places working within brief, little patterns, or, alternatively, skirling around to embellish the tune. Mike was afterwards enthusiastic about the piece, calling it *"a real rouser"*.

By this time the Arts Council had commissioned him to write the music for a documentary film, *Reflection*, and he began work on it after he recorded *The William Tell Overture.* Although pieces of his music had previously been used on a number of films, this was the first time that he composed an original soundtrack.

While Mike had been engaged in the foregoing recording work over the year, he had also taken steps to develop personally, so that by the end of the year he was happier and more assured than previously. He had already beneficially released a lot of his painful feelings about his childhood and its continuing effects upon him through the 're-birth' section of *Ommadawn.* He carried on by dropping drugs, concluding, after some internal debate, that although they might at first inspire creative work, they ended up by hindering real musical development, made sensitive people like himself depressed, and led one *"to the point of insanity"*. He made efforts to overcome his introversion and tried to be more communicative with people. He also became more assertive with various hangers-on he realised he had acquired. He felt that the latter, whom he did not name, had been exploiting him by seeking his financial and personal help to become as successful as himself. *"I've had a hell of a battle and I've lost several friends"*, he commented. *"That I'll have to learn to live with. I guess I'm the worst person in the world at being cruel. Perhaps that's something I'll have to learn too"*. He concluded of all this changes: *"I suppose I'm adjusting to the world, growing up"*. As a result of his actions, Mike became more stable, and he even began to feel that, personally and musically, he was at what he called *"a turning-point"* in his life. A couple of years later, he was to attempt to solidify these changes - with dramatic results.

On 25th January 1977, Mike appeared at the premiere of David Bedford's *The Odyssey* at the Royal Albert Hall. The keyboard players included Soft Machine's Mike Ratledge, Greek composer Vangelis and Deep Purple's Jon Lord. The musicians were augmented by the girls of the 'Queen's College Choir and Wine Glass Orchestra'.

Critical reaction to the concert performance of the piece was more uniformly unfavourable than it had been towards its LP recording. The Guardian's Robin Denselow characterised it drily as the first example of *"rock avant-garde easy listening"*. The Times' reviewer called it, archly, *"very happy and very glamorous, an idle dream of magic and heroism in the warm sun...The piece was well received by an adult audience last night but I presume it is intended for children, rather like the comic-strip version I enjoyed when I was about eight"*.

Meanwhile, Mike's version of *The William Tell Overture* had been prepared as a single, and was released with *Argiers* as the B-side on 11th February. It did not do well, failing to scrape into a chart becoming increasingly dominated by disco music and New Wave bands.

It may have been in the following months that Mike engaged in further collaborative work. He became involved first with Swedish bass and keyboard player Pekka Pohjola, whose third LP, *The Mathematician's Air Display*, was being made for Virgin Records. Not only did Mike play on all the tracks, but the album was made entirely at his Througham studio, where he recorded and mixed the LP with studio technician Paul Lindsay and produced it with Pohjola. It is not surprising then that a German reissue of the record credited it to Mike alone.

The record begins with Mike playing tubular bells on *The Sighted Light*. On *Hands Calming the Water* he takes up on guitar a slow, sad melody Pohjola had played earlier on harpsichord; Mike's sister Sally then hums a solo part and he subsequently accompanies her on guitar. His best work for the album is on the great title track, which he enters in several places before creating a mounting passage in which he gets strong drum backup from Pierre Moerlen. Mike features prominently again on *The Consequences of Indecisions*, which takes up most of the second side. As well as guitar, he sometimes plays glockenspiel; the last of his appearances is the best, when he plays fast spinning phrases with his own overdubbed glockenspiel accompaniment. The LP ends with Pohjola's Oldfield-influenced joke ending, *False Start*, with much speedy piano, muffled shouting, and Sally's singing melting into laughter.

Mike seems next to have played guitar on a track for David Bedford's *Instructions For Angels*. Like Pohjola's LP, Bedford's album was mixed at Througham, although it was recorded mostly in London. The section with Mike was recorded live in Worcester Cathedral. Following flute, Bedford plays the cathedral organ: it has a sheer, awesome sound. Mike enters simultaneously. What he plays is unlike most of his previous work for Bedford. His piercing guitar rises upwards again and again, falls, and returns to rise, his taut, sinewy playing scraping the ceilings of emotion. His solo comprises a basic phrase, repeated nine times. Across his constantly climbing guitar he intersperses occasional finger vibratos or uses his infinite sustain technique to let a final note extend beyond the phrase. The same set of techniques appears on each successive phrase, but with slight variations. On one phrase he bends a note, an otherwise mundane effect whose quivering here is brilliantly effective because the foregoing context has set up a simple repetitive contrast to it. He leaves the following phrase unembroidered, but then plays the longest phrase, created by running two together, at the end of which his guitar clangs like a church bell. The next section is almost equally long, but includes a collection of sharp notes preceded by a quick, twirling embellishment. The penultimate phrase is, again, unembroidered, contrasting thereby with the final expression, another long part that ends on very sharp notes, whose echo is not sustained, but dampened.

Instructions For Angels was released after Pekka Pohjola's LP, in late September or early October. Karl Dallas like it, and observed of Mike's part that he demonstrated that *"even if he had never composed Tubular Bells, he would still be one of our most passionate and accomplished performers on the electric guitar"*.

After working with Bedford, Mike finally recorded some of his own material again, and a single, *Cuckoo Song*, backed with *Pipe Tune*, was released on 25th November.

Both tracks were a direct result of Mike's newfound interest in early music, an LP of which Bedford had given to him at Christmas 1976, and which Mike had said soon afterwards would influence him when he came to record again. *Cuckoo Song* was a version of *Spagnoletta*, a French medieval dance tune by German organist and composer Michael Praetorius. The piece was for two sets of pipes, which Mike replaces with Les Penning's recorders. He sped up the tempo and doubled the tune's length to three minutes, and backed it with acoustic guitar, tambourine and glockenspiel. After a series of alternations between his electric guitar and the recorders which stick closely to the original tune, the guitar swans away simply and gently with Mike's improvised variation.

Pipe Tune is made up of a finished version of a tune from the LP ideas he had been working on intermittently since the end of 1976. It is not unlike *Cuckoo Song*, employing synthesizers to create similar pipe sounds, in Mike's own attempt at the style of early music. Other synths are added from time to time, Mike playing these, like those on the subsequent double album, in a new, swirling style, influenced by that of David Bedford. There is more typical tambourine and tapping percussion, but also another new feature, vibraphones, which Mike was to use a lot on the long form composition. He accompanies his main synth-pipe melody on electric guitar, after which he takes over the tune on guitar and the 'pipes' accompany him. At the end of this he plays a new tune, which, like the main pipe melody, he later incorporated into the long work.

Like *The William Tell Overture*, the single failed to enter the chart.

Mike and Les Penning recorded another piece around the time that they made *Cuckoo Song*. This was Penning's version of *Grenadiers*, a marching tune, which was issued as a single by Polydor.

Tom Newman's *Faerie Symphony* was not issued until towards the end of the year, after Virgin had declined to release it and he had finally managed to sell it to Decca, who he later commented disaffectedly, issued it with little publicity or promotional backing. For some reason Mike was not credited for his appearance on the LP.

Reflection, the Arts Council film that Mike had been working on since 1976 was also released at the end of the year. It featured music provided by himself and classical clarinettist Alan Hacker, with Mike's sister Sally and Katy Hacker as typical Oldfield 'voices'. *Reflection* was an experimental film which attempted to reveal, often through time-lapse photography and computer images, the symmetrical patterns and structures that existed both in nature and in the prehistoric and more modern architectural monuments made by man.

Monthly Film Bulletin reviewer Geoff Brown felt that the film sadly proves how difficult it is to produce the cinema equivalent of a thesis or essay, to find ways of presenting an intellectual argument without degenerating into pretty pictures and shallow words....Unfortunately the use of time-lapse photography and animated diagrams is the film's only successful attempt to elucidate its argument, which otherwise is obscured by the bland philosophical rigmarole of the commentary *("Mankind is the cosmos seeing itself in wonder")*, the heady muzak of Mike Oldfield and the protracted and silly sequence with three figures (shot from above) walking interminably around the Chartres maze before sitting down crosslegged.

(The latter trompe-l'oeil image was one which Mike quite liked, re-using it as a visual accompaniment to his music a couple of years later).

His film and other work over, in December 1977 Mike finally started properly recording the new composition that was later to be titled *Incantations*. This was to be his first major piece for over two years, marking the end of an extensive period of stimulating, if tangential, collaboration with others.

The period had also seen Mike continuing to grow personally, following the catalytic impetus of *Ommadawn* - casting drugs aside, becoming more communicative and developing some powers of self assertion.

Chapter 7

Catharsis (A Sharp Blow to the Head)

Mike was happy with the personal development he had achieved over the past few years. In 1978, however, he was persuaded (by whom he did not say) to go further, and attend a controversial therapy course know as Exegesis, or est (Erhard Seminars Training). He was initially reluctant, but then began to look upon the therapy as a way of sealing all the inner changes he had made. Accordingly, in June he broke from recording, and took the course. It was to act as a powerful agent in transforming his previously reserved and introverted personality, and consequently also the nature and quality of his music.

Est had been originally devised by Werner Erhard, a particularly successful American encyclopaedia salesman and personal trainer. After being expelled from the notorious Church of Scientology, and taking a mind training programme, he started his own therapy course. Since it had been set up in the early 1970's, his est organisation had grown at a huge rate in both size and profits, and by the time

Mike took the course it had just become vogue-ish in Britain.

Mike's course took place in the ballroom of a London hotel, and lasted four days. Throughout, he and the other participants sat on deliberately hard, uncomfortable chairs and were forbidden to talk, move, eat, drink, smoke, or leave, even to go to the bathroom at any time apart from the two short breaks which punctuated the long, sixteen-hour days.

A 'trainer' arrived, and barked aggressively at the audience, telling them that they were there because their lives were *"full of shit"*; they were hurting and confused and did not know how to experience life properly. He told them that their personal world views, beliefs and attitudes, together with the commonplace behaviours which they had been prohibited from engaging in, were the ways they habitually used to shut themselves off from life and mask its reality. He promised them, or, rather, threatened them, that est would destroy their precious attitudes and built them a new, more appropriate belief system. If any of the participants objected to this idea, to the prohibitions, or the harangue, the trainer would address them as *"asshole"* and *"motherfucker"*, and tell them to sit down and shut up.

The physical and mental strictures of the course, combined with several therapeutic processes adapted from more orthodox techniques were used to confuse and finally to break down the individuals' behaviour practices and though patterns, and to replace these with a sense of personal responsibility for the condition of their lives. They were encouraged to see that their problems had been caused by themselves alone. There were no extenuating circumstances. This idea of complete responsibility for oneself, regardless of the role of the actions of other people in the past life of the individual was to strike Mike very forcefully, and he was to propound it repeatedly after the course, denying , as est did, that the otherwise eminently blameable roles of others, and of luck or fate, existed. Unfortunately, he was also to adopt this theme, unhealthily, as a sense of his own personal guilt for the traumatic way he felt his parents had behaved towards him when he was a child.

Among the processes which took place over the days of the course was a meditation session, in which the audience were led in their imaginations to a beautiful beach. Mike like this image, and adapted it for the cover of his subsequent double LP, *Incantations*.

Later, the participants were encouraged to pick one of their major personal problems, which under the same technique of meditation they were made to trace back to its first cause, perhaps in childhood. During this, the members of the audience lay on the floor, writhing, moaning and crying. Afterwards, many of them felt that they had been cleansed of their problem.

At another stage, the group was ordered to stand in rows. The trainer told them that none of their 'shit' could save them now: they were each going to be seen as they really were. The trainer's assistants then marched down the lines and picked an individual at random, into whose eyes one of them stared blatantly and continuously. The individuals' self-consciousness and anxiety, and the bullying attitudes of the trainers produced some extreme reactions: people fainted, broke down, screamed, or vomited.

The final element of the therapy was the trainer's insistence that the mind was just a machine. Because the mind cannot choose what it records or responds to, the participants had not choice about what they had been or had become; they could not be anything but what they were. Instead of spending their lives in misery mistakenly blaming others for what they believed to be wrong with them, they should simply accept responsibility for themselves, realise that they were fine as they were, and be content. Coming as it did after days of continuous, mind-wrenching and physically tiring activity, this convoluted revelation struck the participants as an astounding and life-affirming notion. Typically, they left the hotel and walked into the street renewed, and, in some cases, transformed.

Mike commented: *"You listen to this guy talk...and all your hang-ups and all the things you're frightened of just go - wuuuurgh. It's like having a huge shit, and you've got rid of it. It's all gone, and you can be yourself then"*.

An independent psychological study of people who had taken est found that it gave them an increased sense of responsibility, and a particular awareness of their neurotic, inter-personal 'games', which est said they used as a defence against life and personal responsibility. Participants were found to be more stable than they had been. They had improved self-confidence and personal insight.

In some cases, however, notably of those with mild to severe manic tendencies, participants developed delusions of grandeur, flights of ideas, and expansive moods. Mike appears to have long had a slight form of manic depression, and he was later to exhibit some of these characteristics.

Est was, indeed, to make Mike very strange, as the first thing he did following it demonstrated. Dramatically seized by impulse, he married his est trainer's sister, a young woman about whom almost nothing is known. The following day, suddenly feeling that he had made a terrible mistake, he set about trying to get a divorce. The marriage lasted for two weeks, until Mike's lawyers managed to persuade his dismayed wife to agree to the divorce and to accept hefty financial compensation for the whole experience.

Mike returned to the more familiar territory of studio work, producing, mixing and engineering two pieces by David Bedford, who had been working for him on choral and instrumental arrangements for *Incantations*. Bedford's pieces had first been recorded in London, after which the tapes were taken in Througham. *Star Clusters, Nebulae, And Places In Devon* had been composed in 1971. *The Song Of The White Horse* is of more recent origin, having been written in 1977, as the result of a commission from the BBC for an Omnibus programme, televised on 16th February 1978. A choral work, it was sung by the girls of Queen's College (who also sang on Mike's *Incantations*). To obtain the exceptionally high notes Bedford required at the climax of the piece, the unorthodox composer had the singers inhale helium gas. Virgin never released the planned album: to the composer's chagrin, they decided to drop him, among equally less profitable artists, from the then financially troubled label.

Meanwhile, the fact that Mike had not released a new album for three years gave rise to rumour in the music press, and he had later to denounce as unfounded stories that he was going off to live in Brittany, or that he had wiped the tapes of his new composition when it had almost been finished. He had certainly been finishing off his new LP set, with typical post-est enthusiasm, over one month, September. By then he had been working on the composition for two years, during which time guilt at not having made an album for so long had led him to extend his piece into a double LP.

In 1976 Mike had said that he felt he should be moving into new musical areas; and from the start of his work on *Incantations*, his idea for the piece had indeed been reported to be different to those present on his three earlier albums. This was the case. In the first place, *Incantations* is based almost entirely on keyboards. There is some guitar, but it is usually confined to a background, rhythmic role, or brought in as a more prominent semi-lead instrument, interrupting synth tunes, or alternating with them. Mike's new pervasive, fluttering synths are strongly influenced by David Bedford's particular style of playing; but contained within that approach are occasional twirls, which, unusually, Mike carries over from his technique on guitar.

Another new development is Mike's incorporation of two poems, *Diana* by Elizabethan poet and playwright Ben Jonson and extracts from *The Song Of Hiawatha* by Henry Wadsworth Longfellow - whose popular work has been set to music several times. Mike probably became interested in setting poetry by the many examples of David Bedford.

The first side of *Incantations* begins with the Queen's College Choir singing a rising eight-part harmony arranged by their teacher

David Bedford, who also arranged extensive string, trumpet and flute parts of accompaniments. Throughout the composition Bedford's tight, staccato or quivering strings, wherever they appear, both complement and counterbalance the broad swathes of Mike's mellower, synthesizer, sound. Bedford's trumpet arrangements are particularly attractive later on the first side, where phrases on one trumpet are echoed and completed by a second. The airy flutes are played by Sebastian Bell, who had appeared on Bedford's 1972 LP *Nurse's Song With Elephants*, and by Terry Oldfield.

Sections follow, played here and throughout the composition, usually only on a single lead instrument: either flute, synthesizer or guitar, and backed by bodhran, hand claps, timpani, sleighbells or glockenspiel or by some combination of this small range of instruments.

Compositionally, *Incantations* also differs from the earlier long pieces in that its tunes are more often alternated with each other, or reprised after longer intervals. In addition, tunes are longer, slower and more drawn out than those typical of previous work, so as to fill up the lengthier parameters of the double album.

The choir that appeared at the start of the first side return later on the side to sing 'Diana, luna' several times. (Diana was the Roman goddess of the moon.) These words are not taken from Jonson's *Diana*, but are meant to act as a prefatory statement to the poem's full setting on the last side of the set.

The second side features, among other things, the remarkably hypnotic extracts from *The Song Of Hiawatha*, sung by folk-singer Maddy Prior. These are preceded by the suitably tribal drums of the band Jabula. (Some, possibly early, pressings of the set apparently have an alternate take of *Hiawatha*).

The third side is dominated by Mike's long, screechy, straining guitar solo. This is the only occasion on the composition that his guitar appears with any prominence. The solo is succeeded by a series of alternations between a rock tune and a tune played on two synths, the latter intentionally played like the trumpets on the first side - with the second instrument finishing the phrases of the first. But these and later sections on the remainder of the side, although uptempo and sometimes more raucous than elsewhere on the work, strike one as repetitive and not very original. They also suffer from following the inspirational electric guitar solo: there is a sense of anti-climax. It is a fault of structure: had the solo been placed at the end, the side would have been wholly successful.

All the sides of *Incantations* open with a different variation of the overall, gentle mood. The fourth side begins particularly quietly, flute-like synth notes floating by. Later, remarkably clean and sensually exciting vibraphones begin, played by Gong's Pierre

Moerlen. It is likely that Mike recorded this and the similar guitar-and-vibraphones part on side three after he had undergone est: he was to praise them afterwards because they were in some way for him full expressions of a deeper, non-neurotic personality which he believed est had uncovered. He was to contrast these parts of the work unfavourably with the rest of the composition and with his earlier LPs.

Towards the end of the side Sally Oldfield 'aah's' vocally, nearer the surface of the mix than she had ever been on Mike's previous work. (With the gradual loosening of Mike's personality, he had, as a result of some curious connection, simultaneously become less antagonistic towards clear lyrics and vocals, as first exemplified by the enhanced choral vocals on the 1976 remix of *Hergest Ridge*, then Sally's more prominent vocalising on Pekka Pohjola's 1977 LP, and, here, the choir's and Maddy Prior's reciting of clearly identifiable poetry). Synth replays the theme for the setting of *Hiawatha*, although Prior sings the full words to *Diana*. To make the different metre of the latter fit that of the former, Mike gets Maddy to stretch two syllables out of the vowel sounds. Guitar takes over the tune, with hand claps and sleighbells, and, slowly, the whole thing winds down to the end.

Incantations is a departure from Mike's previous work. It induces not so much catharsis or sense of emotional release, but rather a feeling of reverie and inner peace (no doubt reflecting and expressing all the beneficial changes in the composer's psyche over the years preceding, and during, its recording). There is a new clarity, eloquence and directness. The piece is particularly cohesive, with the same limited set of main and accompanying instruments, and with vocals appearing at regular intervals; Mike also achieves a smooth unity by playing almost all the music on synthesizers, and by making these at times resemble the flute, trumpet and strings also present. The production on the work is notably lucid and distinct, and there is a good deal less overdubbing and none of the admittedly attractive slightly muddy weave of sound typical of the three earlier albums.

For all of these reasons, *Incantations* is, at first, a little disorientating after the earlier LPs; but the musical process has not really been changed so much as it has been refined, and this refinement makes the work comparatively unusual. *Incantations* is subtle, and this subtlety means that it escapes a casual listening, to which it sometimes appears featureless.

After Mike had finished the double LP, a heady energy and enthusiasm, generated in him by est, spurred him to undertake several new ventures, some musical, some not. Free from recording commitments, he started taking flying lessons. He had wanted to fly since he had been a child, when he dreamed of joining the RAF, but he had been partly discouraged by a fear of flying. Est, however, had introduced him to the idea of experiencing even painful feelings, so that he decided that *"the only way to conquer my fear was to experience it and combat it by being in control of my safety"*.

Mike's new personality also caused him to change his image. He shaved off his beard, and had his long, hippie hair cut short - taking the style from contemporary New Wave artists - and dressed in slacks, sports coat, and open-collared shirt - this being exactly the 'uniform' that his est trainers wore.

Having spent most of his career hidden away from his fans in his studios, he decided to arrange with a very surprised Virgin Records for his first ever tour. *"I knew I had to go out on the road and face the people"*, he explained afterwards. A new self-confidence swept away a lot of his disquiet about playing live, which had been partly due to his *"old"*, insecure personality. Mike's apparently sudden conversion to the idea of touring, however, had already begun after *Boxed* had been released in 1976, when he had said that he was coming around to the idea. His feeling then was that if he could only collaborate with sound engineers, and thereby work towards achieving his desired sound quality, playing his music live might be feasible. Est provided him with the impetus to turn theory into practice, and he went on to realise the idea as he had earlier envisaged: when the tour took place in 1979, he had gathered a coterie of engineers and sound assistants.

To play his music, including *Incantations*, Mike planned to have a large electric band, a female singer, a string section, and a choir. By the time he came to tour, there was a remarkable forty-six musicians, and a crew of thirty.

Mike was to concentrate a great deal on the musical and technical aspects of his first live shows, because, he explained, *"I wanted to guarantee it would work; be safe rather than sorry, and I got the best technicians and enough musicians to get the best foundation for future (live) work"*.

When he unveiled his scheme to Virgin, the record company was perturbed at the huge expense they knew it would involve. *"They wanted me to use backing tapes"*, he complained. *"I wanted people. All I'd seen for years was the inside of a studio and machines. I didn't want to go on the road with just a tape recorder"*.

To recoup some of their costs for the venture, Virgin suggested that they provide only half of the money needed, with Mike paying the other half. To offset the costs still further, Virgin also wanted to record the performances for a live album; Mike later commented disaffectedly: *"They have to make their money somehow"*. His comment marked the beginning of a long period of disenchantment and slow-burning irritation with Virgin. At this time, his concern was largely over the record company's financial conduct, and not just over the tour financing. He hated the music of Punk and New Wave bands, who had emerged since 1976, feeling that they were puerile and talentless, and he was annoyed that, in a rush to sign such bands, Virgin were using money which he felt he had earned for them, and were freely offering them highly favourable financial rewards, compared to the terms of the contract to which he was bound. (This concern of his would be supplemented by various other grievances which developed subsequently, and which would bring about conflict between the two parties which would come to a head, dramatically, two years later).

Simultaneously with his decision to perform live, Mike contacted Virgin publicist Al Clark, and, in total contrast to his previously bashful manner, demanded that he be interviewed by every newspaper and magazine he could think of. Clark was astounded. He recalled that, in the past, *"Whenever anyone from Fleet Street phoned to ask for an interview with Mike - which was often - I had to tell them he was too busy working on his new album. After four or five years it began to wear a bit thin"*. Now, Clarke reported, *"Mike's even asked me to arrange interviews with Women's Own and Penthouse. Whatever next?"*

From this time Mike also became more amenable to giving the odd radio or TV interview, and in subsequent years he would actively promote successive LPs, singles and tours with radio and TV appearances both in Britain and Europe.

In order to sort out tour details and be available for interviews, Mike stayed in London, on Richard Branson's houseboat on the Thames. He lived there for most of October and November at least, returning home to Througham only twice during that time.

Living in London allowed him to attend the Virgin staff party held at the end of October to celebrate the opening of the label's night club, The Venue. That he even turned up was surprising, as were the other things that the previously world-shy young man would never have been seen doing before est. Al Clark was amazed to see the diminutive composer talking with weighty concert promoter Harvey Goldsmith, for example: *"He would previously never go near a place like The Venue, and the idea that once there he would find anything to talk about with someone like Harvey Goldsmith would have been preposterous"*. He went on to miss the night's musical entertainment, provided by four minor New Wave acts, because he was up in the balcony with a beautiful model from a soft porn magazine. Later on he mounted the stage - wearing only a nappy! There followed an attempt by himself, some musical friends and even Richard Branson to engage in a spontaneous jam session.

It was around this period that Mike posed for nude and semi-nude photographs which, he said, were meant to make him look like statues by Auguste Rodin. Having these taken was a deliberate device. Mike had previously hidden himself from the world; but one's self, one's ego, is as much a physical, bodily boundary as it is an emotional one: exposing his body was Mike's metaphoric way of forthrightly revealing his new, more open self, and of transforming his public image as a shy, reclusive hippie. One of the nude photos was later used by Sounds for their December 2nd issue.

Fulfilling some of the set of press interviews he had got Al Clark to organise for him, Mike met Melody Maker's Karl Dallas, and NME's Bob Edmands before the end of November. These encounters were to reveal his new est-moulded personality as fervently self-assured and slightly manic. He could not have formed more of a contrast to the reserved and introverted person whom interviewers had found in the past.

Karl Dallas was taken aback when he met Mike: *"I hardly recognised this clean shaven, fresh-faced extrovert who flung his arms around me"*. Mike and his new girlfriend went with Dallas and photographer Barry Plumber to a London restaurant. There, as they waited to be served, Mike took up one of the techniques he had experienced during est and used it to try and create the same unsettling effect in Dallas that he had witnessed then. The victim recounted:

"(he stares) at me piercingly with those steel-blue eyes of his for a minute or more, it seems, challenging me to look away, and I just can't....So there we sit in silence...staring at each other, while the rest of the company shuffles its feet in embarrassment".

The tension was finally broken when Barry Plumer started to pack away his equipment and Mike turned to say goodbye. Dallas was successfully irritated, however.

Mike then demanded that Dallas ask him some questions. The latter demurred, feeling that the situation was unsuitable. *"Right"*, Mike replied authoritatively, like an est trainer, *"Wel'll do it at 8.30. That's precisely ten minutes from now"*. A proper interview did not in fact take place until later in the evening, however. Until then, Dallas reported that Mike turned his attention to his girlfriend.

who turned out to be a model and a would be children's author, a gentle young woman who seemed torn between a fascination with his undoubted charisma, and a resistance to the overpowering nature of the personality he was laying on all of us. I knew exactly how she felt.

After the meal, Mike retired with Dallas to Richard Branson's houseboat, where Dallas, who knew nothing about Mike's taking est, asked him what on earth was going on:

"For a long time", he said slowly, in the measured tones of one dictating a business letter, *"I was determined to have a very bad time in order to work out a few things, including my childhood. I have now completed that process, and chosen to have a good time"*.

Repeating est's main tenet, Mike said of his childhood: *"I've chosen for that to happen...I'm responsible for everything now, rather than saying 'it's all happening to me", and "he did it: and "she did it, it's nothing to do with me". I'm totally guilty, and everything was...my fault"*. By way of explanation for his new outlook, he said to Dallas: *"I'm exactly the same person. I'm just looking at things from a different viewpoint"*.

Dallas still had no idea what had brought about Mike's new attitude, but he soon began to suspect:

I had noticed the whole evening the same disturbing alienness that I had seen in other friends who had turned to Scientology or the Guru Maharaji, and in Communists who had turned to the Church - the hard, burning fire of the convert, disorientation replaced by certainty, the unerring confidence behind the eyes that drilled into mine in the restaurant.

Mike then revealed that he had taken the est course, as a result of a long-growing desire to change.

In the middle of one of Dallas's questions, Mike suddenly spun off - in a manner typical of his post-est behaviour - to describe an apparent personal insight concerning his past music-making, that, although he did not say so, came to him as a result of est. *"The pattern I've been repeating"*, he claimed, *"is to first make people like me, and then make people reject me, which is was what I did with Tubular Bells and Hergest Ridge. With Ommadawn, I had to make people like me again. But then I'd done my game with those two"*. *Ommadawn* wasn't part of his game, he said, especially the re-birth section. When Dallas asked whether the critics had thus been right in dismissing *Hergest Ridge*, Mike agreed - in contrast to what seem to have been his far more real feelings at the time. He then immediately relocated the thread of his mental training, and said of the reactions of the critics and others, *"I get exactly what I want....I can't go wrong. Everything that happens to me, I'm totally responsible for"*.

What he now considered his neurotic game, he explained, had ended with *Ommadawn*. So what had he intended for the soon to be released *Incantations*? He replied by pointing only to those parts of the composition that he had recorded after est, through which he had intended to *"totally express"* himself. What he appears to have meant by this was the expression of a deeper self behind his painful emotions. With a flute solo on the first side, and the vibraphones-and-guitar solos on the last, he felt that he had come close to that ideal. He now considered these elements to be *"the only important parts"* of *Incantations*; *"The rest of it"*, he claimed erroneously, in a comment that must have dismayed Virgin, *"is a load of rubbish"*.

"And all my works have been a load of rubbish", he further announced. This surprising statement is not as shocking as it seems, although Mike was well aware of its value as such, when it is read with his important qualifying statement: his albums, he said, were rubbish by the standards of his fully expressing his deeper self, rather than his hang-ups and emotions, *"all that sort of rubbish"*.

Dallas protested, rightly, that emotions were valuable and important. (Indeed it was the emotional nature of Mike's music, rather than its inventiveness or high melodic content, that lent it its ultimate, lasting value.) Mike, however, drawing on est, said that his emotions were only a part of his total self. Then, repeating est's emphasis on subjectivity to tarnish the reasonably objective nature of Dallas' point, he said, almost condescendingly: *"It's your choice whether you decide to see things like that or not. It's fine, whatever you think, but I see myself as not my body, not my mind, and I'm expressing that essence of me"*.

The most important way in which est had changed Mike was in his new attitude to music-making. Now he was no longer driven to seek a refuge in composing intensely emotional musical sanctuaries. He no longer had to compose, he explained to Dallas. Although he would continue to make music, it was no longer as deep a need as it had been in the past, but was simply an intellectual choice devoid of any emotional considerations. Composing was simply *"not a necessity anymore"*. Through therapy, he had thus inadvertently been deprived, or had deprived himself both of what had been the strongest element of his motivation to compose - his emotional need - and consequently the emotional and sensitive nature and content which contributed strongly to the attraction of his music. Although this was not to detrimentally affect the quality of his music immediately, it was certainly to do so later.

The traits of Mike's new personality appeared again when he met NME's Bob Edmands. Here he demonstrated the flights of ideas typical of est's effects on people with manic tendencies: for example, after again denouncing his own double album as rubbish, he continued, in the same breath, 'We're all the same by the way', and then declared, *"If you also want to be in a state of absolute joy, you can be"*; as Edmands observed drily, *"This comment seems to be yet another conceptual leap"*.

He went on, trenchantly, about responsibility and his not regretting anything in his past, claiming. *"There's no way I can make a mistake. I get exactly what I want even if it is bad, and I always have done"*.

Given all of Mike's expansive, often barely intelligible est-sponsored monologues, it was not surprising that a justifiably weary Edmands was to comment, after the lengthy interview: *"By this time, even my cassette player is beginning to nod out under the sheer oppressive weight of this endless litany..."*

Mike had also talked about his music, for which he had quite new plans. There were three things he wanted to do, he said. He wanted to write and sing *"a really beautiful love song"*. He wanted to compose a piece of disco music, because he had discovered that his body could express itself, and he could dance; in an effect typical of many psychological therapies, a loosening or concentration on mental pains had apparently led him to a new awareness of his body, as the earlier nude photo session also demonstrated. Finally, he wanted to record a really heavy rock track, and massed voices. (He was to realise these ideas in the following year.)

After the interview, Mike was driven off to Bond Street to buy some jewellry. This, coupled with his irritating manner and his fervent, often incoherent monologues led the NME to caption the interview 'Apotheosis Of A Rich Twit'.

At the end of November details of Mike's first tour were announced. He was to perform in Spain, France, Germany, Holland and Belgium, before appearing in England. It was later specified that he would play six UK concerts at the end of April 1979: two shows each at the Festival Hall, Wembley Conference Centre and Wembley Arena. These replaced an originally scheduled single appearance at the Royal Albert Hall; Mike altered this arrangement because he disliked the acoustics of the Hall and the idea of playing in only one venue.

It was also reported that the shows would last two hours and that Mike would be playing excerpts from all his work. Although it is possible that the latter may have been what was originally intended, the shows were simplified to consist instead almost entirely of Mike's most famous piece, *Tubular Bells*, and his most recent, *Incantations*.

Incantations was released to the background of the announcement of Mike's new touring activity. Reviews were mixed. Sound's Hugh Fielder thought that the double album justified its length, because it was different to Mike's previous LPs, and he observed, rightly: *"There's a definite feeling on Incantations that Oldfield is broadening out and opening up new musical areas"*. Melody Maker did not agree on the length of the piece, and felt that it caused Mike to pursue *"one melodic idea to the pinnacle of self-importance (as displayed by making this a two-album set when, in truth, the idea runs pretty thin over one)"*.

Incantations went on to reach number fourteen in the album chart.

On 1st December 1978 Virgin released a four-track extended play collection of Mike's short folk instrumentals. As well as *Portsmouth, In Dulci Jubilo* and *The Sailor's Hornpipe,* there was a new track, *Wreckorder Wrondo.* It is not clear when the latter was made, but it was probably soon after similar early music pieces *Cuckoo Song* and *Pipe Tune,* which were recorded in the second half of 1977. Mike recorded the piece with early music enthusiast Richard Harvey, who had been a member of the band Gryphon. Harvey takes Les Penning's place on the recorder, and his work for the piece earned him a co-writing credit. As the title suggests, the piece is a rondo, in which a main melodic theme is repeated at intervals.

Towards the end of 1978 *Incantations* collaborator Pierre Moerlen asked Mike to play guitar for *Downwind,* the title track of an LP by Gong - now renamed Pierre Moerlen's Gong, after their then main musical force. The band had long since changed direction and personal since the days when they were an eccentric bunch of experimentally-minded hippies led by Soft Machinist Daevid Allen, and they now played a tight and often stimulating brand of jazz-rock. (Their LP also features guest appearances by Steve Winwood, Mick Taylor, and Mike's brother, Terry, on flute.)

Downwind is based on Moerlen's extensive solo work on vibraphones, and, to a lesser extent, on drums, which play to the transient accompaniment of the full band and Mike's forthright guitar, which carries a counter-melody to the instrumental's main clinking vibes part. The guitar and vibraphones recall the same elements on *Incantations,* that piece probably giving rise to this second exploration of the combination.

Not only did Mike play on the PMG track, but a typical desire to perfect his own guitar sound led him to produce it with Moerlen.

Around the time that he recorded with PMG, Mike was also asked to play some (eventually inaudible) tubular bells on *Girl Of My Dreams,* a track by unlikely collaborators, neo-New Wave pub rockers Bram Tchaikovsky.

The release of Mike's *Incantations,* and of the *Take Four* retrospective EP were to mark the end of the Mike's first creative phase. What he was subsequently to record was to break from, or dilute, the moods, style, instrumentation, production, format and recording technique for which he had been noted previously. This was largely a result of his est-sponsored personality change. The past year had been a watershed for Mike personally, which, by inevitable extension, induced changes in his music, most of which are still present today.

Chapter 8

Tour De Force

After he had announced his plans to tour, Mike set about organising the details of what was going to be a huge musical and technical undertaking.

He sought and found musicians whom he could trust with his music, his criteria being, as they had always been, ability and musical and emotional sympathy. Accordingly, he chose players with whom he was familiar, not just as musicians, but also as collaborators and friends: Pekka Pohjola (bass), Maddy Prior (vocals), Pierre Moerlen (drums and percussion), and PMG members Benoit Moerlen (vibraphones) and Nico Ramsden (guitar).

Mike also picked musicians whom he may not have known personally, but whose natural ability or classical training eminently qualified them for their tasks. He added folk performer Phil Beer as another guitarist, and travelled to Ireland to find a bodhrán player, recruiting Ringo McDonough of acclaimed Irish traditional group De Danaan. Additional drummer Mike Frye, and keyboard players Tim Cross and Pete Lemer had all been classically taught, and also had experience of playing rock.

Mike commissioned David Bedford to arrange the orchestra for the live versions of *Incantations* and also of *Tubular Bells*. Bedford's work was considerably lessened because he had already arranged the studio recording of *Incantations*, and had done the orchestral rendering of *Tubular Bells*. The orchestra comprised four trumpets, two flutes, six violins, six violas, four cellos and two double basses. Dick Studt was to conduct.

Mike formed a choir from the girls of Queen's College. He really wanted a full classical choir, *"about a hundred singers"*, but this was financially unacceptable to Virgin, and they made him do with sixteen girls.

The technical aspects of the live shows were also co-ordinated. To present a live sound that was almost studio perfect, Mike arranged for the concert amplification to be in quadraphonic form - probably the first such use of a mode particular to finished recordings. To ensure the best sound balance, he assigned a separate microphone to each of the orchestral instruments, and, to adequately control the sound quality and distribution for the entire ensemble, both rock and orchestral, he was fatefully determined to use a new and untried computerised mixing desk.

To further regulate the sound, Mike travelled to New York towards the end of 1978 to engage the services of producer and engineer Kurt Mankacsi, the studio partner of American minimalist composer Philip Glass, with whose music Mike was familiar and felt a certain degree of musical kinship.

He did not meet Munkacsi solely to talk about his live sound requirement. By the time of his visit he had written *Guilty*, the disco piece he had said he wanted to do, and he subsequently got Munkacsi to produce it.

Guilty was recorded uncharacteristically quickly and simply in New York in December 1978. Mike just booked a studio, used a group of local session musicians, brought in Stevie Winwood on organ, and recorded the track in both single-length and extended versions.

The piece was a shocking change of musical style: disco-rock, but still filtered through his unique musical personality. Despite Mike's unfamiliarity with such music, his piece is excellent, especially its exhilarating main melody. Part of the music is based on his uptempo modification of one of the recurrent elements on *Incantations* (where it is played on strings). From this base, however, it all swans off with synth and horn/guitar sections, drums and bass; the synths sound even richer and more sonorous than on *Incantations*. At times during the quick, swirling music, choir-like vocalists chant the title, Mike's version of est's theme of personal responsibility of one's past. The longer, six minute version repeated sections of the original more often, and also featured Mike's addition of an exciting guitar part.

During his visit to New York, Mike talked to Guitar Player magazine. He explained that the guitars which he had used on his recordings were his old 1966 Fender Telecaster, which he had had since his 1970 band Barefeet, and his Gibson Les Paul Junior, both of which he was very fond of, and a newer Gibson L-5. He was to play the latter extensively during the forthcoming concerts, even though the other two guitars appeared a lot on his recordings. The Junior was, as he himself explained, his *"main instrument"*. It had featured on most of his work, contributing strongly to the wonderful sound of many of his guitar parts for his own and other's music. *"I certainly use the Les Paul Junior the most, even though it's a really tatty old thing. But it's so beautiful, and I like old electrics"*.

Most of the time when he was playing, Mike would fingerpick with his long fingernails, rather than use a plectrum. This was because of the complex recording system he had devised for his 'infinite sustain' guitar technique, an example of which had been his work for *First Excursion*: *"You see with my elaborate distortion set up, I have to damp all the strings that I'm not playing all the time. But I'll use a pick if I'm playing chord"*.

Mike currently possessed three bass guitars, including his old Fender Precision, which he had had since joining Kevin Ayers and The Whole World, and an acoustic bass, a favourite of his, made by noted craftsman Tony Zemaitis sometime soon before the recording of *Ommadawn*, on which it was used. His approach to the bass differed from that to the electric guitar, he explained. The bass was used *"to give a bottom"* to the music. He like its role, enthusing, *"It's nice to give a bottom end to the music and do something creative with it at the same time, too"*. His playing both bass and guitar might occasionally give rise to his creating a bass run that might be some part of the main, guitar tune disguised, although he felt he knew enough to avoid this.

He had a set of acoustic guitars, too. A *"lovely"* Martin six string, which he used primarily as a backing instrument, a Martin twelve-string, and a steel string guitar made for him by Zemaitis. He used the latter as a solo instrument; it could be heard in the acoustic solo just before the bagpipes on *Ommadawn*. He was very careful about the Zemaitis guitar: *"I don't drop it or anything, because it was built just the way I wanted it as far as colour and inlays. But the Martin I'll take into the house by the fire or something, because I'll play that anytime"*. Mike also had two classical guitars: a Ramirez classical, which he found easy to record, and a Ramirez flamenco guitar, which had *"a sharper, more percussive sound"*.

Despite the large amount of guitar playing on his music, Mike said that he did not now compose mainly on guitar: *"There are lots of parts of Tubular Bells that I thought of on guitar, but now I mostly use the piano"*. His then current use of piano as his compositional tool obviously carried over into the music, notably on the synth-dominated *Incantations*, and *Guilty*. He must have continued this compositional practice since then, because almost all his subsequent albums feature a lot of keyboards, to the sad detriment of his guitar, for which he had more remarkable abilities.

Mike described the way he composed: *"I don't actually sit down and say, "Right, I'm gong to compose something". I just love playing things. I play the piano, or I play the guitar. I always improvise. I don't think I'd play anything I loathed. If I find something that I think is nice I'll play it again, and if it seems really good enough I'll put it down on tape. Then I'll think of what else can go with it. One thing leads to another, and then I'll find one more bit and stick that on, just building, building, building - until I've got the whole thing"*.

When it came to record a composition properly, Mike put down a simple percussion timing track, which went most of the way through the piece. The timing track often surfaced as an important component of the finished recording; this was particularly evident with the bodhrán on his short folk instrumentals. After the timing track he added either rhythm guitar or piano, or something that was in tune, so that he could play everything else in tune with it.

Guitar featured regularly in his own music, but Mike did not think much of the guitarist's role in others' music: *"I don't think electric guitar is being used well enough, used as good as it can be"*, he said. *"I think that it can be as expressive and beautiful - if not more beautiful - than a violin or a viola, if it's used properly"*. This was certainly triumphantly borne out in his own work. He pointed out, however, with his particular studio processes in mind, *"You need all the technology to get that sound out"*.

After his American activities, Mike returned to England, to complete the plans for the rapidly approaching tour, beginning rehearsals with the electric band, orchestra and choir in Germany in January 1979.

At this late stage, the plans for the coming tour were by no means without problems - problems which sprang from Mike. Organising a tour was beyond the experience of Richard Branson, who had acted as Mike's manager since *Tubular Bells* had been released. Branson thus bowed out of this role in Mike's affairs. A tour manager was recruited, but Mike sacked him because, he complained haughtily, *"he looked too much like a student"*. As a replacement, Virgin then suggested Sally Arnold, who had managed the Rolling Stones' recent European tour. Time was running out, but, remarkably, Mike was reluctant to employ her, because, she recalled, *"he didn't want a woman in charge"*. She was nevertheless taken on and proved to be perfectly capable.

Sally Arnold's first task as tour manager was to clear up a difficult situation Mike had created. She explained that he originally had picked the prettiest of the Queen's College girls for the choir: *"Unfortunately not all of them had voices to match their looks"*. Mike did not feel up to telling the unlucky girls that, after several weeks of rehearsal, they were to be sacked. Instead, he dropped the matter into Arnold's lap, and left her to explain it all to the girls and their furious parents.

It was a more fortuitous result of the preparatory work necessitated by the tour that Mike came into increasing contact with Sally Cooper, a publicist at Virgin's London headquarters. The pair soon became very close, and Mike later invited her to accompany him on tour.

On 14th February, Mike guested on a live performance of *The Rime Of The Ancient Mariner* at a wide-ranging retrospective concert of David Bedford's works, held at a packed Queen Elizabeth Hall.

He also played *Downwind* with Pierre Moerlen's Gong at Virgin's club, The Venue, on 11th March, where the band were appearing as part of a brief set of shows to promote their *Downwind* LP. The whole performance was recorded for a US radio programme and part of it was subsequently released as *Pierre Moerlen's Gong Live* in May.

Shortly before the beginning his live shows, in response to public demand Mike added two new provincial dates to his English appearances, planning now to close the tour in Birmingham and Manchester in the first week of May.

The huge entourage of electric band, orchestra, choir and crew then embarked on tour. Mike opened his first ever set of live appearances with four concerts in Spain: at Barcelona on 31th March and Madrid on 2nd April Virgin's Al Clark reported that these shows were received with great enthusiasm. From there, the tour went to Paris, and Dusseldorf, where Virgin persuaded Mike to allow a party of English rock press journalists to join him.

One of this group, Melody Maker's Allan Jones, reported that Mike had long since become determined to use a new, custom-made computerised mixing desk for the shows:

"This was one innovation virtually everyone argued against. It was built especially for Oldfield and delivered, with some modifications still to be carried out, after the group had already started rehearsing. Oldfield fell out with the designer. Tom Newman...was brought in to supervise its operation and installation.

Oldfield fell out with him, too. Newman decided to preserve their friendship by retiring gracefully from the front line before too much damage was done to their relationship.

Oldfield continued to be obsessed with the computerised mixing desk. He would use it, and was damned well not going to listen to any arguments against it".

During rehearsals at Dusseldorf, the mixing desk blew up. *"We all told him it wouldn't work"*, Sally Arnold recalled. *"Mike just wouldn't listen to anyone. He had to find out for himself that it wouldn't work"*. Mike later replied, with winning pigheadedness: *"I do listen to people if they offer advice. I just don't find that I take much notice of it"*.

The show at Dusseldorf was seen by NME's Bob Edmands. The first half of the set was devoted to *Incantations, "and this"*, he wrote, *"is admittedly pretty dull. Most of the themes seem four times as long as they need be. Particularly tedious is a vocal rendition of Longfellow's poem Hiawatha"*. The second half of the show, Edmands felt, was *infinitely stronger - a re-vamped Tubular Bells and a majestic version of Oldfield's "disco" single Guilty. The German audience go suitably rabid for Tubular Bells, and Oldfield has beefed up the piece a lot, making it even more impressive than the original.*

Mike had refashioned the music because he was fed up with it as it was, and he wanted to allow more creative space within it for the other musicians he had gathered together.

Edlands thought that the Dusseldorf show had been successful, and that part of the reason for this lay in Mike's new-found confidence.

As a result he does amazingly extravagant things, like smiling at the audience, conducting the orchestra with his head, waving his guitar about and sporting dark glasses for some guitar heroics.

The shows success was also due to the technical details that Mike had gone to such lengths to get right, so that Edmands vouched: *"The sound...is of the highest quality you'll probably ever hear at a rock gig"*.

From Dusseldorf, the party went onto Berlin. Here Mike arranged to talk to Allan Jones, and demonstrated again the still strong effects on est on his personality and mental processes. He turned on Jones at one point, moving his face to within three inches of Jones', giving him 'one of his famous post-Exegesis stares', smiling mischievously and telling the discomfited reporter how much he liked his hair. Immediately on another tangent, he declared that it was his fault that the mixing desk had blown up. It was his fault, he claimed peculiarly, *"Because I had a very unhappy childhood, and I'm paying for it now. I didn't understand my parents. I made them reject me. I made myself have a really bad time. I wanted them to fuck me up. So they did"*. This was all an overlaid, est-inspired reinterpretation of his childhood experiences, rather than a true, balanced representation of his feelings as a child.

He evidenced more of his convoluted and deluded reasoning when he claimed that, subconsciously, he wanted to bore his audiences by performing *Incantations*, and wanted them to reject him. Sections of his audiences had indeed been bored by the live presentation of the long, drawn-out composition. What exactly he meant, though he talked about it at incoherent length, is unclear.

He also debated with Jones about whether or not he should in the future record material other than long instrumental works. *"Why should I suddenly change?"*, he demanded. *"I prefer long instrumental pieces. Why should I suddenly leap on somebody else's bandwagon. What do you want me to do? Go punk? Go disco?"*.

Just before he left Jones, Mike though about his now changed, more extrovert behaviour, and so pinned the journalist down with another of his intense stares, and enquired: *"When you write your article, are you going to describe me as a 'shy, retiring young genius'? That's what they usually write"*. Already somewhat bewildered by the evening, Jones concluded sardonically, *"With that he was off to bed"*.

Mike was up early next morning, posing for photographs besides the Berlin Wall. Bob Edmands asked Mike what he thought of the wall, innocently expecting a comment on it as a symbol of division or oppression. But Mike breezily told the astonished reporter that it was *"wonderful"* and *"tremendous"*.

He went on to give Edmands an interview, but one in which he ran around the journalist, stopping only to listen to questions or to fiddle with the switches of the annoyed Edmands' tape recorder. *"All the while"*, Edmands reported, *"he's grinning widely and laughing impishly"*.

More of Mike's strange, post-est behaviour followed on the night of the Berlin concert. He arrived at the venue with David Bedford, with whom he had been drinking in a local bar, returning in what Al Clark nervously characterised as *"one of his more disquietingly impish moods"*. Sure enough, he cornered poor Bob Edmands again, hugging the embarrassed journalist and telling him that he was frightened of affection. Edmands had almost to fight Mike off. Al Clark later commented ruefully: *"I was quite sure it wouldn't stop there. I was almost convinced he wasn't going to let you off without sticking his tongue down your throat"*.

Mike had just decided, probably as a bizarre form of revenge, to have the journalists actually play with him on stage during *The Sailor's Hornpipe*, thus forcing them to participate in music that he believed they actively disliked. The bewildered reporters were later given various small percussion instruments and shoved on stage by David Bedford; they acquitted themselves quite well, if in a humorous, shambolic spirit.

After the hapless journalists had agreed to the idea, Allan Jones came across Mike in a corridor of the hall. After admiring the jacket Jones was wearing, Mike promptly took off his own expensive tweed, exchanged it for Jones' and went on stage.

Although admiring his own jacket under the lights, Jones found *Incantations* hard going:

"The composition seems to spend an inordinate amount of time running on the spot before it actually gets up enough steam to run; and no sooner does it move into gear then it runs out of ideas. Having established an idea, Oldfield doesn't seem to know what to do or where to go. He just cuts to another line of attack".

He did praise parts of the piece, however, and Mike's *"elegant solo lines"* on guitar, observing: *"The clarity and tone of Oldfield's playing is rather striking"*.

Almost all of the critics agreed that the weakest part of the shows was *Incantations*, and the weakest element of that piece was the setting of Longfellow's poem. *"Poor Maddy Prior!"*, Jones lamented, *"How she ever manages to get through the Hiawatha section without falling asleep and toppling of her perch is beyond me. She's forced to drone on and on, until you think that it can't possibly last another second, and then it continues for at least a further weekend"*.

The performance of Mike's disco single, *Guilty*, was like the two long works, given an orchestral treatment. It was also accompanied by animated images projected onto a screen behind the ensemble. Mike had been led to combine film and music as a result of his introductory experience working on the film *Reflection*; indeed he actually borrowed images from that film. The scenes were done by animator Ian Emes, with whom Mike had worked devising images which, when added to the heady music, would have a hypnotic effect and take the audience to a mental and emotional dimension that they had not entered before. The mind-altering intention of these scenes probably owed something to Mike's meditative experiences during the processes of the est course.

From Berlin the tour continued to Belgium and Denmark, after which it arrived in England. There Mike played eight shows, finishing with the two provincial dates at Birmingham and Manchester. A triumphant tour was complete.

Soon afterwards, Mike and Manor produced Phil Newell put together the live album that had been planned. They used parts of the concerts, all of which, apart from the two final shows, had been recorded by The Manor Mobile. *"We had a lorryload of tapes"*, Mike recounted, *"and at the end of the tour we put together what we considered were the best bits of the whole tour onto a double album....it was a big editing job".*

Mike then quickly started recording a new (and groundbreaking) LP, subsequently to be titled *Platinum*. He did so, Melody Maker's Colin Irwin later reported, because, *"One day his accountant rang up and told him he'd better make some money quick or he'd have to sell his house or his studio"*. The enormous tour had been matched by equally enormous bills; Mike said later that he had bull-dozed right into the tour, *"and I ended up getting ripped-off by lots of people. I knew the tour would lose a lot of money. I thought it would lose about £100,000, and we decided to split it between Virgin and me; we thought, okay, for the promotion, it'll be worth it. But it worked out we lost about £500,000"*. He laughed as he recalled, *"when we finally got all the bills pouring in at the end...it was - phew! - time to start tearing your hair out, because it cost a bomb"*.

Instead of working in the studio in his largely solo manner, Mike gathered a group together. This comprised some members of the electric band he had formed for the tour: Pierre Moerlen, Nico Ramsden, and Pete Lemer, augmented by extra drummer Morris Pert. To these he added four local New York musicians when he returned to America to record some of the album.

The LP was being produced by Mike's old friend and one-time studio partner Tom Newman. Mike had chosen to work with Newman again, because, *"I was looking for a producer who could actually contribute something, so I went back to Tom because I know him well and love his sense of humour"*. Evidently, the pair's disagreement over the computerised mixing desk had been patched up.

While Mike was recording, other, finished work was available. *Guilty* had been on release since 6th April. The 12" version of the single carried the additional, extended recording of the piece. The 7", however, was backed with an excellent guitar section from *Incantations*. The fine single was a commercial, as well as a musical success, reaching number twenty-two in the chart.

Mike's music could also be heard on *The Space Movie*, the first release from Virgin Films. This was a collection of footage from various American space missions. Mike was reported to have been asked to compose an original soundtrack for the film, but this seems not to have been the case. Instead, the soundtrack was made up of extracts from all of Mike's LPs, including a three-minute out-take from *Incantations*. Before going on cinema release, the film was shown on ITV on 20th July.

The double album drawn from the tour was released as *Exposed* on 23rd July. It was excellent, both in terms of performance and sound quality. The major pieces clearly got a fine treatment live. Whatever doubts Mike may have long held about performing his music, the results of his first attempt were very good indeed.

Despite the critics' misgivings at the shows, *Incantations*, which takes up the first LP, was nevertheless livelier and more forcefully engaging than its mild and gentle studio recording. Particularly responsible for this was Mike's expanded role in the live version. In places where he would otherwise have had little to do on guitar if he had stuck to the recorded version, he took on parts originally played by other instruments. Also responsible for the great musical effects were the strings, which sound really alive, and Benoit Moerlen's mesmerising vibraphones.

The live recording of *Incantations* was naturally shorter than the original double album. Parts were cut, but it is not clear if these changes were made for the performance, or when Mike was editing the live recordings. The first, choral 'Diana, luna' phrases, the long guitar solo from the third part of the piece, and twelve lines of *Hiawatha* were omitted.

Mike's transference of *Tubular Bells* to the stage also demonstrated changes from the original, studio treatment. There had to be changes that fully used the electric group (especially bass and drums) and the orchestra. The latter were handled very well, with strings, flutes, and trumpets noticeably adding something to the piece in a way that they had not done on *The Orchestral Tubular Bells*. This is particularly noticeable at the beginning of the second part, and on *The Sailor's Hornpipe*, where a single violin adds the appropriate nautical atmosphere. With such arrangements, and the fuller employment of other players, Mike gave *Tubular Bells* a robust and energetic treatment.

Guilty appears at the end of *Tubular Bells*, incorporating the tune from the last section of the longer work.

Exposed was originally issued in a limited pressing of 100,000 copies, so as to become particularly sought after and thereby gain quick and assured sales which would flow into Virgin and go some way to recouping their outlay for the tour. When copies looked like selling out, Virgin then decided to give the double set a full release. The LPs came in a white gatefold sleeve, packed with photographs from the tour which hinted at its grand scale and spectacle. Mike is pictured many times, playing, posing with his guitar and with his girlfriend Sally Cooper. The set was entitled *Exposed* as a pun on these uncropped photos, and a comment on what one critic had earlier characterised as Mike's new, tortoise-like emergence from his past solitary hibernation from the world.

The set was basically well received by reviewers. Melody Maker's Karl Dallas felt that *"although Incantations had been cut, the joins really don't show, and now that it has been played in, it hangs together much better as a piece. My feeling, at the concerts, that this was actually the summation of everything that Mike has done hitherto, is ...confirmed"*.

He also thought that the live version of *Tubular Bells* was the best of its several re-recordings, commenting favourably on the changes that had been made to it, *"which turn it from a melody of anguished yearning to a tranquil acknowledgement of achievement"*. Sounds' Hugh Fielder felt similarly, and also praised the sound balance of *Incantations,* which he thought was remarkable given the size of the ensemble.

The set went to number sixteen in the chart.

Sometime during the recording that Mike was doing for *Platinum,* he produced a proposed single by James Vane, titled *Judy's Gone Down.* Vane was an early, minor exponent of a post-Punk music and fashion style which subsequently became known as New Romantic; tall, thin and good looking, he wore the movement's hallmarks of make-up and eyeliner. Mike's surprising involvement with Vane, whose music was utterly unlike his own, came about in a roundabout way. Vane had been invited to act in a planned horror film. He was then asked to provide a recording of his singing voice, so he and his band recorded a demo of *Judy's Gone Down.* The tape was sent away to the film company, but he heard nothing, and forgot about it until his manager rang him and told him that Mike wanted to produce the song at his studio. Mike often received requests to compose film soundtracks, and he appears to have been approached by the same company who had recruited Vane, and thus came into contact with the song. Vane and his band re-recorded it, and taped the single's B-side, *Jung Lovers* at Mike's, over three days.

Mike's brother, Terry, later charitably took the tapes around the record companies. Island Records finally took the single and released it in January 1980 to favourable reaction.

Vane was later scathing about Mike, however: *"We don't want anything else to do with Mike Oldfield whatsoever, I don't like him. He charged us a ridiculous amount to record that single, two and a half to three thousand pounds. It cost us the first of the whole single advance to pay him off. Someone like Gary Numan can record an album for about three thousand pounds, and it's probably a better production"*.

Mike broke from his recording work again soon afterwards, when he made a version of the theme music to the long-running BBC children's programme, Blue Peter. He had originally been approached by the programme's producers because they wanted to feature an item showing someone using a recording studio. He recounted: *"Blue Peter wanted to come down to my studio...and film me working so they could show the viewers how I worked, or how any recording studio worked and just the modern technique or multi-tracking, and how that was done, and they chose me to do it"*. As the producers knew, Mike's music was one of the best examples of overdubbing. *"I think it was my suggestion: what better thing to be working on than a version of the theme tune, which I did, and it turned out very well. It didn't take long....just a couple of hours' work"*.

Mike's version of the signature tune, comprising two traditional pieces, is happy and rollicking. The first of these, *Drums and Fife,* was the only tune broadcast as the programme's theme; Mike appears to have added the second, *Barnacle Bill.* He adapted the martial music of the first for synth, piano, guitar, tambourine and bodhrán. The latter was Mike's timing track, but, typically, it also appeared as a main feature of the music; during the Blue Peter film Mike explained how he used the bodhrán as a guide to later overdubbing. *Barnacle Bill* was incorporated well into *Drums and Fife,* beginning after the first statement of the latter, and then opening the music out into something larger. The piano accompaniment to the whole piece is delightful in its quick English folk rhythm.

Mike's most important musical achievement of the year, however, had been his live performances; postponed and avoided for so many years, they had turned out to be generally accomplished. The tour was not long over, however, when Mike returned to recording so that he could make an LP to recover some of his and Virgin's tour outlay. The resulting *Platinum,* like *Guilty,* was to mark further radical change and development, with Mike delving surprisingly well into musical modes which were almost entirely new to him.

PART TWO

Chapter 9

New Sounds, New Styles

Mike made *Platinum* at a number of studios: at Througham; at The Manor, where he had not worked since remixing *Hergest Ridge* in 1976, back in New York, at Blue Rock and Electric Ladyland studios; and at his new home in Denham, a small, pretty Buckinghamshire village not far from the outskirts of London.

He and his girlfriend Sally moved to Denham around September 1979. Througham, he commented a year later, had been *"a lovely place....and it was what to me about four years ago would've been my Heaven: to be miles away from everywhere, and a beautiful place, and trees and fields and cows and everything. And there's a lovely studio in the barn. It had everything I wanted. But I tend to be dissatisfied once I've got what I want, and I felt that I'd moved on from that situation: it was all very well being isolated and happy, but where are the people?...That was what was wrong living so far way and just working in the studio: I was working in an empty room. So... I moved closer to London where it's easier to meet with business people...and meet with technicians, and if you want to go to London to test out a piece of equipment it's very easy to do it, whereas in Gloucestershire it's a whole day's journey in and out".*

The house he found was also convenient because it was only half-a-mile from Denham aerodrome, and he had been learning to fly.

The building was beautiful, and still as relatively secluded as Througham had been, while at £150,000, Mike considered it inexpensive. It was a 140 year old gabled, twelve room farmhouse, which boasted a fine garden and forty seven acres of neatly fenced fields and woodland.

Soon after the couple moved in, their daughter was born. The pair called her Molly, her name derived from Mike's initials and Sally's last syllable.

Mike installed a makeshift 24 track, £160,000 home studio in his new home, where he recorded some of his albums; he was to have a proper studio built for later recordings. He did not produce the LP, but left this responsibility in the hands of Tom Newman, and engineer Kurt Munkacsi. The combination of technicians created a clear, rich, lush production which showed off the kind of music he had composed, and they way he had played it, to great effect.

The resulting album, *Platinum,* differed sharply from all Mike's previous LPs. Its format unusually comprised a single long piece on one side, and a collection of shorter material - including two songs - on the other side.

The music, too, was different: energetic, and optimistic, incorporating a range of completely new styles, such as jazz, disco, contemporary minimalism (in the form of a cover version of a piece of music by Philip Glass), and even punk rock, and it was played through a group, rather than a solo, approach. Whatever the critics might say after its release, the album certainly represented a dramatic and exciting change.

Platinum, the long composition, consists of four separately titled parts. it opens strikingly with *Airborne,* a track inspired by Mike's new found joy in flying, a feeling he very successfully manages to recreate. The track starts off with Mike's broad synth tune, to which sprightly, jumping bass is added; such addition of instruments paves the way for a musical climax within the track. But a larger sense of climax is also created by the mounting nature of each succeeding part of the whole composition, *Airborne* appropriately taking us on a dynamic musical and emotional trip that does not let up until the closing notes of the *Platinum Finale* at the end of the side. To the original synth and bass, Mike adds guitar and vibraphones, the use of which he carried over from *Incantations,* and which was further suggested to him recently by Benoit Moerlen's highly attractive playing during the live shows. At the guitar and vibes we achieve a sense of take off.

The music wobbles eccentrically, and 'disintegrates', to allow for an effortless seguing into the second part, the *Platinum* theme itself. This slide from one part to another, without becoming either too abrupt nor too unified and monotonous, is one of the best features of the whole LP, and one which Mike has not equalled since. Guitar, bass and disco-style drums begin, the rhythm section playing tightly here, and indeed, throughout the recording. A second tune (with now funky bass), and a version of this second tune, follows, sung by Mike himself in the first of several surprising vocal appearances; this is another new development; nor is it the soft, hippy singing of *Froggy Went A-Courting*, or the vulnerable hesitancy of *On Horseback*, but a jazzy, extrovert 'doo-wop' rap, delivered in throaty style. Mike shouts to the band to take it away, and the music speeds off again. There is a strong element of rock parody here (to feature again on the LP).

There is an engaging switch to *Charleston*, which is based on the '20s jazz dance of the same name. Again, Mike's dabbling in such a style is a remarkable new venture. The track opens with attention - grabbing horns, arranged and recorded in New York. The addition of instruments is effectively employed again, featuring a lovely hi-hat foil to the horns and thumping bass. Charleston is one of the odder tracks on the LP: it features some deft, tinkly piano, a neat bass riff, and exaggerated moaning female choral vocals, in the midst of which Mike enters again, whispering some more attractive 'sho-be-do-wop' nonsense. Tom Newman's production makes the most of the latter, switching between channels so that Mike's whispers became quite intimate.

The last part of the long composition, *Platinum Finale*, incorporates Mike's arrangement of *North Star*, the title-track of Philip Glass's most recent, Virgin released LP. The piece reminds us that Mike has been a talented arranger of music, ranging from this piece to his versions of traditional tunes. His version of Glass's track is essentially a simplification and popularisation; his treatment is more rock-orientated than the original, using drums, which had not been a feature of Glass's recording. Mike also developed the choral element of the piece, re-arranged by David Beford, making it less subtle. The choir here may be the 'massed voices' which Mike had said a few months earlier he intended to record. The piece finishes, typically, with an ending Mike plays for all it is worth, drums being withdrawn at the last, the choir and electric guitar remaining in the background.

Woodhenge, which begins the second side of the album, is a short, eerie, atmospheric track, very different in mood to the rest of the album. Although its treatment is in the new musical style, the piece sounds more like something from Mike's pre-theraphy music, perhaps like the music that one imagines accompanied *Reflection*, a film which dealt in part with Stonehenge and other dark, prehistoric sites. The track conveys the sense of a forbidding, mysterious past - an odd, hidden, recurring theme on some of Mike's music, present, for example, in the bodhrán on *Incantations*, and his 'caveman' section on *Tubular Bells*.

The track is a particularly percussive one, depending for its strong effects on ratchety wood - and stone-like sounds, which Mike creates on marimbas, glockenspiel, and deep, ringing vibraphones. He also plays delicate, clinking, echoing guitar, more reminiscent of older material than the strong, remarkably extrovert guitar style characteristic of all the other tracks. Mike plays the piece almost entirely solo, although he did teach Sally to play a part on tubular bells, which clang loudly, like the chimes of a demented clock.

Like the other sections, *Woodhenge* segues well into the next; this is *Sally*, the love song that Mike had wanted to do. If the song is simple and sentimental, it is also gentle and personal. Mike and Sally sing together, the former's modesty about his vocal ability prompting him to get Tom Newman to disguise the vocals so that they sound almost electronic. Mike complements the lyrics with a sweet solo, and also some squashed rhythm guitar (which sounds strongly like a typical sonic device of Newman's). After a repeated chorus Mike plays a bright, speedy break, to the accompaniment of quick, 'ooh-ahh' backing vocals and the sound of crowds cheering him on.

Guitar and drums suddenly double up in tempo in order to allow the track to fit with *Punkaddidle*, a parody of punk rock entwined with an Irish-style jig: a mixture only Mike could have created. Heavy guitar riffs parody punk - of the Sham '69 variety, rather than anything more sinister - onto which Mike plays the skipping jig on synth, Mike subsequently punkily shouting 'Oi!' over reprised crowd noises.. In another example of his penchant for odd endings, Mike's guitar plays along and fades as the synth takes over the tune, until this too fades. The soft ending to a track which had begun more forcefully allowed this piece in its turn to flow smoothly into the last track, Gershwin's *I Got Rhythm*, without disrupting the latter's gentle mood.

I Got Rhythm is not just a cover version but also a kind of statement by Mike about himself and his music at this time. The song, sung well by the rich-voiced Wendy Roberts, is intended to say that Mike is happy personally and confident musically. The track supports Mike's implied claim for musical quality, with some fine acoustic guitar, and the very effective, short, sharp crashes of dampened cymbals. Mike's electric guitar is excellent, as indeed it has been throughout the album, the most consistently fine playing he has ever recorded. Here is burns gallantly till the very end of the song, to whose sentiments of release from past sadness it has added its instrumental affirmation; it then dips suddenly and appealingly, and ends.

Mike's recording songs was an important development. His therapy-sponsored, increasingly positive attitude towards life seems to have led him to loosen a long-standing emotional block against songs which was one of the reasons which had made him so attracted towards instrumental music.

I Got Rhythm ends a musical triumph, an innovative, preconception-shattering record. With it, Mike explored new areas and approaches, stretching imposed, clichéd notions about himself and his music.

Virgin, however, wanted changes instituted to the LP, after they were presented with the tapes. The company took a particular dislike to *Sally*'s sentimental lyrics, and they put pressure on Mike to remove the song and replace it with something else. Mike refused to comply. He thought that *"the song was lovely. I was really knocked out with that whole side until we gave it to them and they hated it"*. He had also originally wanted to call the LP *Airborne, "but they wouldn't have it"*, he later complained. *"They've always done things like that. They even wanted me to put vocals on Tubular Bells"*. He retitled the LP Platinum, *"partly as a joke - you know " Mike Oldfield goes platinum", but also because it's a lovely, strange metal, heavy and bendy, like lead"*.

During the stalemate caused by their disagreement over *Sally*, Virgin pressed 30,000 copies of the LP as it stood, complete with labels and sleeves listing the offending track, because they did not want to miss the important pre-Christmas sales period.

Meanwhile, Tyne Tees Television had approached Mike to record the theme music for a proposed pop show. He decided to do a cover version of *All Right Now*, the famous song by hard rock band Free. He chose the song because it had always been a favourite of his, and he was interested in applying his own musical approach and recording techniques to it.

He re-drafted Pierre Moerlen to play drums and vibraphones, and Wendy Roberts to sing. He had Moerlen play vibes alongside the guitar break, which they do very effectively: the pair's guitar and vibes combinations had always been quite successful. Although Mike introduced vibes and a female singer, he did not alter the original that much, even going so far as to replay Paul Kossof's guitar part, rather than introduce his own, feeling that the former's fast, fiery licks could not be improved.

The pop programme appears to have shot a piece of film

showing Mike and his colleagues playing the song at the former's home studio. *All Right Now* later saw something of a release as a flexi-disc given away with a music magazine.

Mike then decided to go along with Virgin on the issue of *Sally*'s inclusion on *Platinum*, because he was coming to feel that, in the long run, it was in his own best interest to appear to his record company to be co-operative. for some time he had been thinking of renegotiating his contract with Virgin so as to increase his royalty rate, which he felt was not in line with what Virgin had been happy to offer new artists they had signed. He was also keen for Virgin to issue *Platinum* in the US, complaining, *"Nothing of mine has been released in the States for a long time - since Ommadawn in fact. Virgin are currently unwilling to put out Platinum over there in case it won't happen. They say they want to put out the right album at the right time. Meanwhile nothing is being released there and, though I think it's ridiculous, I can't do anything about it"*. By agreeing to the changes to the album, he thought he might garner some good will from the company, and that they might release the LP in the US and look again at his contract. This was not to say that he did not have mixed feelings over the replacement of *Sally*: *"I held out for quite a while, maybe I should have stuck to my guns. The road crew were sufficiently moved to ring me up and plead with me not to take it off. I probably shouldn't have"*.

He co-wrote a substitute song with his guitarist, Nico Ramsden. To sing, he used Maggie Reilly, previously the lead singer with minor band Cado Belle. Mike knew her, however, as the girlfriend of one of his loyal road crew. Her appearance here was to be the first of many for Mike later.

The new song had still to relate to the original, still retained title, *Sally*, so Mike wrote another love song to his girlfriend. This second song, like the first, continued to express his new faith and happiness, and his warm and loving feelings towards Sally, with its theme of leaving together to head into a bright shared future.

The new song had also to fit well with the musical style and sound of the already recorded album. Accordingly, Mike again employed the broad-sounding synths that had appeared prominently on the LP, sang some more 'ooh-aah' backing vocals, and retained a slightly studio-modified version of *Sally*'s original drum track, which had been recorded in New York.

The first 30,000 copies of *Platinum* contained the original track, while the new song (whose real title was *Into Wonderland*) appeared as *Sally* on all subsequent pressings of the LP.

The album was released on 23rd November 1979. It came in a slick black/blue cover, featuring a butterfly, one wing dipped in a pool of liquid metal. There was an inner sleeve to the LP, with two photos of Mike, in one of which he stares fixedly, est-style. The LP marked his third release since the previous November, which meant, as the NME observed, that within a year he had basically doubled his LP output.

The critics were actively hostile to *Platinum*, apparently oblivious to its wonderful melodies, its emotional and musical energy and its many new approaches. Melody Maker's reviewer characterised the LP as typically *"outrageously dull"*, and condemned the title-track as *"classic Oldfield hogwash: sterile, anodyne backing tracks overlaid with a single theme which repeats itself endlessly while Oldfield and his friends play musical chairs with a dozen or so different instruments"*.

Mike's treatment of Glass' *North Star* was said to reduce *"its circling suspense into a flabby, insulated wander around a selection of sound effects"*. *I Got Rhythm* and (the original) *Sally* (*"an infinitely wet ballad"*), were *"unlistenable"*. *Punkadiddle* was considered to be not as bad as the rest because its crowd noises removed it from *"the listless atmosphere of the studio"*.

Mike confessed himself bewildered by the reaction to the LP. He felt that the critics had not noticed what Karl Dallas described as *"the considerable break with his own past that its almost minimalist music"* represented. Mike pointed out that with Platinum he had learnt, for example, *"that you don't have to fill up every single track out of twenty four with millions of overdubs, necessarily. On some parts, there are only four instruments playing. But then the beginning of Incantations was unbelievably complex, in every single key and every single time, and people still said it was boring, so obviously what's in it technically doesn't turn people on or off. Then there's a section in the middle of Platinum where there are more complex chords than I've ever used before. They fit in such a way that they sound normal, but if you look at that chord on the piano, it's most ridiculous, they haven't even got a name for it"*.

Meanwhile, Blue Peter had arranged with Mike and Virgin to have the theme to the TV programme released as a single, to raise money for the programme's Cambodia Appeal. The country was then trying to recover from the ravages of the fanatical rule of Pol Pot and the Khmer Rouge, who had recently been deposed through a Vietnamese invasion. Mike explained that when the Cambodia Appeal was set up the parties decided to release the theme and donate about 85% of the royalties to the relief fund. The single was backed with *Woodhenge* and issued on 30th November 1979.

Soon after its release Mike was forced to re-record the theme's sudden ending. He explained that the usual way to have ended such a piece would have been in the same chord as it had begun. But he hadn't felt like doing that because he wanted to do something slightly different and he finished it abruptly in another chord. The result confused the disc jockeys, who therefore avoided the single. Faced with a potential sales problem, and under pressure from the radio stations, Mike went back into his studio to play the ending the 'correct' way: *"It didn't really take long to do: I put a 'bonk' at the end, I stuck it on, and they were happy then"*.

The single was thus re-released in modified as well as original form. Now that it had been made manageable for radio programmers, it received airplay and entered the chart, where it rose to number nineteen.

In order to publicise the release of *Platinum*, Mike gave a few interviews at Denham over the Christmas period. All the journalists who met him found him now to be relaxed and good natured. He had come to drop the active nature of his hostility towards the music press, having lost the arrogance and intensity characteristic of the kind of immediate effects of est on course graduates, and moved into the second, mild phase typical of participants following longer periods after the course. He was now able to look back detachedly at his extreme post-est behaviour, commenting: *"Someone said it was like I received a sharp blow to the head. And it's true I did go a bit over the top at first"*. In contrast to the various phases of his mental condition in the past, he said he now felt *"nice and averagely neurotic like everyone else"*.

Mike was, in his own words, *"so much happier now"*. One of the main reasons for this was his relationship with Sally, with whom, commentators agreed, he was obviously very close and content.

His learning to fly had also changed him. He had conquered his fear of flying, had gained a pilot's licence, and was also well on the way to becoming a helicopter pilot. Flying was a cathartic experience for him, just as his making music had been, previously. *"Flying is the test if you're all mixed up"*, he said later, *"character-strenghtening. Up there, it's only you. You've got to take the responsibility. I had an oldish flying instructor...and I owe him so much because he insisted I carry on with it. It's got me over so many psychological problems"*.

For all of this, however, Mike's life was not without some difficulties. Most of his interviewers focussed on his current financial difficulties following his tour, the state of which had led the music press to describe him as *"broke"* and *"a pauper"*. He recounted: *"Between Virgin and me we threw half a million on the tour, out of which I personally lost over two hundred thousand, which means that I haven't had any royalties this year. Which means that financially things are quite tight, which is a new experience for me. I know I'm not short of a few bob, but I have to be very careful...Virgin advanced me money to pay for the tour, but even though I never saw that money, from the taxman's point of view I've had it, and I've got to find 60 per cent of that money that I've never had"*.

He confessed: *"I'm very frightened of making a big mistake like that again"*. After *Tubular Bells*, Mike had come to lose his disinterest in, and bewilderment at his success, and it had slowly become an important, and unfortunate, feature of his personality that his sense of personal security became bound up with the state of his finances, as this and later comments showed.

Another cloud on his horizon was a peculiar inability of his to gain the maximum degree of satisfaction from his success. He commented that this had long been a problem for him, and he attributed it to a still remaining lack of self-esteem (a problem that not even est seems to have resolved). *"It's all very silly really. If you've achieved something, you should be able to appreciate it yourself. It's not a matter of self-criticism, it's just merely trying to actually get some sort of kick out of what I am doing!"*

During the first months of 1980 Mike prepared another tour. The financial aspects apart, he had discovered that he liked performing, and he was keen to do so again.

He planned to retain those features of the first tour that he felt were most successful. He thought the films accompanying the music had worked, and together with animator Ian Emes, he developed a set of five film sequences. He was also pleased with the quality of his guitar sound, but had the PA rebuilt so that it was smaller and easier to transport. The quadraphonic sound system and the computer mixer were scrapped.

For the new tour, Mike planned to play with a small electric band, now feeling that the huge entourage he had had previously had not really been necessary. Members of Pierre Moerlen's Gong formed a core group, with Moerlen on drums, Nico Ramsden on guitar, Benoit Moerlen on vibes, and Hansford Rowe on bass. Tim Cross and Pete Lemer played keyboards, Pete Acock played saxes and woodwind, Mike Frye played percussion, and Wendy Roberts and Maggie Reilly sang.

A new set was put together, featuring most of *Platinum* and *Tubular Bells*, part of *Incantations*, *Ommadawn*, *Portsmouth*, *Blue Peter*, and two new short pieces, *Sheba* and *Taurus 1*, later to be recorded for his new LP, *QE2*.

The size of the venues for the second tour was reduced, because Mike wanted to reach people outside London and the few large cities he had played the first time. He was to appear in about twenty English towns, then in Scotland and Dublin.

The tour began in Europe on 12th April, starting with an appearance in Denmark. There followed others in Holland, Berlin, West Germany, Vienna, and another two in West Germany, due to public demand.

When Mike appeared in Vienna he played a traditional polka,

and *The Radetzky March*, a popular tune by Viennese composer Johann Strauss the Elder. Virgin, or some other agency, recorded at least part of the show, *Polka* later appearing as the B-side to a single.

The British leg of the tour started at Ipswich on 4th May. Reviews of the shows were mixed.

After finishing his last show at Dublin, Mike and his band appeared as part of the Knebworth Festival in Mertfordshire in June. Mike's performance was filmed and released by Virgin as *The Essential Mike Oldfield*. The video included brief snippets of an interview with Mike, in which he talked about aspects of the pieces. The performance of *Tubular Bells* is somewhat bowdlerised, as indeed Mike's later live versions of this and other early works were to become. But *Ommadawn* is impressive, principally as a result of its African and regular drums. The latter are particularly striking at the climax to Part One of the piece, with a long, skillful, free-form percussion improvisation. It is also a skill emotional treatment, an element typically provided through Mike's extensive, often lightening fast guitar riffs and solos.

After the live activity was over, and finding himself with nothing in particular to do, Mike went into the studio he had had built while he was away on tour and quickly started recording a new album. It was to be the first disappointing LP of his career.

Chapter 10

Conflict and Decline

Prior to, or during the early stages of the recording of the new LP, Mike, in a remarkable move, approached Virgin and asked them if they had any suggestions for its content. We did so for two reasons. Firstly, and more importantly, after *Platinum* had been released Mike, although he did not recognise the fact, began to fall into a long period of largely uninterrupted artistic decline. This manifested itself initially in his lack of many musical ideas or strong inspiration. Secondly, he felt that be recording idea which Virgin suggested, he might improve his relationship with the record company, which had been soured for him by his dissatisfaction with the terms of his recording contract and the dispute over the content and the American release of *Platinum*. By compliantly recording their ideas for his next LP, Mike appears to have felt that this would be seen by them as a sign of his good faith and desire for mutually beneficial co-operation, and also that it would be difficult for them to decline to issue the new album in the

US if he afterwards pointed out that he had recorded what were, after all, their own ideas. Virgin made perfunctory suggestions that he record cover versions of a current advertising jingle for a brand of breakfast cereal, of Abba's instrumental, *Arrival* and something by guitar instrumental group The Shadows. Mike went on to record *Arrival* and The Shadows' *Wonderful Land.*

Evidence of the artistic decline Mike began to experience was noticeable not only in his lack of inspiration, but also in his now apparently less careful compositional practice for the LP, despite the fact that he was afterwards to claim it as a positive virtue. *"It was the most spontaneous album I've ever done"*, he said enthusiastically. *"I just sat down at the piano and said "Switch the tape recorder on" and I played for a couple of minutes and started overdubbing it"*. Had he devoted as much time and consideration to this LP as he had done to its predecessors, the results might have been better.

Another factor contributed to the poor quality of the LP. Mike wanted to use an outside producer, rather than have to do the job himself. He asked Virgin to nominate someone, and they gave him the name of David Hentschel, generally know for his studio work with Virgin label-mates Genesis, work which was only barely known to Mike. Hentschel's thin and tinny production for the LP only pointed up, rather than counterbalanced, Mike's now shallow music, however.

Despite the sudden decline in his creative power which some of his actions demonstrated, Mike was nevertheless still interested in broadening his musical approach with the album. Instead of having had vocals on his past LPs, he had used his guitar as what he called his 'voice'. But recently he had discovered another means to achieve a similar effect: by singing through a vocoder, a voice box which turned the sound of vocals into that of an electronic musical instrument. He may have become interested in the potential of the instrument following Tom Newman's studio-created modification of his and Sally's voices on *Platinum.* The vocoder must have been attractive to Mike because he was not confident about his own straight singing ability, and because using a vocoder allowed him to bypass not only proper singing, but also formal songwriting; he explained: *"you can just mouth a syllable and make it into your own language. As long as the vowel sounds are nice it doesn't really matter what it means. Any old language will do"*. Mike employed his technique on several of the tracks he recorded.

He also felt like using more percussion than he had done previously, and he later described this as the other main feature of the album, commenting particularly on his new liking for African and other drums. He probably became attentive to the musical possibilities inherent in the increased use of such instruments following his recent live performances of *Ommadawn*, which very effectively showcased a whole battery of drums and percussion. On the album, genesis' Phil Collins played drum kit, David Hentschel steel drums, Mike Frye and Morris Pert percussion, and Mike himself played drum machine, electronic syndrums, bass drum, African drums, and 'Aboriginal Drum Sticks'.

He had the usual array of more typical instruments, too, relying very heavily on his own perfunctory guitar fills in particular. Tim Cross played keyboards and Maggie Reilly sang, while David Bedford arranged negligible strings and choir for a couple of tracks.

Recording at Denham started soon after the tour ended in June, and it may have been wholly or partially complete as early as the time Mike went to perform again, in Spain, during August and September: by 12th September one of the LP's tracks, *Arrival*, was issued as a single. (The latter was backed with the live *Polka*, from the past appearance at Vienna.)

The LP, *QE2*, titled after one of its longer tracks, was released on the 31st October 1980. It came in a cover showing the prow of a ship, in blue and red, complete with an anchor hole cut out of the cover.

Unlike *Platinum*, *QE2* comprises nine quite unrelated tracks. The LP begins with *Taurus 1*, an instrumental piece about Mike himself - his astrological sun-sign is Taurus. One would be hard pressed to find its subject in any way expressed in musical terms. The set finishes with *Molly*, an extremely brief, tuneless, undeveloped instrumental, its ending so irritatingly open-ended that it makes the track more a barren musical device than a piece of music. In between these tracks, one also gets *Conflict*, a percussion-swamped track, which may have been inspired by Mike's friction with Virgin, and the versions of *Arrival* and *Wonderful Land*. The latter are bland and unimaginative treatments, to which, in strong contrast to previous interpretations of others' music, Mike brings little of himself.

All of the material is very lightweight, filled out with lots of now cursory, uncharacteristically flat guitar work, humdrum synths and vocoder lyrics, and supported by cluttered, too rapid percussion. Throughout one also notices that Mike is suddenly unable to make old musical techniques work any longer: attempts at musical climaxes are unconvincing, previously always sterling guitar playing has become mundane, choral-style vocals do not really work, arrangements add little, and even newer ideas, like the wonderful use of horns on *Platinum*, are, on *QE2*, quite uninteresting. But most noticeably, Mike is unable to introduce instruments, effects, or melodies as carefully and skillfully as he used to be able to do; now these elements are brought in for too short a time, run together too quickly, making it impossible for the listener to really absorb them. If in the past Mike drew out musical ideas to their limits, here, as often later, he introduces them at far too fast a rate.

The LP does contain a single decent track, *Celt*. If all the other pieces are unsatisfying, the same cannot be said for this. It is a dreamy, melodic song with inaudible lyrics, written not by Mike, but by keyboard player Tim Cross, and sung by Maggie Reilly. Here Mike's guitar break is excellent, spinning out like a shining thread, demanding that this track, at least, be heard again.

QE2 makes clear Mike's suddenly reduced creative ability and artistic judgement. The music has none of his usual grandeur or coiled dynamism. It lacks both sensitivity and almost any of his previously highly individual musical character. There is none of the customary depth of sound, instrumentation, or emotion: *QE2* skips along the surface of each; one of the great attractions of Mike's music had always been the rich and distinctive instrumental voices, but here instruments are devoid of resonance or qualities of tone - unfortunately, this fault was to appear on almost all of Mike's subsequent LPs.

The larger reason for *QE2*'s poor quality must lie not only in the casual way in which Mike went about gathering some of his material, and in his now cursory compositional practice, or in specific defects, but, more generally, in his personality change. He was now no longer on the energetic, extrovert high that produced the fine, new-style *Platinum*, and no longer driven to seek his only fulfilment in his music nor desperate to carefully construct a complex, highly melodic world of sound in opposition to unpleasant real life, as he had been before *Platinum*. All that was left for him to do was to continue to compose bereft of his strong earlier motivation and emotional need, and to create, consequently, material that was now, and later, devoid of the high melodic content and sensitive and considered nature that was created under, and to alleviate, his earlier prevailing emotional state. By having his mental difficulties removed through therapy, Mike unfortunately necessarily dismantled the inner apparatus that had led him to create great music. The change in musical quality which paralleled his personality change did not occur immediately after therapy, but after the temporary increase in emotional and musical energy it had created in him had dissipated, and Mike became stable, happy, and thereby, musically impoverished. *QE2* was simply the first of his albums composed by a different personality to that which had led to the fine earlier LPs; and after it Mike could do nothing more than go on recording music under his new, foreshortened emotional parameters.

Hardly surprisingly, *QE2* was not well received by reviewers, although after the New Wave had taken root, they were not likely to be favourably disposed to Mike even if he had recorded something worthwhile. The LP, then, was to mark the end of any previous critical regard for his music. Melody Maker's Karl Dallas observed that without his customary angst Mike had descended simply to over-sweet, pretty tunes, and that his music had become all *"surface gloss and facility"*. The NME noticed that, whereas Mike had previously attempted to be cohesive on his albums, *"now he just sticks disparate bits together and hopes we won't notice the absence of even the most basic kind of continuity"*. The NME also pointed out the cursory, automatic quality of the album, and concluded with the devastating comment: *"you're already effectively finished as a questioning human being if you've even considered buying this record"*.

On 28th November, *QE2* tracks, *Sheba* and *Wonderful Land*, were released as a double A-side. A video was made to promote the single, but both this and the earlier *Arrival* failed to enter the chart.

Mike then planned another tour. He did so despite the fact that playing his music live, while enjoyable, was not without its problems for him. *"He's still not entirely at home on stage"*, Melody Maker's Colin Irwin recounted:

"He admits he winces when he hears a mistake, and still can't quite get to grips with attempting to provide a show for an audience rather than a technically perfect performance, but reckons he' s getting there".

He was only going to play in Europe, being doubtful about appearing again in England, where he had played to houses 60% full, a situation he blamed not on the current level of the UK public's interest in him, but on his concert promoters. in reality, what had happened was that his older fans had begun to drift away from him after hearing his new-style *Platinum* and *QE2*, while the younger members of the general music-buying and concert-going public, who otherwise might have become a potential, upcoming audience for him and others of his contemporaries, had long been firmly attracted instead to New Wave artists.

Mike and his band started touring in December 1980, appearing once in Sweden, and then in West Germany. With Christmas approaching, Mike included a performance of the German carol *Silent Night* when he played in Dortmund. Virgin persuaded the BBC's Old Grey Whistle Test to film the show, excerpts being broadcast early in the new year.

Mike returned home before Christmas, where he remained until March 1981, when he emerged for a further set of twenty five concerts in West Germany, where *Platinum* had sold very well.

The live band comprised five members: Mike Frye and Morris

Pert on drums and percussion, Tim Cross on keyboards, Maggie Reilly on vocals, and new recruit Rick Fenn on guitar and bass. Mike was pleased with the group, with whom he was now content to see himself relegated to the remarkable position of just another band member, rather than, as previously, the main person responsible for the music. To each of his musicians he had assigned a percentage of expected tour profits instead of a wage. He was happy that, as a result, the players he had gathered to play his music were 'all completely committed'. The arrangement worked so well that Colin Irwin, who reported on the tour, commented that Mike and the others were very keen to stay together, permanently; indeed after the tour, the group was to continue to record and perform with Mike.

The band's performance impressed Irwin, who saw them in Hanover. This was the last show of a German tour which, the journalist recounted, had confirmed Mike as one of the biggest rock artists in the country. Irwin commented: *"I enjoyed the gig more than I ever imagined possible...the set I saw held a perfect balance of delicacy, tastefulness, and hard, driving rock"*. The concert concluded with a jokey performance of *Nellie The Elephant*, and a thunderous version of *The William Tell Overture*. Mike and the band were joined on the latter by a fiddler and a piper from the tour's opening act, the Battlefield Band.

By this time Mike had developed a firm, if odd, philosophy towards playing his music live. *"For me it's got to have some point, some purpose. Why else go through the mindlessness of being on the road day after day? I want people to go home after seeing my concerts thinking "Yeah, I'll be a better person for that""*. As Irwin told Mike, this was *"an extraordinarily lofty ambition"*. It was also one which sat uneasily with the carelessness characteristic of his recent, and later, studio work.

While Mike may have been happy with his band, his shows, and his personal life, he was, however, still dogged by increasing irritation towards Virgin Records. He suddenly turned on Colin Irwin at one point during the tour and *"gradually started to pour out several years of frustration and anger"*.

Although he had gone to the trouble of trying to curry favour with Virgin, with *QE2*, by this time the record company had not yet issued the LP in the US, and Mike was annoyed because he believed that this was because Virgin were simply demanding too much money for it from potential American distributors. (Virgin did issue the LP in America later in the year, however, and in 1980 they had released *Platinum* there, with *Sally* substituted by *Into Wonderland* and the eerie *Woodhenge* replaced by the more commercial *Guilty*. This package was also issued as a double album, with a live version of *Tubular Bells* and an unusual splicing of the studio and live versions of *Incantations*, so that the latter work also saw something of an American release. Mike managed to get Virgin to call the *Platinum*-based package *Airborne*, his choice of title for the original LP).

He further complained that Virgin were preventing him from fulfilling a desire of his to perform in the US, presumably by refusing to finance him. *"There's lots of places where we could play, where we want to play"*, he said, *"but it's always "the time isn't right" or something. It seems that if there's no profit in it for Richard Branson, then nobody else can work"*.

He felt that, at the same time, the record company had been only too ready to use the money they had made out of him to finance many other activities other than his own, from signing New Wave bands to buying a club like The Venue.

Mike also brought up the subject of his original contract with Virgin, which Branson had typed up with him after he had started recording *Tubular Bells*. He claimed that this contrast meant that he had been, and currently still was, on a low percentage from the large profits generated by his albums. He had signed the document in ignorance, he said: *"I was only nineteen and hardly in any sort of mental state, I just wanted to earn some money to eat"*. He felt that he had been unfairly taken advantage of, and he was now even thinking of leaving Virgin.

Mike had not really expressed his various complaints to the record company earlier because of his previously good relationship with them: *"The trouble is I've always got on well with...Virgin. I like Richard Branson, and we've always been friendly, which isn't always the best way for business relations. Because of that I haven't been as pushy as I should have been"*. His problem with Virgin had developed following his est course, and he also felt that they had rendered him powerless on those occasions when he had mentioned his concerns because they thought of him dismissively: *"It's always been "Oh, Mike Oldfield, he's mad""*.

Given Mike's unexpected revelations, Irwin asked Mike if he objected to his publishing these comments. *"No, I'm fed up defending Virgin"*, he replied strongly. *"I've thought the same way for years but I've always defended them out of some misguided loyalty. You see, I always felt guilty because I wouldn't tour, I wouldn't do all the things you're supposed to do. So I had this guilt that I'd let them down, which was stupid - they've made a lot of money out of me and they still are. I've never said anything about it before, but I'm just so pissed off with them now..."* He was so angry in fact that he had made an important decision: recalling that his recordings their suggestions for *QE2* was a gesture of good faith, he commented: *"Now I'm gonna make another gesture - I'm gonna get a heavy lawyer"*.

After the German tour, which seems to have finished in April, Mike returned home. It appears to have been at this time that he played a little keyboards on *Iona*, a slow, Scottish kind of song by Virgin act The Skids. His working with this New Wave band was unusual, given what one might have expected to be some mutual antipathy for each other's music. *Iona* was released in October as a single from the band's last LP, *Joy*.

During this period Mike also organised yet another tour, his fourth in only two years. Although he planned to include some British venues this time, the majority of his appearances were to be in Europe, whose general public had now become more receptive to him than that at home. He went on to play in Sweden, Belgium, Holland, France, Italy, Greece and Austria. Again he incorporated into these shows pieces which he thought might go down well with various audiences: one Italian date featured *Punkadiddle* segued into *O Sole Mio*, while another in Vienna included a performance of *The Blue Danube*.

During the previous tour, Mike had been notified that he had been awarded the Freedom of the City of London. The award was made in recognition of the effect of the huge sales of his LPs on UK export figures, his charity release, *Blue Peter*, and a free concert he planned to do at London's Guildhall in July, to celebrate the marriage of Prince Charles and Diana Spencer. The show took place on the 28th of the month, the eve of the wedding, when Mike played his own specially composed, and never recorded, royal wedding anthem. Earlier that day he flew his own helicopter to a landing site by the Thames, and went to meet the Lord Mayor of London and sign his nomination papers for the Freedom of the City. He received a scroll, and became entitled to some unusual rights - he was permitted to drive sheep across London Bridge, deposit his family in the city's almslhouse, and, not that the occasion would arise, he could choose to be hanged by a silken rather than by a hemp, rope. *"Of course there is the silly side with the outmoded laws"*, he commented, *"but I tend to look at the positive side. It means a great deal to me"*. The day after his award, The Times carried a photo of the Lord Mayor shaking hands with a smiling Oldfield, dressed in a jacket and then familiar striped t-shirt.

Recognition such as this, by the Establishment (including, subsequently, an entry in the prestigious guide, Who's Who), and continuing support for his work from the quality newspapers, reflected the by then comfortably middle-class nature of much of Mike's following. Unfortunately, this provided the rock press with another reason to sneer at both himself and his music.

Two days after the free concert, Mike appeared at London's

Rainbow Theatre. A Melody Maker reviewer was unimpressed, being irritated by the typical precision and perfection of the performance and what he considered Mike's formulaic musical style, and he concluded: *"staggering professional standards, maybe, but in my book, a sorry waste of time, potential and promise"*.

In August 1981, after taking the legal advice he had mentioned earlier, Mike instituted legal action against Virgin and its associated companies, suddenly issuing a writ for £1 million 'excess profits' which he claimed the record company had made out of him. The emphasis of the huge, thirty page write was on his original contract, which was alleged to be 'in restraint of trade and conferred benefits on those companies that were unconscionable.' Mike also claimed that Richard Branson should have made sure he was independently advised before signing the contract. In addition, he asserted that he was no longer obliged to accept his renegotiated contract of April 1977, by which his royalty rate on future LPs had been increased from 5% to 8%, bringing it more into line with what Virgin had been freely offering their New Wave signings. On the contrary, the writ maintained that the second contract had been made as a result of misrepresentations by Branson and Virgin.

Notice of the action was given to the music press before the record company heard about it, and Sounds reported that *"The move came as something of a shock to Virgin...who first found out about it when eager journalists rang them for a reaction"*. Richard Branson, who had always felt close to Mike, was said to be deeply hurt by the manner in which he became aware of the latter's action. *"We are all rather sad that the first we heard about this situation was through the press"*, he said. *"It's rather bad form issuing press releases before you issue writs"*.

Because Branson had not yet seen the document, he was unable to comment in any detail at first: *"At the moment we're in a position of total ignorance as we don't know exactly what Mike's problems are supposed to be"*. When the writ arrived, a day after the press received the news of the move, Branson did not answer the allegations, but complained: *"When Virgin signed Mike Oldfield he's already been rejected by all the other record companies. He was our first signing and we've enjoyed ten years together during which both sides have obviously done well. In addition his contract was reviewed and renegotiated not so long ago"*. He then pointed out: *"Mike has a new lawyer who has told him that there is little to be lost in "having a go at Virgin". Our advice to them is that they are wasting their time"*.

The dispute was to drag on for two years before solutions were found which were agreeable to both parties.

Chapter 11

High-Flying Sales

Sometime during 1981 Mike made a decision which was to affect the type of material he was to record for several years to come. During a conversation with Richard Branson, with whom he was still on speaking terms, the entrepreneur told him: *"look, no one's into instrumental music anymore. Why don't you save that for film scores and have a go at writing songs"*. Given the poorer sales of *QE2*, and, earlier *Platinum*, compared to his hugely popular earlier works, this struck Mike as a reasonable idea. Accordingly, he hit on the concept of recording LPs with a long instrumental on one side and a few songs on the other. This would allow him to still do what he liked best, namely compose instrumentals, while also yielding the opportunity of recording songs which might make commercial singles and/or tracks which radio stations could pick up to publicise the LPs as a whole. He went out the day after talking with Branson, and bought himself a big Thesaurus, and before he knew it, he said, he was songwriting.

Mike started recording an album at Denham in September 1981, with his favoured tour band. The result, *Five Miles Out*, titles after one of the songs he wrote, was a slight improvement on it's predecessor, largely as a result of the quality of the songs, but also because of the long instrumental, which was harder and more emotionally and musically dynamic than the music of *QE2*.

The beneficial features of the instrumental were partly due to the band's strong playing. They also resulted from Mike's discovery, during his recording work, that he could simulate the states of mental energy which he suffered, and channelled creatively, throughout the first part of his musical career; *"The trick now"*, he revealed after the album was released, *"is to be able to turn on the "disturbances" at will when I'm writing music"*. In this way, he was able to compose material which was more intense and considered than that of *QE2*, which he made while in an emotional no man's land.

Five Miles Out was released on 18th February 1982. It was a highly melodic song, which concerned a frightening flying incident Mike and his band had experienced over the Pyrhenees during the Spanish leg of the 1980 European tour. He recounted: *"We had a brilliant idea on the Spanish tour - see how much a private plane cost. And lo and behold it was a little bit more expensive but not much so we decided to fly out to Barcelona"*. Unfortunately, they had not been given the correct weather forecast and the group flew into a fierce storm. *"We were the only plane airborne in the whole of Spain and because the Piper is such a light plane we weren't carrying the oxygen needed to fly above it. We couldn't land either as we were above the mountains"*. The plane *"was tossed about like a pancake, and there was ice collecting on the propellers and rain on the windscreen and everyone was going aarrggh"*.

Mike turned the experience into a powerful, tuneful song, the vocals of which are attractively shared between himself and Maggie Reilly. His vocals are growled out and his voice is treated so that it sounds as if it is being transmitted over a plane's radio. There is some fine guitar work, and clattering, thunderous drums by Mike Frye and sessionman Graham Broad.

The single was backed with a live version of *Punkaddidle*, a favourite piece of Mike's recorded at Essen, one of the venues of the 1981 German tour. *Live Punkadiddle* was very good, supporting Colin Irwin's favourable impression of the quality of Mike's tour performances. After Mike and the band play the tune, the group fades out, and Mike continues alone, playing crackly, heroic, extended guitar variations, to a later emerging synth foil.

Like its parent album, the single came in a cover which depicted a lone plane flying out of a band of dark cloud towards calmer, sun-filled sky. This was a reproduction of an original painting which

Mike had commissioned from artist Gerald Coulson to commemorate his experience. Mike's father, who had been a glider pilot, and from whom Mike seems to have acquired his love of flying, introduced him to Coulson, who was renowned for painting war planes.

Five Miles Out reached number forty-three in the chart. A month after its release, on 19th March, the album was issued.

The LPs long instrumental track, *Taurus II* is an energetic piece: weighty, crashing, riff-and-drum driven rock, but perhaps far too dependent on its guitars and skillful percussion. It includes a surprisingly weak appearance by Paddy Moloney on uilleann pipes, and a lullaby Mike wrote for his son, Dougal, who had been born sometime previously. The track varies in impact, but if it is sometimes successful, it is not particularly remarkable, and continues to demonstrate Mike's surprising decline in his ability to compose melodic instrumentals.

There is another short instrumental, *Orabididoo*, on the second side of the album. It is an insubstantial and superfluous track, a kind of nursery tune, whose musical mood, like some of that on *Taurus II*, is informed by the fact of Dougal's arrival.

There are three songs, sung by Maggie Reilly. *Five Miles Out* is the best. *Family Man*, too, is good. It is a song of sexual temptation, and sounds very much like Mike's re-write of the scenario presented in Free's *All Right Now*, which he had long liked, and recorded. The gentle *Mount Teide* apparently expresses Mike's sadness at having to leave the named mountain scene, which is in the Canaries, which he visited on the Spanish tour; but, curiously, the only scene actually named in the lyrics themselves in Ireland's Eye, a small island off the Dublin coast, which he may have seen when he came to play in Dublin in 1980.

Although the album was not well received by the critics, the strong single pulled the LP up the album chart, where it reached number seven, undeservedly becoming Mike's most commercially successful album since *Ommadawn*. It went on to sell a million copies in all, a remarkable 300,000 of these in Germany, where all Mike's recent live activity paid off in subsequent LP sales. Europe, Germany in particular, was continuing to be a more important market for his music than that at home.

Meanwhile, Virgin, possibly moved by his past legal attack and its continuing repercussions, finally approved of an American tour, and after the release of the LP, in March, Mike and his band were able to set off on his first and only world tour. The band was augmented by Pierre Moerlen, on drums and percussions, and new Oldfield group member Tim Renwick, on guitar and bass. Mike played a series of well received shows in several American and Canadian cities, after which he travelled to Japan and Europe.

Virgin had also decided to release *Five Miles Out* in the US, and they made promoting Mike's music a priority of their American operations. Despite all this, neither this LP, nor *QE2* or *Airborne* made many inroads with the American public.

At home after the foreign leg of his tour was over, Mike recorded a new single with his band to capitalise on the success of *Five Miles Out* and, later, *Family Man*, which had been backed with *Mount Teide* and released on 28th May, getting to number forty-five in the chart. (It was later recorded by popular American duo Hall and Oates, whose version was much more successful, in both the US and UK charts.) The new single was made up of two good new pieces, *Mistake*, a song, and *Waldberg (The Peak)*, an instrumental.

Mistake is a kind of re-write of *Five Miles Out*, repeating it's theme of travel in bad weather. It is short, straightforward, and uptempo, with a catchy melody, and Mike again sharing the vocals with Maggie Reilly, coming in effectively to accentuate the odd word or phrase, his voice treated similarly to the way it had been on *Five Miles Out*.

Waldberg, again, was also something of a re-write, in its being another homage to a mountain scene, this time once Mike encountered in Bavaria. It also reminds one of *Cuckoo Song*, with its alternation of cuckoo noises and bagpipe-like guitar. That Mike could compose a good instrumental like this, and still record far weaker material for his recent LPs was bewildering.

Mistake was released on 20th August, but despite its quality, did not enter the chart.

The tour carried on, with several shows in Britain, Mike and his band finally finishing up in early autumn.

Chapter 12

Carried Away by a Moonlight Shadow

By late 1982 Mike and Richard Branson had managed to come to an agreement about the claims Mike had made in the previous year about the alleged deficiencies of his contracts. In return for making a further three albums in addition to the remaining three that he had to deliver under the terms of his original contract, Branson agreed that Virgin would give Mike a lump sum in respect of revenue from past sales of *Tubular Bells* which Mike had maintained he would have received had he been on what he considered to be an appropriate percentage; would increase his payments for future sales of the album; and would increase his royalty rate generally. This settlement followed a court case between both parties earlier in the year, which Mike had dropped; he recounted: *"legally I didn't have a leg to stand on. Continuing the action would have meant losing my home and everything else I owned, so I had to grit my teeth and accept that I was stuck with Virgin for a further three albums"*.

Mike seems to have used the opportunity this settlement provided to get Virgin Music Publishers to share control of the potentially lucrative publishing rights to future sales of his songs and music, setting up Oldfield Music. He also created Oldfield Records, his own record label, which was to issue David Bedford's *Stars Clusters, Nebulae, And Places in Devon/The Song Of The White Horse* in the summer of 1983. These were the two pieces Bedford had recorded at Mike's Througham home in 1978, but which Virgin had declined to release. No other LP has been issued by the label, which Mike seems to have set up simply to ensure that his old colleague's work would see release.

Mike began working on his new album almost immediately after finishing touring. He did so because he had another important musical project to undertake: composing the original soundtrack to The Killing Fields, a major British film about Cambodia under the Khmer Rouge regime of the mid-1970s.

For his own LP, Mike had, usefully, already gathered some ideas while on tour. He often did so, he explained afterwards, writing these down on the back of packets of cigarette papers. As he had done for its predecessor, he intended to record a side-long instrumental and a few songs.

The latter featured Maggie Reilly and guest vocalists Roger Chapman and fey, choirboy-style singer Jon Anderson, previously of turgid 'progressive' group Yes. He recruited his guests simply because he knew them both from drinking in the same pub, The Sun, near Barnes. He could have sung himself, he explained, but he was too inhibited about it.

For the instrumental piece, he recruited a guitarist named in the sleeve notes only as 'Ant', and well-respected session drummer Simon Phillips. Mike was to get on especially well with Phillips, who, like himself, placed a great deal of emphasis on technical perfection, and the pair were to work together on subsequent LPs of Mike's.

The song *Moonlight Shadow* was taken from the forthcoming LP and released on 6th May. It was an excellent pop single, among the best ever of Mike's songs. It moves at a fast, dynamic pace, powered by Phillips' drums and Mike's layers of solid acoustic guitar backing. Maggie Reilly's breathless delivery, and the quick running together of lines and verses also makes it compact and speedy. But it is Mike's fine, new-style double guitar break that really shines. Holding back for a few verses to increase one's expectation, he and Ant let fly with two lovely, twangy solos.

Mike said that the subject of the song was the shooting of John Lennon, and was a tribute both to him and Harry Houdini, the escapologist! His lyrics, however, typically focus more on the almost portentious physical details of the moon, the trees and the stars.

The song was released on 7", and also in a pointlessly 'extended' version on 12". It as backed only with *Rite of Man*, a surprisingly tuneless and inane kind of folk song, with Morris Bells and accordion.

A warm, misty video for the single was shot at Mike's home, with Mike and the others playing beside the fire. Such scenes were intercut with those of the killing, which was portrayed as a duel with pistols.

Moonlight Shadow, deservedly, went on to do incredibly well. In Britain it rose to number four in the chart, Mike's highest ever placing for a single. It was an unusual sight indeed for long-time Oldfield fans to watch its continuous rise up the chart, and Mike and his band appearing on Top Of The Pops, a programme for which he had previously expressed scorn. In Europe it went on to sell two million copies, becoming the biggest selling single in Europe in 1983. With *Moonlight Shadow*, which followed on from the high sales of *Five Miles Out*, Mike was to taste again some of the enormous success of the kind that had attended him the early part of his career.

Crises was purposefully released on 27th May 1983, ten years to the month of the release of *Tubular Bells*. To celebrate the anniversary of the latter, Virgin reissued the record, to be sold for one week at its 1973 price, and Mike planned a special anniversary concert at Wembley Stadium in July. The release of *Crises* ten years after his famous and accomplished debut earned Mike a good deal of TV and press attention for his new LP that would not otherwise have been devoted to him.

Crises was hardly an LP to suggest that Mike was as fine a composer or musician as he had been. Like his two previous albums, it was for the most part mediocre. The instrumental title track, in particular, was poor. It's subject was apparently a combination of the themes of the world catastrophe and personal crisis, the latter presumably concerning his disputes with Virgin. It was a cold and hollow-sounding piece, based almost entirely on electric guitars, dull, lifeless synthesizers and Phillip's drumming, with Mike and Phillips playing off each other in a monotonous barrage of harsh sound, unrelieved by varied or imaginative mood, melody or instrumentation. Mike often works hard, there is no doubt, and the piece is energetic in places, but he fails to create anything interesting, churning out ordinary riffs and playing guitar in a limited, rhythmic role. Phillips' drums are often powerful, notably in the over-long closing section, but this heavy-handed climax, like the whole piece, strikes one as a very large filler.

Taurus 3 is another instrumental, a forced Spanish guitar and foot-stomping piece. Mike's motives for composing this piece are highly suspect: Spain had recently become a big market for him, and he may have recorded the track as a means to ensure further airplay there.

Of the songs, only *Moonlight Shadow* is impressive. *In High Places* is a maudlin song written by Mike with its vocalist, Jon Anderson. It expresses Mike's sensory delight in hot air ballooning, which he had experienced on trips with Richard Branson. *Foreign Affair*, sung by Maggie Reilly, portrays travel to an island perhaps as much dreamed of as real. Despite the apparently personal nature of *Shadow on the Wall*, sung by the hoarse-voiced Roger Chapman, the song concerns the contemporary plight of the Polish people under Communist rule; its music and lyrics are too simple and repetitive, and Mike's guitar riffs are mundane rock bluster.

That the music press devoted any attention to *Crises* was primarily the result of the concurrent anniversary of *Tubular Bells*. Their observations were unlikely to alter Mike's antipathy towards them. Melody Maker commented that the title track *"seems scarcely advanced from the original Tubular Bells, a filing cabinet of ideas.*

Just because they're in the same drawer doesn't mean that they have anything to do with each other. Disjointed guitar riffs are (stuck) back to back, but rarely coalesce and it's only Simon Phillips's hungry drumming that lends them any form".

Melody Maker thought that the songs were better than the instrumental, but characterised them as: *"all wispy, rather ordinary songs, usually propelled along by light-hearted acoustic guitars that jangle over soothing synthesizer chords"* and described them, memorably, as blowing *"slackly across the ears with all the earthshaking import of a passing balloon"*. The NME also felt that Mike's *"knack of writing a nifty tune has diminished somewhat"*, and called the LP as a whole *"rubbish"*.

After a four day rest in the south of France, Mike undertook a short European tour, playing in France, Spain and Germany (the countries where he was popular). He had formed a band comprised of those who had appeared on the LP (Ant, Phillips, Reilly, Pierre Moerlen and bass player Phil Spalding), augmented by Grame Pleeth on keyboards and Simon House on violin. The tour had been organised by his companion, Sally Cooper, who had now come to act in the capacity of his tour manager. The tour was brief because Mike had soon to being work on the music for The Killing Fields.

Mike's celebration concert took place at Wembley on 22nd July, where he played *Tubular Bells* and most of *Crises*.

Afterwards he settled down to compose the film soundtrack. To do so he had his home studio converted, probably while he was away on tour, into a private cinema where he went on to watch the film hundreds of times, going over scenes again and again, trying to achieve the closest possible marriage of action and musical accompaniment.

Meanwhile, *Shadow Of The Wall* was backed with *Taurus 3* and released as a single on 30th August. This came out on 7", and on 12" in another needlessly extended version. None of the huge and continuing success of *Moonlight Shadow* extended to its follow-up, which did not enter the chart.

Crises, however, certainly was carried away on the back of the strong first single: the LP reached number six in the UK chart, and within five months of release sold five hundred thousand copies in West Germany alone, *Moonlight Shadow* brought a new, slightly younger audience to Mike, but many of these newcomers, disappointed with the album, were to be temporary fans.

Such commercial success made Mike feel financially quite secure, and, therefore, happier, just as the contrary and been the case after he lost a great deal of money on his first tour. After the large, countries-wide sales of *Moonlight Shadow*, *Crises*, and, earlier, *Five Miles Out*, and remembering his emotionally troubled distant past, he said: *"I worry a lot less now, I've got my philosophy straightened out. I'm much more positive and I've started again. These days, if I feel low, I get out my calculator and work out the accounts"*. Mike's bluntly financial interest in his music was, however, highly unattractive in someone who should have been devoting his attention to its then lamentable artistic mediocrity instead.

By the end of 1983 Mike had just about finished his film soundtrack. His old colleague, David Bedford, orchestrated parts of the music, and composed his own brief choral part, *The Year Zero*. Most of the music, particularly Mike's guitars and extensive keyboards, was recorded at Denham. After which Mike switched his operations to Germany and Switzerland, where he sought asylum as a tax exile. When he had finished, he had recorded a remarkable four and a half hours of music; in the end, the film used only a tiny fraction of this. Mike said of his work: *"I hated working on that film. First of all, I had to get inside what was a very battering and depressing story and then when I'd matched the music to the pictures the flipping director went and edited the footage and put everything out of sync. It was a nightmare! I suppose the end product wasn't too bad but it could have been so much better!"*

After finishing his work on the film in Switzerland, Mike remained there, and, in an anomalous burst of creative energy, went on to record what was to be his best material in four years.

Chapter13

A Temporary Return to Form

Having finished extremely lengthy instrumental labours for the film soundtrack, and encouraged in his song writing by the success of *Moonlight Shadow*, Mike decided to redirect his attention to songs. After some initial work, he had Simon Phillips and vocalist Maggie Reilly and Barry Palmer flown over to work for him (Palmer had previously been the singer with European band Triumvirat),

The first pieces to emerge from recording sessions were the song *Crime of Passion*, and the instrumental, *Jungle Gardenia*, released as a 7" and 12" single at the beginning of January 1984. Both tracks, and subsequent material, were to be a wonderful revelation, capturing Mike on a exciting return to musical form.

Crime of Passion, sung by Palmer, repeats a similar scenario to that of the earlier, highly successful *Moonlight Shadow*, but to even more melodic musical accompaniment. Mike's guitar work is clear and inspirational; as on *Moonlight Shadow*, he creates another double guitar break - one which he lets fly right at the moment of maximum impact. Both lyrically and musically, the song evidences Mike's then continuing but occasional mastery of the pop idiom, a skill that had surfaced from time to time on earlier singles, and which was to find its ultimate - and final - expression on the highly melodic collection of songs which he was to present on the new album.

Jungle Gardenia is a simple, gentle, echoey electric guitar instrumental. Onto a drum-machine kind of backing, Mike lays on a verse and chorus of two guitar styles, one clean and sharp, the other bagpipe-ish, while chimes punctuate the tune at intervals.

Both pieces are, like the later LP, characterised by fine, warm production. The facilities of the Swiss studio must have been responsible for this, and the results point up the over-sharp, harsh sound quality that was typical of all the work done at Mike's Denham studio since 1980's *QE2*.

The cover of the single featured a black-and-white photograph of Mike's mother (although it was not identified as such). This seems to have been less for reasons of some lyrical connection than the fact that the year of the release marked the tenth anniversary of her death.

Despite the song's quality, and its lyrical and musical similarities to *Moonlight Shadow*, the single only reached number sixty-one in the chart.

The months following the release of the single were spent recording further material, and by early June, *Discovery* was issued.

Discovery was a collection of seven songs, with, at the end, a comparatively short instrumental, *The Lake*. The LP is Mike's best work since *Platinum*, showcasing an unaccountable return of his melodic gifts and ability to delight the senses. The music is, like *Platinum*, rich and densely matted, and includes small musical touches on all tracks which cumulatively evidence great care and attention to effects. Much of Mike's guitar work is dazzling: alternately lyrical, trembly, or aggressive; his bass playing is the most solid and rewarding for many years; and his synths are refreshingly deep and warm, for a change. Phillips', Palmer's and Reilly's contributions are equally good; the latter's vocals, which had previously tended towards the over-sweet, here find an affirmative backdrop with the rich music and production. No wonder then that Mike was afterwards to be quite proud of the album.

All the songs are pleasant, if a little lyrically nebulous. Highlights include *To France*, a kind of reverie of Mike's upon the situation of Mary, Queen of Scots, *Tricks of the Light*, and the gentle, concerned, *Talk About Your Life*, all sung by Reilly.

The only successful song is *Saved By A Bell*. This is Mike's attempt to convey his childlike wonder at the physical phenomena of the night sky. He explained a couple of years earlier that, from the age of eight, he and his father would observe the stars through binoculars: *"I used to stay out all night with my father and a flask of coffee. We would park two deckchairs on the lawn, study a map we bought at the London Planetarium, then lean back and take it all in.... We used to trace constellations and items of interest like the Great Spiral in Andromeda, which is another galaxy like our own and can be observed with the naked eye"*. When he had lived at Througham Mike had continued to look at the heavens, but the move to Denham had put paid to some of this: *"You get the glare from London and that spoils observation. In my younger days it was fabulous. You just couldn't avoid gazing at those glorious sights with the whole sky set up for you. I miss those nightly excursions in Gloucester, but it was a luxury I had to forego because of my work"*. Mike's attempt to express his feelings in song form is not at all impressive, however, firstly as a result of his maudlin lyrics, and secondly, by his having Barry Palmer sing, his rock-oriented voice making Mike's sentiments sound a little silly.

The song seems to be about more than just star-gazing. there are other lyrical sentiments which echo Mike's past troubled condition, and the title of the song appears to be partly a metaphor for *Tubular Bells'* catapulting him from obscurity to unexpected success.

The instrumental, *The Lake*, is a very assured, twelve minute piece, one far more accomplished than almost all of Mike's instrumentals since *Platinum*. It was inspired by Lake Geneva, which Mike could see from the studio he was working in, which was situated in the Swiss Alps. The piece, then, is another example of his liking for portraying an impressive physical scene in music, as *Mount Teide, Waldberg*, and indeed, *Hergest Ridge*, had been. Beginning with fluttering synth, which may be intended to suggest sunlight dancing on the lake's surface, Mike moves on to create a strong, well-paced piece, characterised by a mixture of electric and acoustic guitar styles, and backed well by the periodic addition of Phillips' drumming.

Little critical attention was directed to the LP after its release, although one of the quality Sunday papers praised it, particularly *Talk About Your Life* and *The Lake*. Despite the dearth of reviews, the record-buying public liked it, sending it to number fifteen in the chart.

Late in June, *To France* was released as a single, backed on 7" with *In The Pool*, the 12" also having *Bones*. These extra tracks from the Swiss sessions are appealing and uncharacteristically adventurous, given Mike's work of the recent past.

On the first, Mike plays an acoustic guitar tune onto a backing made up of the sound of water flowing, then electric guitar, subsequently played in a wonderfully shaky fashion. Phillips' weighty drums keep time in an enchantingly plodding way, while Mike's bass playing and frog noises are unusual features.

Bones is three minutes of weird, primeval jabbering and banging, to percussive backing. It reminds one of the eerie *Woodhenge* of *Platinum*, and the caveman screaming on *Tubular Bells*, the track being connected to the others in its inexplicable implied interest in man's dark, prehistoric condition.

To France reached number forty-eight in the UK chart, but it was more successful throughout Europe.

After the LP had been issued, Mike gathered a full group together to play a planned fifty date tour of Europe, his being unable to appear in the UK due to his continuing status as a tax exile. His original colleagues Phillips, Palmer and Reilly were supplemented by Phil Spalding on bass and guitar, and new Oldfield band members Mickey Simmonds on bass and guitar and Harold Zuschrader on Fairlight synthesizer.

The set for the tour included almost all of *Discovery* and *Crises*, a reprise of most of *Platinum*, and a very abbreviated, ten minute version of the second part of *Tubular Bells*. When he appeared in Vienna Mike also included his version of *The Blue Danube*.

The months-long series of concerts started in Spain, which was, after Germany, now his biggest market. Further appearances were made in Italy, Sweden, Norway, East Germany, Austria, West Germany, Switzerland, Denmark and France.

It was backstage at the venue for one of his shows in West Germany, in October, that Mike was introduced to twenty-three year old, blonde-haired, blue-eyed Norwegian singer Anita Hegerland, the meeting having been arranged for her by her concert promoter. Getting on well together, Mike and Anita went out to dinner. They were not to meet again until a year later, when they became involved firstly as working partners, and then as romantic ones.

A second single from *Discovery*, *Tricks of the Light*, was issued in September. It came with the instrumental, *Afghan*, on 7", and also an instrumental version of the A-side on 12", both tracks again from the Swiss sessions. *Afghan* is yet another delight, a sparkling and spirited guitar piece. It alternates two tunes, the first on electric guitar, the second on broad, bagpipe-like-synths, to the backing of Phillips' drums and the occasional appearance of the currently ubiquitous acoustic guitar, the latter a rhythmic feature Mike was regularly employing since its successful original introduction on *Moonlight Shadow*.

Tricks Of the Light failed to chart.

Meanwhile, the soundtrack to The Killing Fields, which Mike had composed after recording *Crises*, had been edited onto the film, which went on to have its premiere in New York at the end of October. On 26th November, as Mike came to the end of his *Discovery* tour, Virgin issued an LP of the soundtrack, which David Bedford had compiled from Mike's hours-long tapes. This release was preceded by that of the single, *Etude*, the music which played over the film's closing credits.

As it exists on the film itself, Mike's soundtrack evidences artistic sympathy with the film images, its cold, hard, percussive edge, and orchestral arrangements indicating his attempt to be sensitive to the desolate on-screen action and the warm character interaction respectively.

As an LP, the soundtrack epitomises the deficiencies of all such albums: divorced from its appropriate images, the music is essentially less meaningful, and has more ephemeral than musical value. Musically, it is not particularly melodic, either. One exception to this is *Etude*, which stands well on its own merits. This is a piece which had been composed by nineteenth century Spanish guitarist Francisco Tárrega, for whom,as the title suggests, it was a study in playing technique. Mike did a fine re-arrangement of the piece for synths, electric guitar, and appealing percussion.

Etude did not reach the singles chart, and the soundtrack only made it to number ninety-seven in the album chart, the poorest position for an album of Mike's.

Critical notice of the music as a film soundtrack came when it was later nominated for an Oscar and a BAFTA award. (However, one suspects that this was probably done simply because it accompanied an important and acclaimed film, rather than for any intrinsic qualities which were heard in it).

Whatever about The Killing Fields, *Discovery* and its associated singles material presented a brief, but highly attractive and very much needed reminder of Mike's once great melodic ability. Unfortunately, it was not to last, and the material, both songs and music, which he was to record for the remainder of his second creative phase was to be even weaker than that which preceded the anomalous eruption of quality work.

Chapter 14

A Video Album

After he returned home following the *Discovery* tour, at the end of 1984, Mike recorded another soundtrack which had been commissioned from him, this time for a three-part, three-hour television programme, Sutton Hoo. The series concerned an important archaeological dig which threw new light on both Neolithic and Anglo-Saxon history. Given the thread of his own apparent, perhaps subconscious, interest in man's dark past, which had appeared on several of his pieces over the years, the programme appears to have been well suited to him. It was later broadcast on ITV at the end of August 1985.

Probably as a result of his recent experiences wedding music to film, and having had his studio converted into a private cinema, which he used for his soundtrack work for The Killing Fields and Sutton Hoo, Mike decided to make his next recording into a companion video album. At the cost of £1 million, he went on to buy the latest advanced equipment and set up his own video studio, which opened later in the year.

Because this project would mean that he would not have an album for release for a while, Virgin prepared a double LP compilation of his music and songs, both old and new, for the coming Christmas market. This was issued in October as *The Complete Mike Oldfield.* The last side of the collection featured four previously unreleased live tracks, recorded on Mike's various tours from 1981 to 1984: *Sheba, Mirage,* the lengthy *Platinum,* and *Mount Teide.* Virgin's choice of live material was constrained somewhat by the undesirability of including tracks which appeared elsewhere on the collection as original studio recordings, so they were unable to present live versions of the more popular and important big singles of the early 1980s, for example, which would have been slightly more interesting. Nevertheless, the live cuts they included are good. In complete and mystifying contrast to most of the studio recordings made during the same period as the live shows, consistently solid guitar work by Mike is, happily, much in evidence. So too is the clearly vital role of his various drummers, Mike Frye, Moerlen and Phillips in the effective live presentation of his music. *Mount Teide* is the best of the selections, imbued with more warmth than its studio original.

The compilation reached number thirty-six in the album chart.

Some time around early autumn Mike wrote *Pictures in the Dark,* a song about the power and magic of dreams, for his intended video album. His regular vocalist Maggie Reilly being unavailable, he remembered his meeting singer Anita Hegerland while the *Discovery* tour had been in Germany the previous autumn, and invited her to record with him.

He wanted the song to be a multi-vocal affair, however, and so asked celebrated Welsh choirboy Aled Jones, a Virgin label-mate, to sing too. Mike also had his six year old daughter, Molly, count time, a device he uses as a bridge to the chorus. He originally intended Barry Palmer to sing as well, but although the latter was to receive a full credit on the sleeve of the subsequent single, for some reason Mike himself sang the parts he had intended for him.

Although the song is unusual for Mike in his allusions to Classical Greek and Roman myth, in its slightly oblique melody and his new-style wrenching guitar breaks (a feature he was to repeat over the next couple of years), none of this means that the song is a particularly good one. On release, it scraped to number fifty in the chart.

After it was recorded, Mike made his first home video, with the help of director Pete Claridge. The video combined shots of Hegerland and Jones singing, and himself playing guitar, with computer generated images of opening windows, mazes and spinning household objects.

Although the song, at six minutes, was probably originally meant to be a track on the future video album, Virgin appear to have decided to release it as a single to publicise the concurrent availability of the recent compilation. For its release, in November, Mike added *Legend* on 7" and also *The Trap* on 12". Both of these extremely poor instrumentals sound like incomplete excerpts from soundtracks.

On the home front, Mike's relationship with long-time companion Sally Cooper was beginning to flounder, and after the single was recorded, Mike became increasingly close to Anita Hegerland. The latter recalled: *"I went to his house to record and our relationship just grew from there. We began as musical friends and working partners and by the end of the year we had become involved"*.

Mike's romantic feelings, whether for Anita or Sally is not clear, were voiced on *Shine*, a song he recorded with vocalist Jon Anderson in the first months of 1986. Like *Pictures In the Dark*, it features one of Mike's new, rough, rattling guitar breaks.

By the time of its later release, as a single, in April, Mike had recorded *The Path*, a delicate and restrained acoustic guitar tune, with chimes and a synth background. It was the only piece of worthy music Mike made up to and including his later LP. All formats of the single were backed only with this track.

Shine, however, was lyrically and musically lightweight, and the single flopped deservedly.

On 6th February 1986, Mike made the first of a couple of rare live appearances, when he was invited as one of the guests of neo-progressive group Marillion for their show for Pete Townshend's Double O charity at the Hammersmith Odeon. He came with singer Roger Chapman, bass player Phil Spalding, keyboard player Mickey Simmonds, and new guitarist, 'Joel'. The whole ensemble played a noisy, monotonous version of *Shadow On The Wall*, and, with the addition of ex-Genesis guitarist Steve Hackett, *I Know What I Like*, and old Genesis song.

A few days later, Mike made an originally unscheduled appearance as one of the artists at the Nevado Del Ruiz Disaster Appeal Fund concert at the Royal Albert Hall. The show had been organised to raise money to help refugees from a massive volcanic explosion in Colombia which killed 25,000 people. Mike, Maggie Reilly and Simon Phillips performed an acoustic version of *Moonlight Shadow*. A video of the show was later released in 1988.

In April, Mike and Sally's third child, Luke, was born. The pair's relationship, however, was still in difficulties.

Some time during the summer, Mike was approached to record

an original track for a charity compilation of folk-rock artists. The proceeds were in aid of Broadreach House, in Exeter, a rehabilitation centre for drug addicts and alcoholics, with which Richard Branson was familiar as a result of his efforts to cure Virgin Star Boy George of heroin addiction. Mike recorded *Passed You By*, with folk guitarist Phil Beer, who had played for Mike on his first ever tour. Uncharacteristically, the track harkened back to old material of Mike's like the kind of folk instrumentals he had done in the 1970s. The compilation, *Where Would You Rather Be Tonight?*, was later issued in February 1987.

In October 1986 Mike took delivery from America of a new highly sophisticated mixing desk. It initially gave him a lot of problems, however, so that he decided to move to a studio in West Germany to continue working on his new album, commuting between there and his home. This arrangement put further strain on his relationship with Sally, and as a result of his dissatisfaction with this situation he gave up the idea. The designer of the mixing desk visited his studio to sort out the technical problems, and in the meantime, he took a short holiday with Sally and the children.

This did not improve matters, however, and in late autumn Mike and Sally split up, Mike going to live with Anita Hegerland in Switzerland and France. He said later that his break with Sally was *"totally amicable"*, explaining: *"It was a tough decision but I felt that Anita and I were more suited. Sally and I weren't any good for each other. Quite simply, we made each other unhappy when we were together"*. Mike's long and previously fulfilling life with Sally thus came to an end.

Although there had been no plans to release any more singles until the new LP was available, in May 1987 Virgin issued *In High Places*, Mike's *Crises* song about ballooning, to coincide with Richard Branson's 'Virgin Atlantic' balloon flight, an attempt to break the record for the fastest such crossing of the Atlantic.

By the summer, Mike and Anita had returned to England, renting a house in Marlow, about twelve miles west of Denham, and Mike commuted from there to his studio to finish work on his long overdue LP.

In September, the album's title track, *Islands* was released. It's vocals were by Bonnie Tyler, one of several singers who appeared on the album. The 7" carried the LP track *The Wind Chimes Part One*, with the 12" having the extra *When The Night's On Fire*, sung by Anita. Virgin decided that all formats of the single were to be sold at 7" price, in order to encourage better sales than *Pictures In The Dark* and *Shine* had achieved. Unfortunately, the song's vocals were bland and its music almost non-existent, and insufficient members of the record-buying public could be induced to part with their cash, so that the single made not the slightest dent in the chart.

Islands was released towards the end of the same month, and without its companion video, which was not ready until several months later.

The LP was titled after the often islands-inspired material. The title track is about a real or imagined island experience. *North Point* is about a place in Barbados, *Flying Start* bears Mike's incidental impressions of Kevin Ayers' home island of Majorca, and the side-long instrumental, *The Wind Chimes* is apparently partly inspired by wind chimes from the island of Bali, and includes keyboard samples of the gamelan, a Balinese musical instrument, which Mike must have noticed resembled his own tubular bells.

The songs on the LP are slightly unusual in Mike's metaphorical and indefinably 'spiritual' lyrics, and in their sharing common words and images, as indeed, his later video was to do. *Flying Start* is sung by Kevin Ayers, but it could just as well have been anybody else on material as poor as this. Only *North Point* is anything less than mediocre. Musically, the songs' accompaniments are so economical as to be utterly perfunctory, and Mike's guitar work is negligible and completely uninspired.

The Wind Chimes instrumental is, unusually, in two parts, the first almost entirely orchestral in sound. This and other very minor new approaches on Mike's part fail to lift what must be the dullest instrumental he has ever recorded. The whole thing is ultimately just an 'étude', or study in barren musical technique, of Mike's own.

Islands reached number twenty-nine in the album chart.

After it was released, Mike and Anita started looking for a permanent home, eventually finding a house not far from his old Denham residence. Mike bought the house - at the cost of £2 million - leaving his old house to Sally, explaining: *"I can afford it - and I don't see why I should completely uproot the children. The fact is they should stay in the home they have been living in all their lives"*. The new house was, usefully, close enough to his old one as to allow Sally and the children to visit him regularly.

Mike and Anita moved into their new home in February 1988. It was a large Victorian red-brick building, with seven bedrooms, and large landscaped gardens, which extended over eight acres.

Meanwhile, the LP track *The Time Has Come*, with vocals by Anita, had been issued in November of the previous year. It was backed with an extract from *The Wind Chimes Part Two*, the 12" also having a remix of the A-side.

Flying Start was released at the end of February 1988, both the 7" and 12" only having a second extract from the long instrumental.

For the 12" version of the A-side, Mike did not extend or remix it, instead prefacing it with one-and-a-half minutes of similarly lightweight, understated music.

Both singles sold poorly.

No other tracks were lifted from the LP and released in the UK, but around April a new mix of *Magic Touch* was issued in West Germany, where Mike continued to be popular. The 12" came with the original LP mix, while both 7" and 12" carried the otherwise unavailable instrumental *Music For The Video Wall.*

Because of the personal and technical difficulties he had experienced, the video album Mike had intended to accompany Islands was not ready until June, when it was issued as *The Wind Chimes*. Its belated release meant that it lacked the promotional impetus it would have received had it been released around the time of the LP recording, and it appeared instead almost entirely unpromoted, and unnoticed, by reviewers and public alike. To make the package more attractive, the video came with some old promos like those for *Five Miles Out*, *Moonlight Shadow*, *Pictures In The Dark* and *Shine* tacked on at the end.

Mike directed four of the LP-related video tracks himself, presumably after learning from the previous help of Pete Claridge and Alex Proyas, who collaborated with him individually for three tracks. Most of the videos are shot in the same style, with computer created images added onto live action or landscape scenes, the former element often begin spun into and out of shot. The results are somewhat abstract, the videos appearing to be little more than over-simple experiments in video art; one also gets the impression that Mike is dabbling shallowly in effects, not always to special purpose, a charge that could also be levelled against his music over the previous few years.

Many of the overlaid objects and other images seem unusually symbolic. The videos are full of bird images, drawn from the same images on *Islands*: Mike uses these here to convey his joy in flying and as an abstract representation of personal freedom. (The former interest of Mike's appears in the title track's literal on-screen red arrows, which represent the Red Arrows flying display team which he had yearned to join when he was a child). There are other symbols: during the title track we also come upon a computer picture of an arena, on the floor of which lies the astrological symbol for Taurus, the bull, the whole image being Mike's representation of himself as a performer.

Although Anita features in the videos, singing, Mike himself hardly appears at all except during *Magic Touch*, when he wanders languidly through a country mansion (probably his own), playing guitar. His most personal appearance, in fact, comes when he 'writes' an on-screen message thanking us for watching.

The video project Mike had embarked on marked his entry into a new creative area for him. Unfortunately, his visual work was gimmicky and dull, and his music poor in quality. As the latter, and the non-LP singles which preceded it showed, he was still unable or unwilling make melodic, innovative or even remotely interesting music.

Chapter 15

Turning Point

It was over a year and a half following his last LP before Mike had a new album for release. This was largely because he was having £1 million worth of work done to his house, building a studio onto the side of it. He spent the interim before he could record writing songs (and growing his hair to its old hippy length). Once he was able to proceed, it was the beginning of July 1989 when *Earth Moving* was issued.

The LP was a collection of songs alone. To sing, Mike recruited more redundant middle-aged rock vocalists. His approach, however, was not just rock-oriented, and for the LP he tried to record modern soul-style songs, and so invited vocalists Nikki 'B' Bentley and Carol Kenyon to work for him.

Mike's entry into what was a new musical genre for him suggests that he had an eye on the kind of music which was successful in the current pop marketplace, given the failure of all his recent singles.

Musically, the songs on the LP are given a kind of light Dance cum Adult Oriented Rock treatment. The melodies continue to be aimless and perfunctory, and the music is just a vague background to the lyrics.

Mike's contributions on keyboards, guitar and drum programming are so negligible as to be rendered non-existent. The LP continues the generally uninterrupted downward trend of his work over the years, so that by this time Mike's individual musical 'voice', the element which originally made his recordings so unique and clearly identifiable as his alone, had finally become so completely diluted as to make him a virtual absentee in the proceedings; with *Earth Moving*, Mike finally reduced himself to the position of a very minor and unremarkable session player on what was supposed to be his own work.

The only in any way notable feature of the album is the still surprisingly 'spiritual' nature of some of the lyrics. There are songs entitled *See The Light* and *Bridge To Paradise;* Runaway Son is a kind of re-write of the New Testament Prodigal Son story; love is sent from heaven, and the beloved of one song is 'holy'. All of the songs imply some nebulous past of impending self-transformation and salvation. Whether these are deep personal expressions by Mike of his own feelings is, however, not conclusive, although some of the songs are known to be personal: *Far Country* is about Anita Hegerland and *Innocent* was written for Mike and Anita's daughter, Greta, who had been born the previous June.

The release of the LP was preceded by that of the title track. The 7" came with *Bridge to Paradise,* while the 12" and CD featured a disco mix of the A-side as well as the regular version of the song. Mike's creation of a disco treatment of the song was another obvious concession to the current pop market, where single were often helped into the chart on a wave of disco and club play. But *Earth Moving* did not chart.

The parent LP reached number thirty in the album chart, but, not surprisingly, failed to spark the remotest interest beyond the traditional hard core of Oldfield fans, and quickly dropped out of the ratings.

To promote *Earth Moving,* Mike gave a rare interview to Steven Wells of the NME. This was an unusual action, not only because Mike and the music press had not shown any interest in each other for many years, but because the NME was the most radical of the music papers and the one least likely to accord him any standing. Nevertheless, the interview turned out to be playfully aggressive; Mike, prepared to be attacked, turned on his 'manic' persona, and engaged Wells in continual banter about the state of current music and about Punk rock, which he blamed for his fall from critical and commercial acceptance. *"The way I see it"*, he said, *"the early '70s and late '60s were a golden era.... I don't think music should stay the same for Christ's sake, but Punk was the worst thing that could have happened. Why shove that down the throats of young people?.... What puzzled me was why Tubular Bells didn't inspire lots of other people to try the same thing. I suppose you've got Jean-Michel Jarre and Vangelis but I thought they were both crap. Punk Rock just came along and destroyed everything. How many great instrumentalists have there been in the last ten years? How many of them can actually play their instruments? I mean, take away the drums from 90 per cent of modern music and what are you left with? Total shit"*. Mike went on in this vein, but his assertions were questionable; his belief that Punk destroyed his career, for example, ignored the larger factor of his producing poor music in the matter of the shrunken audience for his work.

To impress on Wells that he was not a limp, introverted old hippy, Mike also revealed that he had once hit Richard Branson in the throat for looking at his girlfriend, and a couple of other 'rock 'n' roll' stories. This attempt to alter his public image, as he had tried to do during his est period, worked temporarily, the resulting published interview convincing many among the NME staff that Mike was an amiable madman.

His grievances against what he regarded as the poor state of modern music apart, Mike was otherwise content. He was happy in his new life with Anita, another, more homely interview with coffee table celebrity magazine, Hello! revealed. The pair were expecting their second child, and he liked his 'peaceful' house and gardens, which the family shared with Greta's nanny, their gardener, and Mike's spaniel, CD.

His separation from Sally, he felt, *"seems to have worked out all right in the end, Sally has gone back to work at Virgin as artist liaison manager - a job she loves - and, as we live so close, we keep in touch all the time. I see the kids every week - they love coming here and they get me to ride them around the grounds on my motorbike"*.

In September 1989, *Innocent*, with vocals by Anita, was taken from *Earth Moving* and released as a single. The 7" was backed with the previously issued disco mix of *Earth Moving*, while the 12" and CD had a treatment by Germany remixer Bob Kraushaar. Like *Earth Moving*, and all of Mike's singles over the past four years, *Innocent* was commercially unsuccessful.

No more tracks were issued in the UK, but *Holy* was retitled *One Glance is Holy*, given three different mixes, and issued in West Germany.

The decline in sales of his recent albums featuring songs and the complete commercial failure of his songs when released as singles sparked a turning point in Mike's career soon after the release of

Earth Moving. He had been recording such material following the initial advice of Richard Branson, and the subsequent prompting of Virgin, who felt in the 1980s that completely instrumental music was no longer popular. Mike had decided to go along with them; but after the release of his last LP, he thought the better of this policy, and decided that it was time he return to something similar to his original work. Accordingly, he began recording ideas in his studio for a purely instrumental work. He visualised this as an *Ommadawn* II kind of composition of a similarly personal nature.

Mike's decision to concentrate on instrumentals again marked the end of his second creative phase. Although he had initially produced some occasionally worthy commercial work during that period, it had generally been an artistically unsuccessful time. With his next album, the completely instrumental *Amarok*. Mike began what was to be a new creative phase, and the three recordings he has since made have been, pleasantly, far more artistically and aesthetically rewarding than most of the work which preceded them.

PART THREE

Chapter16

A New Synthesis

Some time during the last months of 1989, Mike decided to record a session for Radio One. His action was an unusual one, probably intended, not just to promote his own work, but to present his music in an arena which he felt was swamped with poor artists; to present what he viewed as his own high standards in music.

For the session, Mike played a short version of *Tubular Bells,* and a section of music for what was to become *Amarok.* He may have been experimenting with the former because he had begun to think again about recording a *Tubular Bells II,* when his contract with Virgin expired. This was an idea he had originally considered for 1983, the tenth anniversary of the original LP, but had postponed because he did not want to give Virgin the satisfaction of releasing such a potentially profitable recording, having had a number of disagreements with them at that time.

The session was to alter Mike's conception of the recording he was doing for *Amorok*. He recalled that when he had been taping the version of *Tubular Bells*, *"The BBC engineers were pretty impressed to see someone coming in with all these instruments and playing everything by hand - it only took three hours. So I thought, "Blimey, why have I been sitting punching buttons on computers all these years? This is really fun!" - and as a result of that I did the whole of Amarok that way"*.

What Mike went on to do was combine the more computer programmed and sampled approach of his second creative period, which he had been using on the recording, with the multi-instrumental, multi-layered approach for which he had been noted during the early part of his career. The result of this combination of approaches was to create a new synthesis of musical elements from Mike's old and new phases on the album and the following work.

Given this approach, and the fact that he wanted to make a kind of *Ommadawn* II, Mike brought in a number of old or *Ommadawn* related colleagues to work on the project. Tom Newman produced the LP, Bridget St. John and Clodagh Simmonds became again once-typical choral vocalists, Paddy Moloney played tin whistle, Julian Bahula, of African band Jabula organised a group of African musicians, and William Murray (who had written *Ommadawn's* horse song with Mike) wrote a parable for the LP cover. Mike himself recreated some of his attractive old playing styles and instrumentation: there is his once so characteristic skirling or mandolin-like electric guitar, lots of Spanish and acoustic guitar, Hammond organ, and even tubular bells, which he coyly described on the LP cover's long list of instruments as 'Long Thin metallic hanging Tubes'.

Such older musical elements and personnel were incorporated with features from Mike's newer instrumental approaches: the wrenching, rattling guitar style he had been using since 1985, keyboard samples of extraneous sounds, and his dropping into the music various enigmatic words and phrases.

Mike used the latter feature, which are either sung or spoken by himself or the vocalists, to reflect some of his current feelings. He said something a couple of years later about the kind of music he was making which is particularly relevant to *Amorok*: *"Instead of making albums like I did, dredging something up from inside me and saying, "There you go, listen to me being miserable, grumpy and unhappy", I'm saying, "Hey, listen. Look at me. I'm happy, I feel great. Mmmmmm.""*

The rich, warm work is a mosaic of contrasting styles and instrumentation, linked together through the reprises of central musical and instrumental themes, such as a recurring flamenco guitar tune or periodic abrupt interruptions of Mike's loud, wrenching, new-style electric guitar. On the whole, the piece is enjoyable and accomplished, and certainly far more melodic than work of the recent past. Some good guitar playing by Mike is a much needed and attractive surprise. But most remarkable of all is the re-emergence of Mike's individual musical voice; this work is different in some ways to his early recordings, but, like the latter, it carries a musical colouring immediately recognisable as his alone.

The second side, which flows seemlessly from the first - Mike utilising the compositional opportunity provided by the CD format - closes with his attempt at a humorous ending. Impressionist Janet Brown imitates then Prime Minister Margaret Thatcher commenting on the music and dancing as African drummers lay down an Ommadawn-style metronomic beat and Paddy Moloney plays a jolly Irish tune on tin whistle.

After it was recorded, Mike titled the work, like *Ommadawn*, the album which accounted for a large part of its spirit, after an Irish word: in this case *Amarach*, which means tomorrow. His choice of title, and the Thatcher character's comment that endings are just beginning seem unusually philosophical, and suggest that Mike sensed he was entering a new period of creativity.

He also decided to package the album like *Ommadawn*, the front cover again being a photograph of himself pictured through a rain-streaked window, taken by William Murray. The latter's parable went on the album insert; its moral seems to be that good music is in the ear of the beholder, a point Mike repeated elsewhere on the cover, with his two-fingered warning: "This record could be hazardous to the health of cloth-eared nincompoops'.

The album was released at the beginning of June 1990. While Q magazine thought that some of the music was interesting and noted that it contained elements typical of Mike's early work, it characterised the album as *"a thing of only patchy delights"*.

Soon after the LP was issued, Mike appears to have had a peculiar crisis of conscience over what he viewed, typically, as the lamentable state of modern music, and, in what he announced as a protest against *"the over-commercialisation, mechanisation and mass production of modern music"*, he took to living in a small tent somewhere on the land which surrounded his house. He would sleep there for several nights, making cups of tea on a camping stove, eating meals cooked and brought to him by Anita, and returning to the house for an occasional shower. A sillier and more ineffective 'protest' can hardly be imagined. Mike, remarkably, seemed only dimly aware that this might be the case: *"I know this protest looks a bit odd, but what else could I do?"*, he said limply to the only journalist who visited his tent.

Like previous outbursts against current music or the music

industry, this one coincided with another grievance he had against Virgin. Although he considered *Amarock* to have been his best album in many years, the LP only reached number forty-nine in the chart, spending only two weeks in the ratings before disappearing. Although 30,000 copies were bought in Germany, it only sold between five and six thousand copies at home. Mike felt that this and previous LP's poor performances were due to what he viewed as Virgin's less than wholehearted promotional efforts for his recordings. He was particularly annoyed that, after he had presented the album to Virgin, the company's managing director told him that he did not know how to go about selling instrumental music. Mike subsequently concluded that he would have to do the job himself, commissioning a radio commercial for the LP, composing his own jingle to go with it, and setting up a £1000 treasure hunt related to the album; the advertising campaign had little effect on sales, however, and the prize was never claimed.

The episode confirmed in Mike his decision to leave Virgin Records after his next, last album for the label. He would try and get a deal with another company, and record *Tubular Bells II* for them. He felt that another label might put heavier financial backing into his work, and that a successful sequel to his famous debut might relaunch his musical career.

Chapter 17

Experimenting Again

For his last album for Virgin, Mike retained the services of Tom Newman, formed a band, and recorded a set of songs and a side-long instrumental. The group comprised long-time associate Simon Phillips on drums, Mickey Simmonds (who had previously played for Mike on 1984's *Discovery* tour, and again for his appearance at Marillion's charity show in 1986) on Hammond organ and piano, and new collaborators Dave Levy on bass and Andy Longhurst on keyboards. Mike played guitar and main keyboards.

The LP, *Heaven's Open* was issued in February 1991. While it was quite different to *Amorok*, its instrumental, *Music From The Balcony* continued to combine elements from Mike's old and new musical styles, and, generally, continued to show that Mike was genuinely stretching himself. It was not the throwaway Mike's final contractual obligation might have led one to expect.

Music From the Balcony is a decidedly experimental, almost minimalist piece, with far less musical substance or activity than *Amarok*, but, rather, clicking synth patterns, sound effects and zoo noises. Such passages are interchanged with, again, some more 'old-style' guitar from Mike, and, most surprisingly, some modern-jazz-tinged rhythms. During the latter, synths and guitar play some unusual chords while the percussion plays in a complex tempo. One gets the impression that Mike is trying to create some music that has no precedent anywhere, something that is entirely new. The jazz element appears to have led Mike and Tom to bring in celebrated jazz saxophonist Courtney Pine, to play a little sax or clarinet in the reprised jazz sections.

While the piece lacks strong melodies, it is nevertheless surprisingly successful as, instead, an exploration of rhythms and technique. As an étude, then, this is an example, perhaps the only example, of Mike's creating something which actually works well. This is in contrast to those études which epitomised the character of most of the instrumentals from the second phase of his career.

The songs on the album are better than average. They are sung - at last - by Mike himself, who reveals himself as having a reasonably accomplished style of vocal delivery. He is certainly more interesting than the session singers he had too frequently employed to sing his lyrics over the years. His singing also makes the songs a little more personal than usual, although they still tend towards the nebulous. (*Make Make* appears to be a criticism of Virgin, but the lyrics are so obscure that nothing enlightens us, whatever it may all mean to Mike).

The songs are accompanied by broad, contemporary dance-influenced keyboard sounds and Phillips weighty drums; Mike makes only brief appearances on guitar, but these are quite attractive. *Gimme Back* is an unusual song for Mike in its light reggae feel.

The LP was preceded in January by a 7", 12" and CD single of, the title track, backed with an extract from the instrumental. Apparently as some sort of joke, both this and the album were credited to 'Michael' Oldfield, their production to 'Thom' Newman.

With the release of *Heaven's Open*, Mike was free of his contract with Virgin Records. Just over a year later, Virgin was sold to EMI for £500m. Although relations between Mike and Richard Branson had been tense for some years, Branson rang Mike on the day of the sale and thanked him for making it all possible. Mike was happy that Branson was so gentlemanly, but said of Virgin: *"I'm very glad they've been sold to EMI. They did so well out of me and then they let me down; there was just no support from them. I'll never forgive them; I'm so glad to see them disappear"*.

Chapter 18

Tubular Bells II

Mike spent much of the rest of 1991 thinking about ideas and approaches for *Tubular Bells II*, taking on a manager, and setting about organising a new recording deal. He recruited Clive Banks, a highly rated figure in the music industry and the manager of Courtney Pine and the hugely successful Simple Minds. Touting *Tubular Bells II*, Mike was subsequently signed to Warners.

He became involved in a couple of other activities during this period. Still thankful for his therapeutic experiences with est, he set up TONIC, his own charity, which was intended to raise public awareness of the benefits of psychotherapy and sponsor individuals who would otherwise not be able to afford it.

He also added some guitar to a track for his old colleague Kevin Ayers' new LP. Ayers' career had declined sharply in the late 1970s, as a result of the poorer quality of his material, and his own lethargy when it came to promoting his music. He preferred to live in sunny Majorca, running a bar there, and releasing the odd LP on

Spanish or independent labels. His subsequent album, *Still Life With Guitar* was released in 1992 by Permanent Records. On *I Don't Depend on You,* Mike played only a few notes at intervals - although these are notably in the style he had frequently employed on Ayers' LPs of the early '70s.

When he came to record *Tubular Bells II,* Mike shifted his operations to America, renting a large house in Beverly Hills, Los Angeles, and bringing over Tom Newman, whom he had originally intended to produce the album, and Trevor Horn. Mike had liked Horn's late 1970s electronic pop band, Buggles (famous for *Video Killed The Radio Star*), and later met Horn, learning in conversation with him that he was an admirer of his own production work and *Incantations.* Horn became a celebrated producer in the 1980s, chiefly for his work with Frankie Goes to Hollywood.

Recording started at the house in September 1991, and lasted nine months. As well as transporting his many instruments, several of which had appeared on the original *Tubular Bells,* Mike went to the trouble of shipping over his trusted mixing desk, the piece of advanced hardware he had bought in 1986, rather than rent equipment in L.A..

In making *Tubular Bells II,* Mike did not plan to make a piece of music in the style of the original LP, as one might have expected. Rather, he wanted to record a new treatment of its material: sampling or replaying elements from it, or using some of the same instruments he had employed on it, and combining these approaches with new instrumental sounds and techniques, and bits of new music, so as to remodel the original tunes and create something which sounded the same, yet different. He did not reprise everything of the original LP, but most of its main sections.

The process involved a kind of layering. Mike would start off with the tunes as they had been recorded originally, and then add or subtract elements, changing the instrumentation, tempo, mood or texture, gradually moving further away from the original material with each finished take, yet retaining something of the tunes as they had been first recorded. This procedure is amply illustrated on the B-side of the later released single of *Sentinel* (the reworked first piano tune of *Tubular Bells*): *Early Stages'* is a demo version of the more advanced result, a kind of 'middle layer' of the process; a piece which is different to the 1973 original but which has not yet been transformed into the end product. On the subsequent album, Mike often alters the original material out of all recognition, while on some sections this is much closer to the surface of the finished work.

As an aid to work such as this, Mike kept a notebook to categorise what he thought of the results of various stages, grouping sections under headings like 'Brill', 'Good', 'So So', 'Some Life' and 'Rubbish'.

"I couldn't make it too clear or too far away from the original so I had to draw a very fine line", Mike commented. *"I had to ensure there were cross-references and points where the two works converge, albeit momentarily, without making them too similar. Hopefully I got the contrasts right"*.

As for the mood of the recording, Mike felt that it was more optimistic and positive, a celebration of life rather than a retreat from it. *"Tubular Bells addressed the human being as a multi-faceted beast who feels happy and sad, hateful and loving and just about every other emotion you can think of. The second instalment is perhaps a slightly more sophisticated and considered version of that but be assured the lifeblood is the same"*.

Like *Amorok* and *Music From The Balcony, Tubular Bells II* combined approaches from Mike's old and new musical phases: computer samples of the original LP mixed with live playing, his old guitar style coupled with the new. As Mike said of the recording, he felt that he had had twenty years after his debut to grow as a musician, and the sequel was for him an ideal way of putting everything he had learnt into context.

Mike felt that Trevor Horn was a great help during the recording work. He commented that an element of frustration had crept into his guitar playing during the last years of his association with Virgin, for example; *"Trevor's trying to encourage me to play with more feeling. I was getting a lot of anger into my playing and he's say, "Play that with a bit more love""*. Mike also observed that he still had a tendency to add many overdubs, an element which was not so surprising given the multi-instrumental nature of the original album; but, he said, Horn noticed this and would go through all the additions and sort out those which were worthy of retaining: *"you can cram things so full of stuff that it sounds like musical goulash - you have to strip it away and let beautiful things hang there"*.

Recording was finished in June 1992, and the album was mixed the following month. Afterwards, Mike retired for a break to St. Paul De Vence, near Nice, and there gave several interviews to promote the forthcoming LP.

Warners packaged the LP in an updated version of the cover of the original, and they and Clive Banks set about a heavy promotional campaign for it, the album being released on 31st August.

Tubular Bells II comes as fourteen, separately titled, more clearly sectional pieces than the original; the 'caveman' section becomes *Altered States*, the Scottish tune, which is different to the original, is titled *Tattoo*. Generally, the better parts of the first album are the better parts of the sequel; *Sentinel*, in particular, still has the power to mesmerise in its new treatment. Also highly attractive is *Weightless*, the first tune of the second side of the LP, which is very beautiful indeed. The only piece of completely new music is *Moonshine*, a kitschy country hoe-down tune, which replaces *The Sailors Hornpipe*.

The LP as a whole is generally a pleasant and enjoyable experience, with mellow instrumentation and production. Mike's musical approach continues to demonstrate some of the interest in new sounds, tempos and rhythms which he had recently developed. Not surprisingly, however, it lacks the cathartic power and purpose of the original, and as a result, it is sometimes one-dimensional by comparison.

Overall, this most recent treatment of *Tubular Bells*, like earlier attempts, does not surpass the original, but it does succeed in extending and developing it, and adds new slants to much of the material. As a composition in its own right, however, it is not as challenging and attractive as the more artistically pleasing, but far less commercial *Amarok*.

Reviews of the LP were lukewarm, critics smelling a hype.

Warners were determined that the LP would be a success, however, and had expended a good deal of effort and money advertising and promoting the album, ensuring a huge number of advance orders. In its first week of release, *Tubular Bells II* went straight into the chart at number one.

The record company also released *Sentinel* as a single in early September. This came with an attractive promotional video featuring Mike. The single rose to number twelve in the chart, having captured the imagination of the general public, and further encouraging LP sales.

Clive Banks organised a special live premiere of the piece, an imitation of the Queen Elizabeth Hall concert which had been a feature of the launch of the original LP. The show, in aid of the Prince's Trust charity, took place on 4th September, at Edinburgh Castle. Mike, together with a large ensemble of largely unknown session musicians, played a note-for-note copy of the recording. Television rights were sold to a number of European channels, and the show was broadcast in the UK on BBC 2. *Tubular Bells II* was thus beamed directly into millions of homes, and this added another impetus to sales. A video of the concert was released in October as *Tubular Bells II The Performance*. It was also planned that Mike would play the sequel live again at the Royal Albert Hall from 5th - 8th April 1993.

In early December, a second single, *Tattoo* was issued. It was backed with Mike's seasonal *Silent Night*, the CD also carrying a live version of *Sentinel*, from the Edinburgh show to publicise the release of the video. The single sold poorly, however.

With all the promotion, Tubular Bells II quickly sold over 300,000 copies in the UK alone.

Mike Oldfield was, once again, a success.

AFTERWORD

Whether or not Mike will be able to continue to be as commercially successful with subsequent recordings for Warners as he was with a sequel to his celebrated debut remains to be seen. After relaunching his career with *Tubular Bells II*, Mike may, in fact, simply find himself in a reprise of the situation which followed the original LP: making albums which gradually sell less and less well, until he becomes an even more marginal figure in the British music scene that he had been.

Equally uncertain is the future for Mike's artistry. Certainly, the recordings of his third creative phase have, so far, been more aesthetically accomplished and rewarding than those of the preceding period, but as the latter phase repeatedly demonstrated, Mike is perfectly capable of producing consistently dull, bland music.

It was never like that during the years of his early work. Then, Mike's music bowled one over with its irrepressible melodies and the internal dynamism of their rich multi-instrumental settings, its admixture of very joyful and intensely melancholic moods and its general cathartic power and highly emotional undercurrent. Mike's guitar work deserves special mention, because it was as a highly individual electric guitar stylist that he particularly shone, with fierce, heady effects and explorations of delicate, ringing tones and timbres.

The recordings of Mike's second phase, however, were generally those of a composer and player whose work had become musically and emotionally shallow, perfunctory and anonymous. This work usually included only the odd hint of his apparently now absent or, simply, curiously dormant talents - LPs graced by a single fine track, and only two really worthwhile full albums. Mike's songwriting, initially promising, became lyrically nebulous and musically lightweight.

The reason for Mike's artistic decline appears to lie largely in his therapy-sponsored personality change of the late 1970s. If genius is pain, to use one reviewer's lofty metaphor, then it seems that after Mike threw off the mental burdens he was carrying when he made his great early recordings, he no longer needed to compose appropriately emotional, considered and cathartically melodic music, and went on, instead, to make a series of basically empty technical exercises.

Given Mike's only recent emergence from a period of decline, with his last three albums, one awaits the future of 'Oldfield music' not with unbounded hope, but, nevertheless, considerable interest.

RECORDINGS

ALBUMS:

Tubular Bells (Virgin V 2001)
Side One/Side Two (inc. *The Sailor's Hornpipe*)
5.1973

Hergest Ridge (Virgin V 2013)
Part One/Part Two
8.1974

The Orchestral Tubular Bells (Virgin V 2026)
Part One/Part Two
1.1975

Ommadawn (Virgin V 2043)
Part One/Part Two, On Horseback
10.1975

Boxed (Virgin V Box 1)
Tubular Bells; Hergest Ridge; Ommadawn; Collaborations (Phaecian Games, Extract from Star's End, the Rio Grande/First Excursion, Argiers, Portsmouth, In Dulci Jubilo, Speak)
10.1976

Incantations (Virgin VDT 101)
Part One/Part Two/ Part Three/Part Four
11.1978

Exposed (Virgin VD 2511)
Incantations; Tubular Bells; Guilty
7.1979

Platinum (Virgin V 21421)
Airborne, Platinum, Charleston, North Star-Platinum Finale/Woodhenge, Sally, Punkadiddle, I Got Rhythm
11.1979

QE2 (Virgin V 2181)
Taurus 1, Sheba, Conflict, Arrival/Wonderful Land, Mirage, QE2, Celt, Molly
10.1980

Five Miles Out (Virgin V 2222)
Taurus II/Family Man, Orabididoo, Mount Teide, Five Miles Out
3.1982

Crisis (Virgin V 2262)
Crises/Moonlight Shadow, In High Places, Foreign Affair, Taurus 3, Shadow On the Wall
5.1983

Discovery (Virgin V 2308)
To France, Poison Arrows, Crystal Gazing, Tricks Of The Light, Discovery/ Talk About Your Life, Saved By A Bell, The Lake
6.1984

The Killing Fields - Original Film Soundtrack (Virgin V 2328)
Pran's Theme, Requiem For A City, Evacuation, Pran's Theme, Capture, Execution, Bad News, Pran's Departure/Worksite, The Year Zero, Bloodsucking, The Year Zero 2, Pran's Escape - The Killing Fields, The Trek, The Boy's Burial-Pran Sees The Red Cross, Good News, Etude.
11.1984

The Complete Mike Oldfield (Virgin V MOC 1)
Arrival, In Dulci Jubilo, Portsmouth, Jungle Gardenia, Guilty, Blue Peter, Waldberg (The Peak), Wonderful Land, Etude/Moonlight Shadow, Family Man, Mistake, Five Miles Out, Crime Of Passion, To France, Shadow On The Wall (12" version); Excerpt from Ommadawn, Excerpt from Tubular Bells, Excerpt from Hergest Ridge, Excerpt from Incantations, Excerpt from The Killing Fields (Evacuation)/Sheba, Mirage, Platinum, Mount Teide (all live)
10.1985

Islands (Virgin V 2466)
The Wind Chimes Part One, The Wind Chimes Part Two/Islands Flying Start, North Point, Magic Touch, The Time Has Come
9.1987

Earth Moving (Virgin V 2610)
Holy, Hostage, Far Country, Innocent, Runaway Son/See The Light, Earth Moving, Blue Night, Nothing But, Bridge To Paradise
7.1989

Amarok (Virgin V 2640)
Amarok
6.1990

Heaven's Open (Virgin V 2653)
Make Make, No Dream, Mr Shame, Gimme Back, Heaven's Open / Music From The Balcony
2.1991

Tubular Bells II (WEA WX 2002)
Sentinel, Dark Star, Clear Light, Blue Saloon, Sunjammer, Red Dawn, The Bell / Weightless, The Great Plain, Sunset Door, Tattoo, Altered State, Maya Gold, Moonshine
8.1992

EP

Take Four (Virgin VS 238) 7"
Portsmouth, In Dulci Jubilo / Wrechorder Wrondo, The Sailor's Hornpipe
Take Four (Virgin VS 23812) 12" White Vinyl
12.1978

SINGLES

Mike Oldfield's Single (theme from Tubular Bells)/Froggy Went A-Courting (Virgin VS 101) 7"
6.1974

Don Alfonso/In Dulci Jubilo (For Maureen) (Virgin VS 117) 7"
2.1975

In Dulci Jubilo/On Horseback (Virgin VS 131) 7"
11.1975

Portsmouth/Speak (Tho' You Only Say Farewell) (Virgin VS 163) 7"
10.1976

The William Tell Overture/Argiers (Virgin VS 167) 7"
2.1977

Cuckoo Song/Pipe Tune (Virgin VS 198) 7"
11.1977

Guilty/Excerpt from Incantations (Virgin VS 245) 7"
Guilty/Guilty (long version) (Virgin VS 24512) 12" Blue Vinyl
4.1979

Blue Peter/Woodhenge (Virgin VS 317) 7"
11.1979

Arrival/Polka (Virgin VS 374) 7"
9.1980

Sheba/Wonderful Land (Virgin VS 387) 7" Double A-Side
11.1980

Five Miles Out/Live Punkadiddle (Virgin VS 464) 7"
Five Miles Out/Live Punkadiddle (Virgin VSY 464) 7" Picture Disk
2.1982

Family Man/Mount Teide (Virgin VS 489) 7"
Family Man/Mount Teide (Virgin VSY 489) 7" Picture Disk
5.1982

Mistake/Waldberg (The Peak) (Virgin VS 541) 7"
Mistake/Waldberg (The Peak) (Virgin VSY 541) 7" Picture Disk
8.1982

Moonlight Shadow/Rite of Man (Virgin VS 586) 7"
Moonlight Shadow/Rite of Man (Virgin VSY 586) 7" Picture Disk
Moonlight Shadow (Extended Version)/Rite of Man (Virgin VS 58612) 12"
5.1983

Shadow On the Wall/Taurus 3 (Virgin VS 625) 7"
Shadow on the Wall (Extended version)/Taurus 3 (Virgin VS 62512) 12"
8.1983

Crime of Passion/Jungle Gardenia (Virgin VS 648) 7"
Crime of Passion (Extended Version)/Jungle Gardenia (Virgin VS 64812) 12"
1.1984

To France/In the Pool (Virgin VS 686) 7"
To France (Extended Version)/In the Pool, Bones (Virgin VS 68612) 12"
6.1984

Tricks of the Light/Afghan (Virgin VS 707) 7"
Tricks of the Light/Tricks of the Light (instrumental), Afghan (Virgin VS 70712) 12"
9.1984

Etude/Evacuation (Virgin VS 731) 7"

Etude (Full length version)/Evacuation (full length version)
(Virgin VS 73112) 12"
11.1984

Pictures in the Dark/Legend (Virgin VS 836)
Pictures in the Dark (extended version)/Legend, The Trap (Virgin VS 83612)
11.1985

Shine/The Path (Virgin VS 863) 7"
Shine/The Path (Virgin VSS 863) 7" Shaped Picture Disc
Shine (extended version)/The Path (Virgin VS 86312) 12"
4.1986

In High Places/Poison Arrows (Virgin VS 955) 7"
In High Places/Poison Arrows, Jungle Gardenia (Virgin VS 95512) 12"
5.1987

Islands/The Wind Chimes Part One (Virgin VS 990) 7"
Islands (extended version)/When the Night's On Fire, The Wind Chimes Part One (Virgin VS 99012) 12"
Islands/When the Night's On Fire, The Wind Chimes Part One (Virgin VSC 99012) Cassette Single
Islands/When the Nights On Fire, The Wind Chimes Part One (Virgin CDEP6) CD
9.1987

The time has come / Final Extract from The Wind Chimes Part Two
(Virgin VS 1013) 7"
The Time Has Come (Remix) / The Time Has Come (7" Version), Final Extract from The Wind Chimes Part Two (Virgin VST 1013) 12"
11.1987

Flying Start / The Wind Chimes Part Two (Edit) (Virgin VS 1047) 7"
Flying Start (12" Version) / The Wind Chimes Part Two (Edit)
(Virgin VST 1047) 12"
2.1988

Moonlight Shadow (Extended Version) / Rite Of Man, To France,
Jungle Gardenia (Virgin VDT 7) CD
6. 1988

Earth Moving / Bridge To Paradise (Virgin VS 1189) 7"
Earth Moving (Disco Mix) / Earth Moving (7" Version), Bridge To
Paradise (Virgin VST 1189) 12"

Earth Moving (Disco Mix) / Earth Moving (7" Version), Bridge To *Paradise* (Virgin VSCD 1189) CD
7.1989

Innocent / Earth Moving (Club Version) (Virgin VS 1214) 7"
Innocent (12" Mix by Bob Kraushaar) / Innocent (7" Version), *Earth Moving (Club Version)* (Virgin VST 1214) 12"
Innocent (7" Version) / Innocent (12" Mix), Earth Moving (Club *Version)* (Virgin VSCD 1214) CD
9.1989

Heaven's Open / Extract from Music From the Balcony (Virgin Cat. No. unknown) 7"
Heaven's Open / B-side unknown (Virgin Cat. No. unknown) 12"
Heaven's Open / Other tracks unknown (Virgin Cat. No. unknown) CD
1.1991

Sentinel (Single Restructure) / Early Stages (WEA 4509-90930-4) 7", Cassette
9.1992

Tattoo / Silent Night, Sentinel (Live) (WEA 4509-91409-2) CD
12.1992

The Bell / Sentinel Restructure (Trance Mix) WEA 4509-92259-4) 7", Cassette
5.1993

ODDITIES + ALBUMS

Tubular Bells (Virgin HE-44116)
1973
Half-speed re-mastered.

Tubular Bells (Virgin QV 2001)
1974
The first quadraphonic mix, different to that with *Boxed*.

Tubular Bells (Virgin VP 2001)
1978
Picture Disk. Stereo version of second, *Boxed*, quadraphonic mix. Issued in two versions: one includes the noise of an aircraft.

Hergest Ridge (Virgin VR 13-109)
1974
Promotional LP, banded into tracks for radio play.

The Orchestra Tubular Bells (Virgin VR 13-115)
1975

PROMOTIONAL LP, BANDED

Various Artists V (Virgin VD 2502)
1975
Includes 6 minute version of *Don Alfonso*

Ommadawn (Virgin PZ 33913)
1975
Promotional LP, banded.

Ommadawn (Virgin QVQS 2043)
1976
Never fully released quadraphonic version, in a different mode of the quad system to that usually employed.

Platinum (Virgin V 2141)
1979
Only the first pressing, matrix number V 2141-B-1, includes the original *Sally.* Later pressings replaced this with *Into Wonderland* - which is nevertheless also credited as *Sally*

Impressions (Tellydisc TEL 4)
1979
TV-advertised, mail-order only compilation. Features a different version of *I Got Rhythm*

Airborn (Virgin VA 13143)
1980
The double album version of this US release couples the later pressing of *Platinum* with a different live version of *Tubular Bells* to that on *Exposed*, and an unusual segueing of the live and studio versions of *Incantations*.

Five Miles Out (Virgin VVIPD 106)
1990
CD re-release, distributed through the budget label, Pickwick. Includes otherwise unavailable lyric booklet.

Crises (Virgin CDV 2262)
Release date unknown
Some of these CD pressings include a booklet with a short anniversary interview with Mike.

Discovery (Virgin CDV 2308)
1984
CD includes an otherwise unavailable lyric booklet.

The Complete Mike Oldfield (Virgin VJD 25019/20)
1985
Japanese CD. Includes otherwise unavailable lyric booklet.

Islands (Virgin CDV 2466)
1987
CD features the addition of *When The Night's On Fire*

Islands (Virgin VI 90645)
Release date unknown
US release. Features vocalist Max Bacon, not Tim Price, on *Magic Touch*

ODDITIES

EPs

In Concert 80 (Virgin 696009) 7"
Punkadiddle, Excerpt from Tubular Bells/Guilty, Blue Peter
1980
West German promotional release . Includes booklet.

In Concert 82 (Virgin 104678) 7"
Mistake, Waldberg (The Peak)/Family Man, Mount Teide
1982
West German release.

SINGLES

Tubular Bells/Tubular Bells (Virgin VR 55100) 7"
1974
US single imported into the UK as the theme from The Exorcist.

Spanish Tune (Virgin VS 112) 7"
7.1974
One-sided promotional release, taken from *Hergest Ridge*

Mike Oldfield's single/Froggy Went A-Courting (Virgin 13245 AT) 7"
Mike Oldfield's single/Froggy Went A-Courting (Virgin 1348 AT) 7"
1974
On these Dutch and West German releases Mike sings an additional verse of *Froggy* which on the UK release was sung by Bridget St. John.

Guilty/Excerpt from Incantations (Virgin VV 45002) 7"
1979
Portuguese pressing, on yellow vinyl.

Guilty/Excerpt from Tubular Bells (Virgin 600 115) 7"
1979
West German issue of live material. On yellow vinyl.

Blue Peter/Woodhenge (Virgin VS 317) 7"
1979
Pressing A4 features the original sudden ending, pressing A7 the re-recorded version.

All Right Now (TT 362)
1982
Flexi-disc release, given away with Flexipop magazine.

Moonlight Shadow/Rite of Man (Virgin VS 586) 7"
1983
Later pressings fade out Mike's exclamation at the end of the B-side.

Magic Touch/Music For The Video Wall (Virgin 109872) 7"
Magic Touch (remix)/Music For The Video Wall, Magic Touch (7" version) (Virgin 609872) 12"
1988
West Germany-only release.

One Glance Is Holy (single edit)/One Glance Is Holy (remix) (Virgin 112761) 7"
One Glance Is Holy (Hard and Holy Mix), One Glance Is Holy (remix)/
One Glance Is Holy (single edit), One Glance Is Holy (instrumental mix) (Virgin 612761) 12"
1989
West Germany-only release of *Holy*

RECORDINGS WITH OTHERS

ALBUMS

Kevin Ayers And The Whole World ***Shooting At The Moon*** (Harvest SHSP 4005)
May I?, Rheinhart and Geraldine, Colores Para Dolores, Lunatics Lament, Pisser Dans Un Violon/The Oyster And The Flying Fish, Underwater, Clarence In Wonderland, Red Green And You Blue, Shooting At The Moon.
10.1970
Mike plays electric guitar on bass on all tracks except *Pisser* and *Underwater*

Kevin Ayers ***Whatevershebringswesing*** (Harvest SHVL 800)
1.1972
Mike plays electric guitar on *Song From The Bottom Of A Well* and *Champagne Cowboy Blues*, and electric guitar and bass on the title track.

Kevin Ayers And The Whole World ***BBC Radio 1 Live In Concert*** (Windsong International WINCD 018)
1992
Mike plays electric guitar on *Why Are We Sleeping?* Session recorded 1972.

Kevin Ayers ***The Confessions Of Dr Dream And Other Stories*** (Island ILPS 9263)
5.1974
Mike plays electric guitar on *Everybody's Some Time And Some People's All The Times Blues*

Kevin Ayers ***June 1, 1974*** (Island ILPS 9291)
6.1974
Mike plays electric guitar on *Everybody's ....Blues* and acoustic guitar on *Two Goes Into Four*

Kevin Ayers ***Odd Ditties*** (Harvest SHSM 2005)
2.1976
Mike plays electric guitar and bass on *Gemini Child, Puis Je?, Butterfly Dance, Stars* and *Lady Rachel.* The LP is a compilation of singles and other material.

Kevin Ayers ***Still Life Guitar*** (Permanent Records PERM CD5)
2.1992
Mike plays electric guitar on *I Don't Depend On You.*

David Bedford ***Nurse's Song With Elephants*** (Dandelion 2310 165)
2.1972
Mike plays bass on the title track.

David Bedford ***Star's End*** (Virgin V 2020)
10.1974
Mike plays electric guitar and bass.

David Bedford ***The Rime Of The Ancient Mariner*** (Virgin V 2038)
9.1975
Mike plays electric guitar.

David Bedford ***The Odyssey*** (Virgin V 2070)
9.1976
Mike plays electric guitar on *The Phaecian Games* and *The Sirens*

David Bedford ***Instructions For Angels*** (Virgin V 2090)
1977
Mike plays electric guitar on the title track.

Edgar Broughton Band ***Edgar Broughton Band*** (Harvest SHVL 791)
1971
Mike plays mandolin on *Thinking Of You*

Edgar Broughton Band ***Bandages*** (Nems 6006)
1975
Mike plays electric guitar and harp on three tracks.

Lol Coxhill ***Ear Of The Beholder*** (Dandelion 69001)
1971
Mike plays electric guitar on *A Collective Improvisation, Vorblifa-Exit* and *The Rhythmic Hooter.*

Tom Newman ***Fine Old Tom*** (Virgin V 2022)
2.1975
Mike plays electric guitar on *Suzie, Ma Song and Sad Sing*

Tom Newman ***Faerie Symphony*** (Decca TXS 123)
1977
Mike plays electric guitar on *The Dance of Thenna Shee* and *The Unseelie Court.* He is uncredited.

Lea Nicholson ***Horse Music*** (Trailer LER 3010)
9.1975

Lea Nicholson ***The Concertina Record*** (Kicking Mule SNKF 165)
8.1980
Mike plays electric guitar, bodhrán and sleight bells on *Kopya,* a track which appears on both LPs, but for which he is credited only on the second.

Pierre Moerlen's Gong ***Downwind*** (Arista 1080)
8.1979
Mike plays electric guitar on the title track.

Pierre Moerlen's Gong ***Pierre Moerlen's Gong Live*** (Arista SPART 1130)
5.1980
Mike plays electric guitar on *Downwind.*

Pekka Pohjola ***The Mathematician's Air Display*** (Virgin V 2084)
1977
Pekka Pohjola ***The Consequence of Indecision*** (Happy Bird B 90133)
1981
Two editions of the same recording, although the second, a reissue on picture disc, is credited to Mike, not Pohjola. Mike plays electric guitar on *The Mathematician's Air Display* and *Hands Calming The Water,* electric guitar and glockenspiel on *The Consequences Of Indecision* and tubular bells on *The Sighted Light.*

Sallyangie ***Children Of The Sun*** (Transatlantic TRA 176)
Strangers, Lady Mary, Children Of The Sun, A Lover For All Seasons, River Song, Banquet On The Water/Balloons, A Midsummers Night's Happening, Love In Ice Crystals, Changing Colours, Chameleon, Milk Bottle, The Murder Of The Children Of San Francisco, Strangers
11.1968
Mike and his sister Sally sing and play acoustic guitar.

The Skids ***Joy*** (Virgin V 2217)
11.1981
Mike plays keyboards on *Iona*

Bram Tchaikovsky ***Strange Man, Changed Man*** (Radar 17)
3.1979
Mike played inaudible tubular bells on *Girl Of My Dreams.*

Various artists ***Canterbury Tribute*** (Cat. No. unknown)
1974
Limited edition transcription LP of a US radio show on the late 1960s music scene in Canterbury. Includes a live track by Kevin Ayers And The Whole World, on which Mike plays guitar.

Various Artists ***Where Would You Rather Be Tonight?*** (Sunrise A4011M)
2.1987
Mike performs with Phil Beer on *Passed You By*.

Robert Wyatt ***Rock Bottom*** (Virgin V 2017)
7.1974
Mike plays electric guitar on *Little Red Robin Hood Hit The Road*.

RECORDINGS WITH OTHERS

SINGLES

Only those single releases which feature tracks which do not appear on LP are listed.

Les Penning ***Grenadiers/The British Grenadiers*** (Polydor 2058 892) 7"
1977
Mike plays on the A-side.

Sallyangie ***Two Ships/Colours of the World*** (Transatlantic Big T Big 126) 7"
9.1969
Mike plays acoustic guitar on both tracks.

Sallyangie ***Lady Go Lightly/Sweet Child*** (Label and Cat. No. unknown) 7"
Release date unknown
This single certainly exists in the form of a US demo; it is not clear if it received a regular, or UK, release. No details of Mike's involvement are known.

Sallyangie ***Child of Allah/Lady Go Lightly*** (Phillips 6006 259)
12.1972
Issued three years after Sallyangie had officially broken up. The extent of Mike's participation, if any, is unknown. Sally Oldfield later re-recorded the song for her 1979 LP *Water Bearer* (Bronze BRON 511)

PRODUCTION AND ENGINEERING CREDITS

David Bedford ***Star Clusters, Nebulae, And Places In Devon/The Song Of The White Horse*** (Oldfield Records OM1)
1983

Mike produced and engineered both pieces.

Henry Cow ***Legend*** (Virgin V 2005)
5.1973
Mike engineered a small part of *Nirverda for Mice*

Henry Cow ***Unrest*** (Virgin V 2011)
5.1974
Mike engineered *Ruins*.

James Vane ***Judy's Gone Down/Jung Lovers*** (Island WIP 6538)
1.1980
Mike produced both tracks.

FILM

Reflections
57 Mins 16mm Colour 1977
Directed by Laurence Moore
Distributed by Concord Films (Hire), The Arts Council (Sale).
Original music by Mike Oldfield and Alan Hacker. Vocals by Sally Oldfield and Katy Hacker. This is the only film which features music of Mike's which is not also available on LP.

VIDEOS

The Space Movie (Virgin Video VVA 016)
90 Mins VHS 1983 1 1979 1
As well as previously released material, this film contains a short alternate take from *Incantations*.

The Essential Mike Oldfield (Virgin Video VVD 011)
70 mins VHS 1980
Guilty, Tubular Bells, Ommadawn
Filmed at Knebworth Festival 21.6.1980. Includes interview.

The Wind Chimes (Virgin Video VVD 353)
60 mins VHS 1988
The Wind Chimes, North Point, Islands, The Time Has Come, Flying

Start, Magic Touch, Five Miles Out, Moonlight Shadow, Shine, Shadow On the Wall, Pictures In The Dark.

Tubular Bells II The Performance Live At Edinburgh Castle (Warner Music Vision 4509 90686 3)
65 mins VHS 1992
Sentinel, Dark Star, Clear Light, Blue Saloon, Sunjammer, Red Dawn, The Bell, Weightless, The Great Plain, Sunset Door, Tattoo, Altered State, Maya Gold, Moonshine, Reprise
Filmed 4.9.1992

Various artists *Colombian Volcano Concert* (Castle Hendring 2 086)
60 mins VHS 1988
Includes Mike performing an acoustic version of *Moonlight Shadow*, and a brief interview snippet.

Various Artists *It's Christmas* (PMI MVP 9912023)
40 mins VHS 1989
Includes the promotional film for *In Dulci Jubilo* (1975)

BIBLIOGRAPHY

Baker, Barry, 'Rock veteran Oldfield attacks "machine music" of the Kylie generation', Daily Mail 25th June 1990

Bedford, David, and ***Cornelius, Cardew,*** 'A Conversation', The Musical Times March 1966

Bedford, David, 'Eighteen Bricks left On April 21st' (Universal edition, London, 1967)

———, 'The Garden of Love' (universal edition, London, 1970)

———, 'The Rime Of The Ancient Mariner', Gramophone April 1976

Bell, Max, '*"I should be getting royalties when I'm 80 or 90"*', NME 27th September 1975

Beller, Miles, 'Exorcising Demons', US 3rd August 1982

Benoliel, Bernard, 'Oldfield - With and Without Bedford', Tempo No. 120 March 1977

Black, Johnny, 'Mike Oldfield *Amarok*', Q August 1990

Breen, Joe, 'A Man And His Music', The Irish Times 28th May 1980

Brewer, Mark, '*"We're gonna tear you down and put you back together"*', Psychology Today August 1975

Brown, Geoff, 'Reflection', Monthly Film Bulletin January 1978

Carr, Roy, 'Remarkable lack of levitation in Oxford outback', NME 23rd March 1974

Clark, Al, 'Mike Oldfield *Tubular Bells*', NME 16th June 1973

——, 'The Bells of Oldfield', NME 21st July 1973

——, in *Mike Oldfield Boxed* (Virgin Records, London 1976)

Clark, Stuart, 'Tubular Bells: The Sequel', Hot Press 10th September 1992

Corr, Alan, 'Tubular Bells and Killer Seals', RTE Guide 28th August 1992

Dallas, Karl, 'Chimes of Freedom', Melody Maker 23rd June 1973

——, 'Oldfield: high on the ridge...', Melody Maker 24th August 1974

——, '*"I Can't Stand People Who Play Things Blandly..."*', Melody Maker 28th September 1974

——, 'Star's End', Melody Maker 26th October 1974

——, 'Balm For the Walking Wounded', Let It Rock December 1974

——, 'Beyond the Ridge', Melody Maker 25th October 1975

——, 'Portrait of a genius', Melody Maker 25th October 1975

——, 'David Bedford', Melody Maker 5th February 1977

——, 'David Bedford "*Instructions for Angels*"', Melody Maker 8th October 1977

——, 'This is the year of the expanding man....', Melody Maker 25th November 1978

——, 'Pierre Moerlen's Gong *Downwind*', Melody Maker 10th February 1979

——, 'Oldfield: Pedalling Recycled *Bells*', Melody Maker 4th August 1979

——, 'Boy genius "not broke" shock', Melody Maker 29th December 1979

——, 'Mike Oldfield *QE2*, Melody Maker 1st November 1980

Denslow, Robin, 'The Odyssey', The Guardian 26th January 1977

Edmands, Bob, 'Getting it together in the country and finding true happiness', NME 1st November 1975

——,'Apotheosis of A rich Twit', NME 25th November 1978

——, Tubular Tortoise Leaves Shell', NME 21st April 1979

Ellicott, Susan, 'Retuned Tubular Bells', The Sunday Times Magazine 23rd August 1992

Eskine, Pete, 'This scene of frenzied activity...', NME 1st September 1974

Fielder, Hugh, 'David Bedford *The Rime Of The Ancient Mariner*', Melody Maker 4th October 1975

——, 'Bedford Gets His Sea Legs', Sounds 11th October 1975

——, 'Ongoing approaches to fresh musical scenarios', Sounds 25th November 1978

Flood Page, Mike, 'Oldfield At Star's End', Sounds 17th August 1974

Gilbert, Paul, 'Mike Oldfield *Crises*', Melody Maker 28th May 1983

Gill, Andy, 'Mike Oldfield *QE2*', NME 8th November 1980

——, 'Mad? US?', Q October 1992

Graham, Paula, 'James Vane', Zig Zag April 1980

Griffiths, Paul, 'Music in London; New Music', The Musical Times January 1975

——, 'The Odyssey', The Times 26th January 1977

Grossman, Stefan, and ***Tom, Mulhern,*** 'Mike Oldfield A Rare Interview with the English Guitarist, Studio Wizard, and Composer of *Tubular Bells*', Guitar Player January 1979

Hammond, Ray, 'The Virgin's Manor', Sounds 29th January 1972

Harrison, Max, 'Music in London', the Musical Times November 1970

Humphries, Sue, 'Mike Oldfield English Paradise For The Man Whose Musical Touch Turned to Gold', Hello! 19th August 1989

Ingham, John, 'Omma believer', Sounds 1st November 1975

Irwin, Colin, 'Sinking A Few With The Sensitive Boy Genius', Melody Maker 1st November 1980

——, 'The Age of Disillusion', Melody Maker 11th April 1981

Jenkins, Mark, 'Instrumental Innovator', Music and Equipment Mart February 1991

Jewell, Derek, 'Flickering Star', The Sunday Times 10th November 1974

——, '*The Rime Of The Ancient Mariner*', The Sunday Times 7th September 1975

——, 'Mike Oldfield: on the tubular route', The Times 5th December 1976

——, 'A Fallen Pop Idol Rises Again', The Sunday Times 29th May 1983

——, 'Biography' in Mike Oldfield 10 1973 - 1983 (Virgin Music, London 1984)

John, Andy '*"Under No Circumstances Do I Want to be Normal"*', Superpop 5th January 1980

Jones, Allan, 'Bedford sets sail with the Ancient Mariner', Melody Maker 4th October 1975

——, 'The Greatest Tour He Ever Sold', Melody Maker 14th April 1979

Jonssen, Marianne, 'Saved By The Bells', Vox October 1992

Kent, Nick, 'Ayers and Graces', NME 6th July 1974

Lake, Steve, 'Overture in Glass Ashtray Major', Melody Maker 9th March 1974

——, 'Son of Tubular Bells', Melody Maker 16th March 1974

——, 'Icing - with nothing inside', Melody Maker 24th August 1974

——, 'Bedford: not so gloomy Star', Melody Maker 16th November 1974

Lamb, Tim, 'Mike Oldfield', Record Collector No. 128 April 1980

WSM, 'Rime of the Ancient Mariner', Gramophone April 1976

Peacock, Steve, 'Kevin Ayers Wants to Dominate the Whole World - Then Again He Doesn't', Sounds 14th November 1970

——, 'Kevin Ayers and The Whole World "Shooting At The Moon"', Sounds 14th November 1970

——, 'Lol's Way of Being Free', Sounds 29th May 1971

——, 'Gong: The Return of The Banana', Sounds 26th October 1971

——, 'Kevin Ayers *Whatevershebringswesing*', Sounds 23rd January 1972

——, 'Something in the Ayer', Sounds 9th June 1973

——, 'A Young Virgin Will Never Let You Down', Sounds 9th June 1973

——, 'Music Triumphs Over Madness', Sounds 11th August 1973

——, 'How To Make a Model Glider (And compose a rock symphony)', Sounds 2nd March 1974

——, 'Kaleidoscope Mind', Sounds 24th August 1974

——, (untitled interview with David Bedford), Sounds 21st December 1974

Schiffer, Brigitte, 'Rock Und Pop in Londons Konzertsalen', Melos December 1970

Shawe-Taylor, Desmond, 'Music', The Sunday Times 10th November 1974

Smith, Robin, 'Oldfield's Overture', Record Mirror 18th December 1976

Snow, Mat, 'Mike Oldfield *Crises*'', NME 18th June 1983

Stokoe, Carolyn, 'David Bedford' in British Music Now ed. Lewis Forman (Paul Elek, London, 1975)

Sutherland, Steve, 'For Whom the Bells toll...', Melody Maker 8th August 1981

Truman, James, 'Mike Oldfield *Platinum*', Melody Maker 1st December 1979

Valentine, Penny, 'Will it go round in circles?', Melody Maker 25th November 1978

Wells, Steven, 'Morrissey? Who's He', NME 5th August 1989

Williams Richard, 'Kevin Ayers', Melody Maker 18th April 1970

——, 'Ayers Apparent', Melody Maker 25th April 1970

——, 'Fresh Ayers', Melody Maker 4th March 1972

'Mike Sues Virgin', NME 8th August 1981

'Oldfield Sues Virgin', Sounds 15th August 1981

'Public NME', NME 30th June 1990

'For Whom the Bells Toll', RTE Guide 28th August 1992

The following material was sent to the author without source details:

Beacon Radio ('Beacon Radio, Latest Hits and Greatest Memories, broadcasting to the West Midlands and Shropshire'), Interview with Mike Oldfield (1980)

Bonici, Ray, in Mike Oldfield The Concert tour booklet (1980)

Dellar, Fred, 'Who Wants To Be A Millionaire', Smash Hits (1979)

Gardner, Mike, 'Fear of Flying' (1982)

Thomas, Nigel, 'Music Scene Turns you on To Mike Oldfield', Music Scene (1974)

Other music titles available from Britannia Press Publishing:

This is the Real Life... Freddie Mercury

ISBN 0-9519937-0-4 Hardback Limited Edition £14.99

ISBN 0-9519937-1-2 Paperback Limited Edition ....£ 8.99

ISBN 0-9519937-3-9 New Edition ....£ 5.99

U2 The Story so Far

ISBN 0-9519937-2-0 Paperback ....£ 8.99